JUSTIN'S FOUNTAIN

EUGENE H. STRAYHORN JR.

Copyright ©2025 by Eugene H. Strayhorn Jr.

ISBN 978-1-966540-45-8 (hardcover)
ISBN 978-1-966540-44-1 (softcover)
ISBN 978-1-966540-46-5 (ebook)

All rights reserved. No part of this book may be reproduced or transmitted in any form or by any means, electronic or mechanical, including photocopying, recording, or by any information storage and retrieval system without express written permission from the author, except in the case of brief quotations embodied in critical reviews and certain other non-commercial uses permitted by copyright law.

This book is a work of fiction. Names, characters, places, and incidents are the product of the author's imagination or are used fictitiously. Any resemblance to actual locales, events, or persons, living or dead, is purely coincidental.

Printed in the United States of America.

CONTENTS

CHAPTER 1

Flames curled around Tower One of Liberty Commons as the inferno tightened its grip. Gouts of fire danced along the roof's ridgeline and leapt into the night sky, turning the underbellies of the low-hanging clouds bright orange. The fierce heat shattered windows, showering shards of glass down upon the three companies of firefighters that had answered the alarm.

My name is Justin Moore. I designed the three-story residential complex that was burning. The masterwork into which I had poured six years of my life was being incinerated. Liberty Tower One stood for everything I believed in as an architect: intelligent design, the efficient use of space, cost containment, and utilization of the most modern building materials. My goal had been to design a safe, livable, and affordable environment for the residents who would call Tower One home. All that was now going up in smoke.

Up and down the crowded access road, red and blue lights flashed atop fire trucks and police cruisers. A media van broadcast a live feed for a local network.

It was hard to believe my eyes as I staggered toward the grassy quadrangle at the heart of Liberty Commons. Chaos surrounded me on all sides. I watched helplessly as plumes of sparks erupted into the night sky. Truck engines revved, and pumps arced streams of water into the burning building. Firemen furiously fought the raging blaze. Having fled the flaming building, people milled around in stunned disbelief. Some cried. Others searched frantically for loved ones. Many stared at nothing.

Then, a bloodcurdling sound reached my ears—the screams of those trapped inside. Wails of unimaginable anguish echoed in my brain. Shrieks rose in a crescendo until suddenly snuffed out. Even after the voices fell silent, the reverberations resounded in my mind—over and over and over again.

Flames like banners fluttered high above condominium balconies. Heat blistered the paint off exterior walls. Smoke and ash billowed upward in thick, toxic plumes. When the wind changed, I caught the scent of burning flesh. My stomach roiled, and I vomited onto the grass.

Dear God, how could this be happening? What had gone wrong? Why had the fire suppression systems failed? Incredibly, I sensed that I might be somehow responsible.

Not till eleven months later would I begin to understand what had been lost that fearsome night.

Know thyself. I suspect many people would agree this is sage advice—a realistic knowledge of self bridges the gulf between foolishness and wisdom. Understanding who we are allows us to avoid life's potholes.

Why, then, do so few people comprehend their own nature? Could it be because there is a horrific price to pay for such knowledge? Coming face-to-face with your identity strips away all excuses and leaves you no place to hide.

I remember the first time I understood with absolute certainty who I was or, more precisely, what I was becoming. My epiphany came to me in an alley behind the Tempest Bar. I remember that I was sprawled atop a pile of boxes. An angry longshoreman with fists like wrecking balls and arms long enough to scratch his knees without bending down had punched me in the center of my chest and sent me flying.

Branford Gardens—the urban slum to which my wife and I had recently been exiled—is four square blocks of brutal, dead-end misery thirty miles south of Chicago. More than a few tough guys live there, and I had picked a fight with one of the toughest. No doubt he had resented being labeled an imbecilic knuckle walker, not that he had understood my phraseology, but he had caught my drift.

Our fight had been deplorably one-sided and remarkably brief. In addition to knocking the wind out of my lungs, the brute's thundering blow had dispelled the alcoholic haze that had cocooned me.

Abruptly sober, I floundered atop the rubbish.

Upon looking in the direction of my feet, I discovered that I had unwittingly latched on to a battered cardboard box that I now clutched in my hands. The scuffed and water-stained container was large enough to hold a small kitchen appliance. One of its top flaps had been torn half away. Grime smudged its imprinted logo, rendering it unreadable.

At first, I couldn't imagine why I should focus my attention on an empty box. Then, an unwanted rush of clarity came upon me, and I realized that the box represented me. It showed me who I was and where I was headed. That cast-off cardboard container declared what I was becoming: frayed, hollow, unrecognizable—empty. No longer fit to embrace anything of value.

A shiver ran through me as my revelation pierced me to the quick. For what seemed an eternity, I lay there bitterly cold, totally sober, and unendurably sad. The battle with the longshoreman having been forgotten, I stared at that beat-up box. No longer could I deny my past, keep it walled off behind bulwarks of guilt and regret.

Then, an even more unsettling thought came to me. The ebb and flow of my life was actually starting to make sense.

The naked bulb above the back door to the Tempest Bar cast a yellow glow into the alley connecting Lois and Myrtle Avenues. Its feeble light painted mounds of trash in jaundiced shades of gray. As I floundered atop the pile of boxes, I noticed a ribbon of sky overhead, an inky void squeezed between shadowy rooftops. Two stars peeked through like pinholes in a black shroud. They contributed nothing to the night's illumination.

My first attempt to stand failed. There was nothing solid to grab on to.

From my horizontal orientation, I glanced around. The alley's details, unnaturally sharp, began to emerge. A second-story window frame shed flecks of walnut brown paint. A puddle rippled beneath a leaky spigot. A scrap of paper stirred, then lifted in the chill October breeze. In a few months, winter gales would churn Lake Michigan to froth and hurl spears of ice and snow inland.

One o'clock in the morning is when the urban pulse skips a beat. Between ten and midnight, citizens with jobs either leave to work the night shift or trudge wearily home. The bars close at two in the morning, disgorging inebriates onto the sidewalks. Between one and two, a curious peace settles over Branford Gardens. This is the interval I hate most because it's when I feel most disconnected, unless, of course, I happen to be thoroughly plastered, which was no longer the case thanks to a brutal longshoreman.

With unwelcome lucidity, I again regarded my cardboard crystal ball. A fresh wave of revulsion swept through me. I let out a grunt of disgust and looked toward Mace, who stood several feet away. Or was his name Trace? Not that it mattered.

My newfound best friend had latched on to me several hours earlier—instant pals united by a common goal: consume as much rotgut as possible. Regrettably, our limited resources had petered out before our ability to stand upright, leaving us broke and a little wobbly.

I could tell Mace was feeling the cold. His shaking hands tugged the lapels of his threadbare jacket closer together. His denim trousers, frayed at the cuffs and worn through at the knees, seemed incapable of retaining warmth, not that his gaunt body could generate much. His off-brand sneakers sported so many holes they might as well have been sandals. Layers of grunge caked his thighs, and dark lines marked the limits of his broken and bitten fingernails. I found it hard to discern whether he was staring at me or gazing into space. The dullness of his expression gave no hint—a human stump rooted in the soil of urban blight. Yet something about his countenance seemed prophetic. Could this be a future me come back to deliver a warning?

I glowered at the empty cardboard box, hating what it implied. Like Adam after biting into the apple, I recognized that I was forever changed, though I could not yet fathom how. As a chill not born of the cold rushed through me, I thrust the box aside.

I snarled up at Mace, "Help me up."

My new best pal blinked. Between us, grunts and gestures had served as conversation. He stayed put and made no offer to help. To my chagrin, I found I knew nothing about the man except that he stank. Even from a distance, I could smell his stale sweat and bad breath, and that was saying a lot, the alley being a stone canyon of stench. Moldy trash and rotting garbage created an olfactory nightmare.

Three months earlier, right after my wife and I had relocated to Branford Gardens, the reek had seemed unendurable. Now, the odors were merely revolting. The thought that I could become accustomed to such stench filled me with disgust and spurred me to action.

Shoving boxes aside, I thrust out my arm. My palm encountered the rear wall of the Tempest Bar. Rough textures dredged up a dormant memory.

As the founder and lead architect of a premier architectural firm no longer in existence, I had favored bricks as a building material. Seen from afar, their grooves and striations blend in sensuous patterns. Up close, individual bricks are as scarred and distorted as the human soul.

Cautiously, I twisted sideways and stiffened my arm. With care not to bury myself deeper in the pile, I threaded one foot between boxes until the thin sole of my worn-out wingtip found the asphalt. I planted my foot and lurched upright. The change in orientation brought a moment of unsteadiness. With my palm still pressed against the bricks, I closed my eyes and let the sensation pass. When I opened them again, I saw I was facing Myrtle Avenue.

Then, I noticed something. Like cardboard monuments, piles of boxes bracketed the back doors of most establishments. There were dozens of empty cartons, some large and sturdy, others less pretentious. The variety was intriguing. Empty liquor cases, partitioned by interlocking dividers, lay scattered at my feet. Farther down the alley, thin flower boxes had been haphazardly cast aside, no doubt abandoned after the florist shop had gone out of business. Diagonally from there, a pair of oversized shipping crates stood tilted on end, monoliths holding up the rear wall of the appliance repair shop.

In the distance, a flash of movement caught my eye. I peered in the direction of Myrtle Avenue. Having lost interest, my opponent, the longshoreman, was nearly out of sight. A sense of incompleteness, like a thought interrupted, gripped me.

"Hey," I bellowed with false bravado, "come back here! I ain't done with you yet."

The man saluted me with one finger in a gesture of disdain but kept on walking. How could I fault the man for deserting the field of battle? As with most of his predecessors, I was an appalling adversary. Combat, as I was learning, is a tricky business. Enthusiasm is a poor substitute for skill. Regrettably, I was born with a fighter's will, not a fighter's reflexes.

I drew my hand away from the brick wall and realigned the lapels of my corduroy windbreaker, the only serviceable coat I owned. As I attempted to square my shoulders, a sharp pain stabbed the middle of my chest. Then, I recalled seeing the blow coming and being unable to slip aside. The punch would leave a fist-sized bruise, another battle token to distress my wife, Hannah.

Her sudden image reminded me of a comment she had made during our recent arguments. Looking at me straight in the eye and with great sorrow, she had declared, "You can't be that stupid. You know what's going to happen. In my opinion, you don't fight to win. You fight to lose. You want the beatings. You need them."

I cringed anew at the truth of her indictment. The sudden lucidity that had come upon me now made clear what she'd been trying to express: guilt is the direst of all human emotions. Allowed to fester, it strangles the mind and warps the soul, a truth I can verify from personal experience. Without self-forgiveness, there can be no defense against the ravages of personal blame.

Self-forgiveness. The concept mocked me.

I squeezed my eyes shut. A towering inferno rose in my mind. Flames, dreadfully familiar, seared the insides of my eyelids. I tried not to listen, but gut-wrenching screams sickened me, hideously rising in volume until they were horribly stilled. I could feel the heat. Through sightless eyes, I watched two innocent souls throw themselves out of their third-floor window. Even in that wretched alley, I could smell, nearly taste, the acrid smoke—the burning flesh. Through the lens of my memory, I watched helplessly as people died. There was nothing I could do. Nothing…nothing…or was there?

In the deepest reaches of my being, I desperately yearned for closure. I needed to rid myself of the nightmare.

My eyes snapped open, and I stared at the piles of boxes. Perhaps if I were to recreate the tragedy but engineer a different outcome, I would keep the fire from consuming my architectural masterpiece this time. This time, I would put the fire out.

Admittedly, it was a crazy idea, but it had seemed perfectly reasonable at the time.

≈ ≈ ≈ ≈

The oversized shipping carton I balanced atop my head wobbled precariously as I carried it toward Myrtle Avenue. Mace grunted as I passed by, his way of asking, 'What are you doing?' I suppose he had finally figured out my behavior was a trifle odd. The load I carried made it impossible to turn my head or even to gesture effectively. So I continued without comment. He wouldn't have understood anyway. Besides, I doubt I could have offered a satisfactory explanation, the matter being too painful to discuss.

After squaring the oversized carton end to end with its twin, I stepped back to look. I visualize the blueprints I had drafted for Liberty Tower One. The building had stood three stories tall. The second- and third-floor condominiums were less spacious than the common areas. I would need smaller boxes for the upper floors.

After several trips hauling cardboard containers, I again found myself behind the Tempest Bar, where my gaze fell upon the grimy box that had triggered my unwanted epiphany. To my surprise, it seemed special, but as I reached for it, I could tell it was perfectly ordinary. I set the box aside, well out of harm's way. In its place, I grabbed a liquor carton, also with a damaged flap, and a second container of similar size.

As I straightened up with a box in each hand, my foot dislodged an apple from a rubbish heap. It tumbled across the asphalt and came to rest beside Mace's shoe.

He looked down and then grinned, as if handed a precious gift. Bending at the waist, he picked up the apple. His thumb sank in to the first knuckle when he tested it for firmness. With a grunt of disappointment, he tossed the fruit aside, too rotten even for his taste. "I'm freezing," he muttered, "and thirsty. Let's go."

"I'm not finished," I replied.

"Finished with what? Looks like all you're doing is hauling out the trash." He inclined his head toward the end of the alley. "Won't help, you know."

"What won't help?"

"Collecting the garbage. There'll be more tomorrow. There's always more garbage."

I regarded my companion. In the pallid light, I could almost make out his features. "Mace, how long have you lived here in Branford Gardens?"

I sensed his sudden tension. His scowl warned me that I was at risk of crossing an invisible line. Reticence is a trait I had encountered in other members of our shared fraternity, a trait with which I was rapidly becoming familiar. I elected not to press the issue.

Mace hunched his shoulders against the bitter wind. "Come on," he said. "I really need a drink."

I arched an eyebrow. "You got any money?"

He shoved his hands deep into his pockets and shook his head.

I nodded in confirmation. "Yeah, well, neither do I. Remember what the barman told us? No gold, no booze. Now, do you want to help or not?" I suppose my desire for companionship, no matter how shallow, prompted the invitation. Misery shared seems less oppressive.

"Screw this," Mace snorted. He turned toward Lois Avenue at the opposite end of the alley. Our "best pals" relationship was over. I imagined he would seek out a steam grate or build a nest beside a dumpster unless he had the good fortune to latch onto another patron.

Momentarily, I thought about inviting him to my apartment, but facing Hannah alone would be challenging enough. A man is known by the company he keeps. My wife would take one look at Mace, and I, too, would be homeless.

I watched my erstwhile pal shuffle off, head down, back bowed. I felt a pang of sympathy. "Traitor!" I called out after him, softly enough so he couldn't hear. "Deserter," I whispered. There was no need to burden him with my anguish.

I hefted the boxes and marched in the opposite direction. There was work to be done.

≈ ≈ ≈ ≈

Unit 1 of Liberty Commons was taking shape. With thirty condominiums per floor, sixty families had briefly called the tower home—243 souls. My original plans had specified four identical structures surrounding a quadrilateral courtyard. Only one tower had ever been built.

Liberty Commons was to have been my magnum opus, the crowning achievement of Heartland Designs, the architectural firm I had founded and into which I had poured my heart and soul. Ultramodern building materials had kept costs to a minimum. High-capacity solar panels and wind-capture technology had helped meet the tower's energy needs. A novel work-to-own program enabled low-income families to experience pride in ownership. When completed, the Liberty Commons Project would have housed over a thousand souls and stood as a shining example of compassionate engineering. But that dream had turned to smoke, consumed by flames that seared the night sky.

I regarded my cardboard construction and promised myself that the outcome would be different this time. I knew my actions were irrational, but when everything has been taken from you, all that's left is fantasy.

The grocery cartons I had stumbled upon at the opposite end of the alley proved especially suitable. Neatly stacked together, they had seemed out of place, the nearest market being two blocks away. Someone must have set them aside after moving in, hoping to reuse them upon moving out, which to me seemed wishful thinking. To the best of my knowledge, not a single soul had escaped Branford Gardens in the past three months. This neighborhood was the bottom rung, the end of the line. Still, truth be told, I, too, harbored the illusion that one day, Hannah and I would regain what we had lost.

Had it been only eleven months since our nightmare had begun?

I studied the structure taking shape. An eddy of a breeze tugged at the red and blue flap of a FedEx box, but I was untroubled. My buildings were designed to last. All that remained was to place the roof, and I recalled having seen a long shallow container, the sort used to ship mattresses. Opened lengthwise, it would do nicely.

Upon reentering the alley, I noticed Mace walking away, head down, huddled in upon himself. I tried to think if the man had ever laughed or smiled even once. Admittedly, our fellowship had been brief. Still, he had seemed utterly devoid of humor, as if every ounce of levity had been leached out of him.

After shoving a mound of rubbish aside, I squatted down to recover the half-buried box I had been seeking. Then I paused. What was Mace's story? I wondered. What had triggered his downward spiral? How many of his dreams had been shattered? Surely, he hadn't always been the same hollow shell with whom I had shared a pint of rotgut.

Mace was poverty's legacy. He was what remains when everything of worth is stripped away.

Pathetic, I thought. *Utterly and wretchedly pathetic.*

Then I saw myself squatting there in that filthy alley: freezing, painfully sober, rummaging through piles of garbage to build an edifice to a conflagration so horrible it had burned all other thoughts from my mind.

"Good thing I'm not like Mace," I said with a snort. I threw back my head and tried to laugh. What came out was a harsh, raspy whimper that faded to a sorrowful lament.

The time had come. My cardboard version of Liberty Tower One was complete. With a critical eye, I inspected the finished project. Standing there with my hands on my hips, I pictured the dedication ceremony hosted by Heartland Designs. The celebration had been a huge success. Every VIP in Manchester, including the mayor, had sought to bask in the limelight. A week later, all that had changed.

The fire had begun in the main wiring shaft, resulting from a confluence of unrelated screwups. An apprentice electrician, pressed for time, had committed a fundamental error. Rather than fetch a wire of proper length, he had haphazardly spliced two shorter spans together to form the main high-voltage feed. Electrical current had arced across his shoddy coupling, heating the junction to ignition temperatures.

The framing subcontractor, hassled by cost overruns, had omitted several critical fire-suppression baffles. Installed horizontally between studs, the baffles partition a wall and limit the vertical migration of a fire, keeping it confined. By crippling such an essential fire-defense mechanism, my subcontractor had unwittingly transformed the primary wiring shaft into a chimney.

Excited by the thrill of ownership, the Tower's new residents had turned on every light in celebration.

Overheated, the electrical tape wrapped around the apprentice's splice had ignited. Clawing its way upward, the blaze had turned the main wiring bundle into a candlewick. Intense heat had seared the insulation off vital circuits and shorted out the remaining fire-suppression systems in no time. Without power, smoke alarms and overhead sprinklers were useless.

By the time the first whiffs of smoke had blossomed from blistering walls, the fire had reached the building's upper stories. Snaking outward from the central core, flames had cut off escape routes and filled corridors with lethal gasses. Manchester's fire marshal would later declare it a miracle that anyone had made it out alive and that only seven people had lost their lives. Seven people! Seven!

I stared blankly down Myrtle Avenue, fresh tears spilling from my eyes.

A frail mist, too insubstantial to be called fog, had settled in, blanketing the neighborhood. Pale auras surrounded streetlamps. Tendrils of vapor drifted upward from a nearby steam vent. The frayed hem of a curtain fluttered outside an open window, the residence having long since been abandoned. A feline shadow disappeared into the alley from which I had gathered my boxes, a feral cat hunting, I presumed.

Like a shroud, a damp quiet lay over the neighborhood. Soon, the chaos would return. Yes indeed, it was time. This night, I would answer the question why, or I would cease to exist.

I fished in my pocket for the box of matches that, weeks ago, I had pilfered from a bar, having come to treasure the warmth of metal trash cans set ablaze. I put the matchbox to my ear and shook it, praying there was at least one left. I was rewarded with the sound of precisely one match rattling around inside. After opening the matchbox, I knelt and cupped my hands against the wind. With the greatest care, I struck the match and advanced the burning sliver toward a dry tangle of cardboard strips I had fashioned beside the base of Tower One, near the middle. The tinder ignited. I watched tentative flames feed upon the torn scraps of paper, gathering strength and transitioning from orange to translucent blue.

I stood up and watched as the fire began chewing a hole in the side of the first oversized box. Then, like a living thing compelled by purpose, it seized its prey, though for a moment, nothing special seemed to happen. I watched hesitant flames scale the vertical exterior. They appeared weak, fragile—insignificant. I shed my coat and prepared to batter the fire to extinction without mercy.

Then, to my horror, I saw through the hole. Illuminated by the flames, the box's interior was a rat's nest of shredded paper. The fire had found a home.

A spear of despair pierced me to the marrow of my bones. Intuition told me it was already too late. Still, with mounting dread, I repeatedly flailed the wall of my Tower, the tail of my coat flattening against the cardboard. The blaze outside retreated, but the inferno inside flared anew, fanned by my efforts. I considered ripping the oversized box away, but the outcome would have been the same. No matter what, my creation would be destroyed.

Frantically, I looked around. My gaze scrabbled across brick façades and probed the recessed niches of concrete porches, searching for a water source. Then I remembered the faucet in the alley, but I had neither a bucket nor a hose to douse the inferno, and it was too far away to carry water in cupped palms.

Smoke billowed from the structure's roof. Like charred wraiths, embers lofted skyward, glowing edges bright against the darkness. The crackle and snap of the fire taunted me. In desperation, I again assaulted the burning structure, my arm repeatedly traversing great arcs, willing the blaze to retreat. Each swipe showered sparks into the night.

Volcanic tongues of flame erupted from the roof. Fire danced upon the sizzling corpse of what I had designed. In shared tempo, shadows cast on brick walls writhed and gyrated, partners in a ghoulish fandango. Illuminated by chaotic light, the edges of buildings appeared to undulate, shadowy and insubstantial. The neighborhood had devolved into a festival of madness. The screams inside my mind shrieked, "Save us!"

But as before, there was nothing I could do. Nausea swept through me. I felt woozy, and my knees tried to give way. Rather than accept that all hope was lost, I wildly flailed my arm, keeping pace with the music of the fire, desperately seeking to retain a fragile grip on what little sanity was left to me.

A hand touched my shoulder and gently rested there.

CHAPTER 2

Dazed and half mad from forcing myself to relive the terror, I failed to respond to the touch at first. The pressure on my shoulder increased. Slowly, the hand turned me around until I stared into the face of a man I did not recognize. His black hair, neatly trimmed, showed a touch of gray at the temples. A broad forehead conveyed a look of distinction, as did his nose and mouth, which were well proportioned. His dark eyes regarded me, though mostly with concern.

Then I noticed his lips were moving. They seemed to form phrases, like lip-synching a song or uttering silent prayers. *How odd*, I thought. I continued marveling at the strange occurrence until I realized he was speaking to me. I labored to hear beyond the heartbeat throbbing in my ears. Gradually, his words became distinct.

"Are you all right?" the man was saying in a voice tempered by a Hispanic accent.

Incapable of answering directly, I mumbled, "Who are you?"

"Patrol Sergeant Green. Call me Hector. Let's step over here, shall we? It's all right. The fire will burn itself out." He took hold of my elbow and urged me away from the middle of the street. His grip prevented me from resuming my efforts to pummel the blaze.

Patrol Sergeant? Then I noted his uniform, dark blue with a gold shield on his chest. Looking west toward Polk Street, I was bemused to see a white squad car with distinctive blue and green accents parked at the curb.

As my head began to clear, I noticed that Hector's partner, a rookie by his starched look, had stationed himself on the sidewalk five feet away. His thumbs rested atop his woven leather belt. Its buckle reflected the light of a nearby streetlamp, as did his shoes, polished to a black luster. I judged him to be in his early twenties, two-thirds my age. A nervous twitch spoiled his efforts to seem at ease. Whereas Hector's eyes offered sympathy, the rookie's were—what, apprehensive, wary…afraid? The man was worried—not a desirable trait for a cop.

Not that I could blame him. Branford Gardens punishes the poorly prepared, as Hannah and I had learned shortly after settling in. The weak could expect neither mercy nor pity. I wondered on what account the rookie had drawn such a rough first assignment. I decided that he must have pissed off somebody important.

Hector, upon noting that I was staring at his partner, sighed. "That's Patrol Officer Romansky." He confirmed my suspicions and added, "It's his first week." He lowered his voice and leaned closer. "He won't bite, not while I'm around." The patrol sergeant released his grip on my elbow and stepped back. "Are you all right?"

I nodded.

The patrol sergeant seemed unsure. After giving me a quick once-over, his demeanor became more solemn. "Usually, the force is grateful when citizens get involved, but what you did was foolish. You could have been burned. That pile of rubbish made quite a blaze. Are you hurt?" Glancing down, he pointed at my hand. "What's that?"

"My coat." I lifted the soot-stained garment for his inspection. A spot of light caught my eye. The streetlamp's glow showed where the fire had burned through the lapel. Hannah would be miffed, to say the least. Knowing her as I did, I assumed she would do her best to mend the damage. It was the only serviceable coat left to me.

"No, there." Hector indicated the back of my hand where a blister the size of a quarter was forming. "You need to get that looked at."

"I'll take care of it at home."

The sergeant was startled. He had probably assumed I was homeless, like the majority of nocturnal denizens. "You live around here, do you?"

"Two blocks that way." I inclined my head to the east, toward Monroe Creek.

"How long have you lived there?"

"Three months."

"Strange we haven't seen you around the neighborhood."

I regarded the smoldering tower, no longer recognizable, and considered that if not for my distress beacon, he wouldn't have encountered me this night either. I refrained from mentioning that fact but shrugged instead while I watched the wind scatter flecks of blackened ash across the asphalt.

"What's your name?"

"Moore."

"First name?"

"Justin."

"Justin Moore? Do we know you?" The cop's dark eyes narrowed.

Rather than ease his curiosity, I lied. "I can't imagine why you should." For weeks, my face had been plastered across the front page of every newspaper in Illinois, and though nearly a year had passed, people still remembered. I knew because far too often, I had witnessed their remembering, that casual first glance, the probing second look, and then startled recognition. Worse was the revulsion that routinely followed. Seeing it invariably made me heartsick.

"If we're done here…" I turned to leave.

"Hold on." Hector gestured for me to stay put. "One more question."

Here it comes, I thought, but what followed was not what I had expected.

The cop spoke in an offhand manner, maybe deceptively so. "I imagine this was the work of kids. They're always pulling stunts like this. Comes from having too little supervision at home, stressed parents trying to make ends meet, or for whatever reason they're never home—divorce, alcohol, or they stop caring. The bottom line is that it's the kids who suffer. They get into trouble because they lack discipline. Anyway, did you happen to notice who started this fire?"

The fading embers of my tower lay in a dwindling heap. Eddies of smoke thinned, then vanished, swallowed up by the night. I briefly watched a last bit of cardboard flare, fanned by a sudden gust. My creation was gone. My dreams lay in ashes. In the back of my mind, I perceived that Patrol Sergeant Green was offering me an opportunity to disavow my involvement. I could have said something like, "No, but you're probably right, kids," and simply walked away. That is precisely what I would have done a couple of hours earlier. But then it occurred to me that if I continued to embrace the status quo and refused to face my demons, nothing would change.

Except something had changed. An empty box had shown me that to have any chance of putting my life back together, that is to make sense of the horror I had experienced, I would have to stop hiding from the truth. Redemption would never be found in a bottle or come from starting street brawls or shutting out the one person I truly loved.

"I did," I admitted softly.

Hector stiffened. "Excuse me? I'm not sure I heard you correctly."

I squared my shoulders and faced the officer straight on. "I did. I'm the one who started the fire."

Patrolman Romansky took a step forward. Out of the corner of my eye, I noticed that his right hand now hung at his side, near the handle of his service revolver. I'm sure he regarded me as a disheveled pyromaniac intent upon burning down the neighborhood.

"Why would you do that?" Hector inquired blandly.

"It seemed…necessary."

Hector nodded, as if mulling over my choice of words, and then suddenly, there it was, that probing second look. I wanted to run, to climb back inside my shell, but I stood my ground and waited. The cop glanced from me to the heap of ashes and back again, causing my stomach to roil.

A small light came on behind Hector's walnut brown eyes, and the corners of his mouth drew down in disgust. "Oh my god," he breathed out softly. "I know you."

The sergeant and I stood facing each other. We hugged the brick wall of the boarded-up florist shop to escape the wind. My mental chaos had receded, so I felt less distracted and better able to follow trains of thought. Horrible images lingered, but rather than compel my attention, they waited to be summoned, which I struggled mightily to avoid. Abruptly, I realized I was chilled to the bone. With shivering hands, I put on my coat, which made no appreciable difference. I wiggled my feet, though I wasn't sure I could feel my toes.

After the shock of recognition had worn off, Sergeant Green began peppering me with questions, mainly seeking requisite details: my date of birth, address, how I had come to be mucking about in the alley. After studying my driver's license and verifying my identity, he relaxed. There was less tension in his voice. Perhaps he had concluded I wasn't much of a threat, or possibly because he sensed I was less distraught.

Patrolman Romansky sidled closer as if to join the interrogation, yet remained beyond arm's reach, watching intently. I considered making sudden movements to test his reaction but decided that scaring the man would be foolish. For all I knew, he might pull his service revolver and shoot me. The one detail I failed to mention was my encounter with Mace. I could find no good reason to involve him.

As the sergeant's questioning wound down, the look on Patrolman Romansky's face became even more somber. Now armed with an arsenal of facts, he donned his most officious persona and said sternly, "Sergeant Green, would you like me to call this in?"

"Call what in?"

"This crime—that we've apprehended a perpetrator."

With exaggerated patience, Hector replied, "To what end?"

"It's protocol. We're going to arrest him, aren't we?"

"On what charge? Littering?"

The patrolman blinked with incredulity. "Sir, this is a clear case of arson." For emphasis, he stabbed a finger toward the ashes.

"Arson, is it?" Hector pursed his lips. With a sidelong look, he eyed his partner. "Well now, let's see. Perhaps we should abandon our patrol duties and return to the station with our prisoner. There, you can fill out all the necessary paperwork and carefully record every item that's been destroyed. Then, early tomorrow morning, you can come back here and interview the shop owners, ensuring you document how they feel about having their trash hauled out of the alley and burned. Also, you'll need to confirm their willingness to press charges. Of course, it will mean they'll have to give up one or more days to appear in court. So what if they lose revenue? After that, you can speak with the district attorney and accurately present the crime you've described. I'm sure he'll be most eager to prosecute this terrible violation of the law. While you're at it, why not ask the judge how he feels about using up valuable court time?"

Patrolman Romansky pressed ahead, undeterred. "This man is a criminal. Justice must be served."

Hector's mocking grin became a look of dismay. "Go wait in the car. Let me deal with this." Before the patrolman could protest, the sergeant cut him off. "That's an order, Romansky."

For a moment, the patrolman seemed inclined toward insubordination. The set of his jaw proclaimed that he knew he was right and was, therefore, obliged not to back down. However, the man wilted when the sergeant leveled a withering scowl at him. Without further protests, he turned and walked away.

"Rookies," Hector spat. "They send me the misfits, you know, the ones they think can't hack it. Nothing's worse than a cop who's screwed up inside. He'll either get himself killed, or his partner, or an innocent. I've seen it happen. So I get to see what makes them tick. You'd be surprised. It's not tough to predict how they'll respond once you know them well enough. The hard part is understanding how they came to be that way."

He exhaled a long sigh and looked straight at me.

"Often as not, they can't help being their own worst enemy."

The cop's air of familiarity sparked a sudden sense of uneasiness. I wondered where his comments were headed and if they were aimed at me.

With a critical eye, Hector said, "So tell me, what are we to do with you?"

"Am I on my way to jail?"

"Not tonight unless you plan on getting into more trouble."

"Not me," I declared flatly and with only a minuscule twinge of uncertainty. "I'm cold, I'm tired, and I've had about as much catharsis as I can stand."

"Is that what this was? Catharsis?"

"Honestly? I don't know. Like I said, it seemed necessary."

For a time, Patrol Sergeant Green stood lost in thought. Light from the streetlamp cast his face in shadowy relief as he stared at the scorched pavement. When he spoke, I perceived genuine empathy in his voice.

"I can't imagine living through what you have."

He turned to face me.

"I remember a conversation I overheard. A couple of the arson investigators had been keeping tabs on your case—professional interest. One guy, Sergio, a real hard ass, said you needed to be put away for life. The others were convinced the coroner's inquest would clear you, which it did. Right?"

I shrugged in confirmation.

Hector said, "Yeah, I remember the day the verdict came in. People like Sergio were furious. More than one newspaper was screaming for blood. As I recall it, their editorials were vicious. I wonder, how does one deal with having so many people believe you are a murderer—or worse?"

Memories came flooding back. Again, I wanted to hide, to be anywhere else.

The sergeant persisted. "Tell me how it felt. What thoughts went through your head?"

"About like you'd expect, okay? Do we have to do this?"

"I'd like to know. How did you feel inside?"

I squared my shoulders and faced the officer. "The worst part," I admitted, feeling compelled to tell the truth, "is knowing Liberty Tower One should have been built differently. I should have foreseen the fire."

"You think so?"

"That was my job. I failed to appreciate what could happen."

"Do you believe in fate, Mr. Moore? What some call predestination?"

I shook my head. "I believe in choice and consequence. I made bad choices. People who trusted me suffered the consequences."

"If fate isn't a factor, how can we be responsible for choices that have unpredictable results? You follow? Is it right to be held accountable for what you cannot foresee? Negligence is failing to provide whatever care a reasonably prudent person would exercise under similar circumstances. The law doesn't expect people to be clairvoyant."

"We have imaginations. We construct mental scenarios. It's called planning ahead. Recognizing risk is how we avoid catastrophe, and that's what I failed to do."

"I don't recall the particulars, but didn't the coroner and the fire marshal both rule that the fire was an accident resulting from a series of unlikely events?"

"Yes."

"So tell me, how should we defend against every bad thing? If we tried, would anything ever get done? Seems to me that you have to accept some risks. No venture is ever completely safe or secure."

"Thanks for trying, Hector, but I've rehashed this argument repeatedly."

"I see. Well, that still leaves us with my original question."

"Which is?"

"What are we going to do with you?"

"What do you mean?"

"Obviously, you need help." The sergeant took a step back and eyed me up and down. "I mean, is this really how you want to be?"

I thought about defusing his query with a flippant retort, but no humor was left in me. I remembered Mace.

"Well?" said the sergeant.

"Well, what?"

"Well, what's your answer? What are you going to do about it? If you were insane or a danger to yourself or someone else, I could run you in and make you see a doctor. As it is, you seem sane enough, though evidently, you're not coping very effectively."

I remained silent. How could I explain what I did not yet comprehend, that I sensed the beginnings of a transformation, and that it was real? I must have conveyed some sense of assurance when I declared, "I'll be all right," because after giving the matter additional thought, the sergeant nodded as if there was nothing more to be gained from continuing our discussion.

He gestured toward the patrol car. "Look, I'd offer you a ride home, but I must wet-nurse the rookie there. It might be best if you and he avoided each other for now."

"Thanks, but I'd rather walk anyway. I've got a lot to think about."

"Oh, indeed you do. You plan on going straight home?"

"Yes."

"Good. Don't let me bump into you again tonight."

"You won't."

I watched the sergeant climb into the passenger side of the patrol car. After exchanging curt words with his partner, who glowered at me, they drove off.

My blister stung in protest when I shoved my hands deep into my pockets. I headed home.

Night sounds came to me as I crossed Hayes Street. In the distance, two voices, both male, quarreled. Slurred insults provoked angry retorts. I assumed that unless someone backed down, there would be violence, a common-enough occurrence in Branford Gardens, as I had painfully discovered.

Farther down the street, a truck engine wheezed to life, sputtering in protest at being pressed into service at such an unreasonable hour. A door slammed two blocks to the south, beyond Octavia, followed by the hurried sounds of someone running.

A gust of wind brought the scent of lilacs as I stepped onto the curb. The women of the night were gathering in anticipation of the bars closing. More than once, they had sought to entice me. Sadly enough, I had been tempted. Only the certainty that Hannah would find out had saved me.

Infidelity is betrayal, and betrayal inflicts wounds that never heal. Confessing adultery to my wife didn't sound like the good time the whores had promised.

Near the middle of the block, I halted beneath a storefront awning. Tilting back my head, I noticed a single bright star peeking through a gash in the fabric. Because of the night's dampness, a shimmering halo surrounded the glittering star.

Out of the blue, I recalled wishing on stars as a child. But what to expect for now? What one thing above all else was most vital? I could not decide. I was broke, my marriage was crumbling, and I would never again resume the career I loved. My life was in shambles, and I had no idea how to rebuild it.

I can't do this alone, I wailed in silence. "God, if you hear me, I need you." It was the first time I had prayed since the fire. I looked around to see if anyone had noticed. No one had. I turned and continued on.

Did I expect Providence to rescue me? Could I lay claim to any hope beyond what I created for myself? These and other questions dogged me as I plodded homeward.

Through the haze, I saw my destination a block ahead, the three-story apartment building on the corner where Myrtle Avenue deadened into Beach Street. Small windows decorated its otherwise featureless walls. No doubt the architect's priority had been to limit heat loss. In the regions surrounding the Great Lakes, winters could be notoriously severe. Rather than functional simplicity, however, he had designed a massive brick cube.

After moving in, it had become apparent why the landlord had discounted our rent and why the third-floor apartment above us was still unoccupied. A stark façade was but one of the building's many shortcomings. Another was that the rooms were dark and gloomy on even the brightest days. On overcast days, Hannah was forced to turn on every lamp to function, which was a problem, given the cost of electricity.

Her eye specialist had broken the news as gently as possible. Her condition would progress. Over time, she would go blind. The bottom line is that there was no cure for retinitis pigmentosa. We had started her on vitamin A supplements and other nutrients as palliative care, but when the money had run out…

What does it say about a man who can't provide medical care for his wife?

An upwelling of shame seized me as I trudged the three concrete steps to our front porch. I braced my body straight-armed against the metal railing. My fingers tightened against the cold steel, stretching tender skin around the blister. I ignored the sting. Instead, I gritted my teeth and tensed my muscles, determined to break free of the downward spiral of anger and self-loathing that could so quickly suck me in. That path ended only in a bottle.

Seeking a distraction, I peered into the darkness.

The emptiness of the sizeable vacant lot across the street called to me like an invitation to lose myself in nothingness. Only a few details were recognizable. In daylight, the triangular-shaped plot of ground had seemed ugly, thick with weeds and strewn with trash. At night, it exuded an inherently evil quality.

Why, I wondered, did the lot exist at all? Why hadn't the urban sprawl swallowed up such a prime bit of real estate ages ago? I tried to imagine what might be built on the lot and how the terrain might best be exploited. In my mind, I worked out potential routes of ingress and egress. I laid out suitable building sites, worked out drainage issues, and decided where the utility easements would run.

Gradually, my despair eased. Could it be that I was finally starting to think more rationally? I fervently hoped so.

Feeling less distraught, I entered my apartment building.

Our building's interior was darker than the night I had abandoned. A low-watt bulb lit the third-floor landing two flights overhead, but hardly any illumination filtered down to ground level. Both the entryway and the lowest flights of stairs were inky black.

After my eyes had adjusted as best they could, I inched forward until my hand found the railing. I headed upstairs.

Halfway to the second floor, I paused to listen. All was quiet. The family in the first-floor apartment was undoubtedly asleep.

Their name was Mallow. A week or so after Hannah and I had moved in, the wife, Judy, and her eleven-year-old son, Ricky, had stopped by to introduce themselves. As I recall, Judy had mentioned that Tony, her husband, worked as a night clerk; I don't remember if she had revealed where.

Since that initial visit, our paths had crossed only rarely. It suddenly occurred to me to wonder if the Mallows might be avoiding us. Was it that they, like other inhabitants of Branford Gardens, tended to mind their own business, or had they, too, become aware of my history?

I strained to catch any sounds that might be coming from my apartment. Upon reaching the second-floor landing, I eased forward and looked to where I thought the bottom of the door should be. No light spilled out above the threshold. I tiptoed across the landing to press my ear against the hollow-core door. Nothing—not a sound. All seemed serene.

Good, I thought. What I needed was rest, not confrontation. I would be better equipped to deal with Hannah's concerns in the morning.

As noiselessly as my cold numb fingers would permit, I inserted my key and unlocked the deadbolt.

The 10×18 foot space that passed for a living room was as dark as the landing except for a smidgen of light trickling in from the recessed fixture above the kitchen sink. I tiptoed forward but then stopped.

Fully clothed, Hannah lay full-length on the couch.

Straining to see, I realized she was wearing a pair of faded jeans and a red plaid flannel shirt. Her head rested on a throw pillow. Locks of hair the color of corn silk flowed across the arm of the couch. In the wan light, her features were as beautiful as ever. I could hear the rhythmic rise and fall of her breathing.

Falling asleep on the couch, fully dressed, was something Hannah never did. There had to be an explanation.

Panic seized me when I noted the suitcase on the floor beside the kitchen table.

CHAPTER 3

Hannah must have sensed my presence. Her eyelids fluttered open, and she stirred. I remained motionless near the middle of the room, unwilling that a sudden movement might frighten her. I stilled my breathing and waited. When her head lifted off the pillow, I said softly, "Don't be alarmed. It's only me."

"What time is it?" she said thickly, squinting in my direction. As she sat up, she swept a hand through her hair. Blonde tresses settled in layers around her shoulders and descended in waves to the middle of her back. It was a gesture both intimate and familiar. During our nine years of marriage, I must have seen that same quick sweep a thousand times, and even before that, all the way back to our college days when we first started dating. Often, it appeared when I interrupted her. Head down, focused on this or that, she would look up, comb her fingers through her hair, and smile. It was an automatic mannerism, like a reflex, but I found it sexy, like when she rested one hand atop the other while engrossed in conversation, or how she tended to tug on an earlobe when feeling insecure. This time, there was no smile.

"I don't know. Perhaps a little after two, I think."

I really missed wearing a watch. Not only did my wrist feel naked, but without a watch, the passage of time seemed uncertain, not the orderly march that had previously demanded my unwavering allegiance.

I crossed the room and shed my damaged coat. When I tossed it through the door to our bedroom, it landed on the floor, on my side of the bed. The soot stains and the hole in the lapel could wait.

Hanna sniffed the air. "Is something burning?"

"It's nothing." I tried to sound nonchalant. "There was a trash fire. I helped put it out."

Coming fully awake, she said, "Were you hurt?"

Nothing could be gained by drawing attention to the blister on the back of my hand or the fist-sized bruise forming in the center of my chest. In time, both would heal. "I'm fine."

"You're sure?" I could tell she wasn't convinced.

"Yeah, really, I'm okay. What about you? Why are you sleeping on the couch?" I stepped forward and reached for the light switch on the wall.

"I'd rather you didn't do that."

"Really?"

"Yes."

"As you wish." I drew my hand away from the switch and returned to the middle of the room. The light from the kitchen was sufficient enough that I could make out Hannah's features. "I'm sorry you waited up. You need your sleep, you know. The doctors have explained why it's important."

"We have to talk. Please, sit down." She shifted her body sideways to brace the small of her back against the couch's armrest, one leg curled beneath her—a defensive posture. Pale light from the kitchen bathed her complexion in shades of alabaster.

I complied, mindful to preserve a neutral zone between us. I, too, angled my body. Drawing my right leg up and draping my left leg over the ankle, I rested my right arm along the back of the couch. Though Hannah sat just out of reach, I could sense her through my fingertips. We faced each other like bookends on an empty shelf.

"Talk about what?" I made eye contact in anticipation of what I thought was coming. "What we don't need right now is another fight." No sooner had I voiced the words than I regretted my lack of sensitivity. Prejudging intentions is stupid, no matter how strong your premonition.

Rather than take up the gauntlet I had so thoughtlessly cast down, Hannah waited. She seemed to be gathering her composure. Gracefully, she settled one hand atop the other in her lap. "I'm moving out. I wanted you to know why."

There it was.

Only moments before, the notion had been unthinkable. The real possibility that our marriage might not survive was staring me in the face. I wanted to scream, to demand that she recant her declaration. But I knew why or thought I did—prejudging again. Rather than speak, I remained mute, paralyzed with dread.

Then I pictured the cardboard box, that tattered container I had clutched in my hands. Every cheerless detail seemed sharp and immediate. The image mocked me. Without my wife, I would be alone, worthless—completely and utterly empty.

In due course, we migrated to the kitchen table, a mundane assemblage of glass and chrome that we had rescued from a second-hand store. I made a fresh pot of coffee, which ordinarily would've been a treat. Usually, we brewed three, even four pots from the same grounds. I've never quite figured out why meaningful conversations generally occur in the kitchen.

For half an hour, we chatted like distant cousins at a family reunion, avoiding thorny issues like my drinking, my fighting, my habitually staying out till the wee hours of the morning. Most of all, we avoided discussing money or our lack thereof. Neither of us, I suppose, felt inclined to provoke an argument and thereby hasten what we knew was coming.

Hannah uncoiled her fingers from around her coffee mug and pressed both palms flat against the glass tabletop. She tilted her head as she looked in my direction. "I can see you're exhausted. It's time for you to get some sleep."

"Good idea. No doubt you're as tired as I am. We'll both feel better in the morning."

"No. I have to leave." She slid her chair back from the table.

"At this hour?"

"Putting it off won't make it easier."

"You're not serious? After all we've been through? Look, Hannah, I need you now more than ever. I can't do this alone."

"Do what?"

"Change—get my life back. Make sense of everything that's happened. You're important to me. I depend upon you for what little stability I have left."

"I know that, but I can't stay here." My wife stood and carried her coffee mug to the sink.

"We can work this out," I pleaded. "I know we can."

"So you've said before, but nothing changes—nothing ever changes." She began scouring the blue porcelain mug with vigor.

"You're wrong. Something has changed. Something happened tonight. I feel different—here inside." I tapped the center of my chest, which was a mistake. I winced as the pain spread outward from where I had been punched.

"What happened? Did our rent money run out before you were good and thoroughly drunk?" She froze and stared into the darkness outside the window above the sink. "I'm sorry. I promised myself I wouldn't do that." She rinsed the soap off the mug.

"We did run out of money, but that's not why I'm sober. I experienced something, something that's hard to describe."

My wife froze for a moment. "We—"

"A fellow I met, a derelict. His name is Mace, I think, but this isn't about him. Please, come sit down. We need to talk. You were right about that."

"Talk about what?" Hannah spun to face me. Water from the mug splashed onto the patterned linoleum. "All we ever do is talk, if you call arguing talking. Do you think rehashing our marriage will change anything? Will dredging up the good old days make everything all right? Reliving the past fixes nothing, and I've had enough. I can't do this anymore."

The starch seemed to bleed out of her. Her shoulders sagged. She reached for the floral hand towel beside the sink and began drying the mug. Her weariness was evident in her green eyes.

Seeing her feel so depleted tore at my heart. "Don't you think I know how you feel? Believe me, I understand how hard this has been on you, having to live with losing everything: your furniture, home, possessions—everything you care about."

"What I care about is you. But yes, you're right, I have lost something. I've lost you. For eleven months now, you've closed yourself off. You keep me at arm's length, never let me inside. We've become strangers."

"It won't continue," I declared solemnly and meant every word.

"Right." Hannah returned the hand towel to its hook. She deposited the coffee mug in the cupboard near the stove. When she turned around again, our eyes met, and her beauty possessed my soul, like on homecoming night when we were first introduced. I recalled that moment and how captivated I had been…and still was. She was even more attractive in many respects because her beauty seemed to flow from within.

"You can't go," I said.

"Watch me."

"Then at least tell me why you're leaving. You said you wanted me to know."

Her demeanor eased a little. "I did say that, didn't I?"

"I could probably guess, but it might be best if you tell me the reasons."

Hannah sighed. "I suppose you're entitled." She returned to take her place at the table with her back to the window. The muted light fixture above the sink again haloed her head.

I raised a hand to interrupt her. "Before you begin, I think it's important for you to know that I still love you. Maybe I haven't said so in a long time, but I do. Hopefully, you'll keep that in mind."

"I know you love me, just as you know I love you. And that's why I'm leaving."

"What?" I found the notion incredible. "You're leaving because you love me? Seems an odd way to show it."

"I'm leaving because I can no longer stand by and watch you destroy yourself. I die a little every time you get into a fight, every time you come home drunk. Knowing the history of your troubles doesn't help. If you choose to commit slow suicide, so be it. That's your prerogative, but I won't be here to hold your hand, not for that. I can't. I don't have the strength. So, I need to let you go."

"You've thought this through, have you?"

"For weeks now, I've thought of nothing else."

I pondered her explanation. "Do you remember I told you that something changed tonight, that I feel different inside?" I touched her hand softly, letting my fingertips make only the slightest physical contact. She did not reciprocate, but neither did she draw her hand away, for which I was grateful. "Well, it's true. I won't even try to explain. I doubt that I could. But for the sake of everything we've meant to each other, everything we've shared, for all that's yet to come, I ask you to trust me in this. Please, I beg you. Give me one more chance. I will do better. I mean it. I mean it from the bottom of my heart."

Hannah tilted her head back and stared at the ceiling. "I knew this would happen. I could see it coming." Still, she left her hand in place. At the points where my fingers made contact, I sensed her resolve begin to weaken.

Encouraged, I continued, "I need you. It's as simple as that. Change doesn't come without purpose, without a reason to endure. If you leave…look, if I lose you, nothing will matter enough to make the struggle worthwhile."

I summoned every ounce of honesty within me and opened myself as completely as possible.

"You are my bones and my blood. Every breath I take is you. You are my truth. You are the reason I exist."

The pain and sorrow I had sequestered in the dark recesses of my being suddenly burst forth. Anxiety became panic, and a tidal wave of guilt tore my heart. I began to cry. Tears of lament flowed in torrents—not hesitant, uncertain drops, but terrible sobs filled with anguish. Grief seized my soul, and I wept bitterly.

"I am sorry!" I wailed. "I am so, so sorry. Forgive me, Hannah, please. Please forgive me."

She rose and moved to stand beside me. I angled my chair away from the table and blindly groped for my wife. She took my head and pressed it tightly against her. My arms circled her waist, and I clung to her in desperation. In that posture, we held each other while regret poured out of me in great rushes.

"It was not your fault," she said in a voice barely above a whisper. "You need to accept that it was not your fault."

Daylight trickled in through the flimsy curtains that barely covered the narrow window in our bedroom. Gradually, I came awake. Tatters of a dream lingered in my mind. I had been wandering through a deserted building with many rooms. Corridors branched in odd directions. I thought I knew where I was supposed to go, and it seemed vital that I get there, but the route kept shifting. Every hallway led away from my destination. The more I pressed forward, the more confused I became until I was hopelessly lost. I wanted to stop, but a sense of urgency drove me onward.

With a start, I realized I was lying in my own bed. For a moment, I could not recall how I had gotten there. Troubled by the gap in my memory, I shoved the last fragments of my dream aside and tried to concentrate. Details surfaced—I was seated at the kitchen table, unbearably distraught.

A tide of jumbled emotions came rushing back: sorrow, fear, humiliation—a deep regret. I struggled to sort them out but was hindered by dull feelings of physical distress. My whole body ached. A pounding discomfort had settled in behind my eyes. Snippets of conversation returned. Then I recalled that Hannah had announced she was leaving. The memory jolted me fully awake. I reached for her, but my hand found only empty bedding. Steeling myself against the throbbing, I turned my head to look. The sheets and blanket on her side of the bed were smooth and undisturbed. She had declined to join me in slumber.

I eased my legs over the edge of the bed and sat up. The world swam in front of my eyes. I buried my face in my hands. My wife was gone, and I was alone. At that moment, I truly wanted to die. I would have sat there forever, except a full bladder compelled me to action.

When I stepped to the closet to fetch my robe, I noticed my coat neatly draped on a hanger. The hole in the lapel had been mended and most of the soot removed. My wife had done a credible restoration job, though a few singed fibers testified to the heat of the blaze I had battled.

"A goodbye gift," I muttered hoarsely. Hannah's parting act of kindness redoubled my sense of loss.

As I stumbled to the bathroom, I passed the apartment's second bedroom, which we had converted into a studio for Hannah's sculpting. My wife's latest creation caught my attention. About three feet high, an exquisite marble statue sat on her workbench. As her eyesight had dimmed, her senses of touch and proportion had increased. I paused to admire the angelic cherub. With wings outstretched and arms extended toward heaven, the little angel gazed upward as if longing to return home. To my mind, a slight parting of the lips, the faintly fissured brow, and the doleful gaze perfectly captured an expression of childlike lament. It was Hannah's finest work, and it was nearly finished.

The diminutive angel on Hannah's workbench awakened a glimmer of hope within me. She would never abandon a piece into which she had poured so much of herself, and that meant, in the near future, I would be seeing her again.

My spirits lifted, but only a little. I entered the bathroom to empty my bladder. Stepping out of the bathroom, I was greeted by a vision that filled me with optimism. My wife was seated on the living room couch in the same posture as the night before. I had been so engrossed in my sorrows that I had failed to notice. Or perhaps I hadn't seen her because I hadn't expected her to be there.

She wore the same plaid shirt and denim jeans. Viewed in profile, the dusky circles under her eyes spoke of tears shed during a sleepless night. She did not acknowledge my presence but continued gazing at the blank living room wall, lost in thought.

"You're still here," I noted, unable to conjure up anything more compelling. Stating the obvious was a talent I had inherited from my mother's side of the family. Even so, uttering banalities seemed preferable to mutely gawking from the doorway.

"I couldn't just leave. I had to make sure you were okay."

I glanced toward the kitchen. "Have you eaten? What time is it?"

"No, and I don't know."

"You're still angry. I thought we… Last night, didn't I say I was sorry?"

"I heard every word you said, and that's a big part of the problem. I was all prepared for you to dance around the issues like always. But no, you had to…. It wasn't what I expected. Anyway, I'm not angry. I hurt. There's a difference."

"Yes, there is. Did you sleep?"

"I couldn't." Hannah gave me a look that declared her insomnia was my fault, yet her manner seemed a little less edgy.

"Mind if I sit down?" A chill pierced the thin fabric of my robe, and my bare feet were cold, but I was loathe to return to the bedroom to finish dressing, not with her suitcase still packed and waiting in the kitchen.

A look of consternation furrowed Hannah's brow. "What did you mean when you said something has changed, that you felt different inside? How can you expect me to believe that one minute you're a self-abasing drunk, and the next you're this new person? Pardon my skepticism, but it doesn't compute."

I stepped forward to indicate the vacant end of the couch. "May I?"

Hannah shrugged her consent.

I snuggled up against the armrest, hugged both arms to my chest, and covered one foot with the other for warmth. "Do you remember when I first mentioned going into business for myself in graduate school? Remember how eager I was to start my own architectural firm and how I was convinced that Heartland Designs would succeed? You laughed when I boasted I could read the future, but my dream was real, and I knew it. I knew that I could make it happen if I applied myself. Well, whatever this thing that came upon me last night is, it's like that, except in a negative way and more intense. It was a warning. I was shown what I'm becoming, and it scared the hell out of me. I do not want to be that person—worthless and empty."

"Justin, you have so much potential. Even now, you could have a great future, yet you insist on throwing it all away. You can't blame yourself forever. It's high time you put the tragedy behind you. People died. Yes, it was terrible, but get over it. Get on with your life. I miss you. I want you back, and I believe in you. I believe you can do anything you set your mind to. Sometimes you amaze me. I wish I had a fraction of your talent."

"What are you talking about? With your sculpting, you create beauty in ways that are beyond me."

"This isn't about me. What I'm saying is you need to go to work. You need a job. Do something that will challenge your skills. Maybe it won't be designing buildings. Maybe that phase of your life is over, but you can be productive again."

"That's what I'm trying to tell you. It's what I want; I know I can make it happen. I can see it. By the way, do we have any aspirin? My head is about to explode."

"No doubt, considering all the booze you swill." Hannah winced as if stung by a twinge of conscience. "Sorry. You're not the only one who's picked up some bad habits. There may be some aspirin in the medicine cabinet. Would you like me to look?"

"No. I can get it." I rose to my feet. "While I'm up, do you want anything?"

"A glass of water—if you don't mind."

"Water? Wouldn't you rather have coffee?" I said.

"There isn't any."

"Really?!" The prospect of suffering a hangover without caffeine intensified my depression. I shuffled into the kitchen.

After fetching a glass of water for my wife, I set off to locate the aspirin. Luckily, the bottle I found contained a few flaky tablets. I refrained from checking the expiration date since I didn't care. They disintegrated when I spilled them into my palm.

Hanna was in the kitchen when I trudged back into the living room. I joined her there. My stomach heaved at the thought of food, but as I drew near, I noticed that, rather than fixing breakfast, Hannah was standing beside the kitchen table, waiting for me.

She indicated a stack of envelopes and other papers arranged in a neat pile on the table's glass surface. "I think that's all of them."

"All of what?"

"Our unpaid bills, overdue notices. Here's the checkbook, for what it's worth. There's nothing in our account."

"Why do I need this stuff?"

"You're the bookkeeper now."

"What are you saying?"

"I'm saying I can't stay."

"I thought we settled this last night. You're my wife. I need you. I can't put it any more plainly than that."

"And what if you don't keep your word? What if this is all talk, like before? Don't you see? If you disappoint me again, you'll lose me forever. I love you too much to keep watching you fail."

"That hurt."

"I'm sorry, but it's true."

Due to my wounded pride, I was about to turn away but stopped myself. I spread my hands. "Look, you just told me you believe in me. If you mean what you say, why leave?"

"Because I need proof. You'll have to show me you're different, not just say it."

"The truth is you don't trust me."

"I can't afford to trust you. I care for you too much to watch our marriage slowly die. I want you to succeed with all my heart, but you'll have to take the first steps yourself."

A ray of morning light shone through the window to touch Hannah's green eyes, evoking a sparkle.

Instantaneously, I was transported back to an Easter morning when we were still attending church. I had noticed that same sparkle during the sunrise service, just as the sun had peeked over a low mountain ridge. I recalled the air being crisp, clear, and cold enough for puffs of vapor to annotate our conversation. Hannah had stood half facing me as she was now. The jade-green glint in her eyes had literally taken my breath away. She was then, and still was, the only woman I have ever truly loved, but her mind seemed to be made up.

I could tell this was an argument I wouldn't win, and there was no point in discussing the matter further. There had been occasions in our marriage when Hannah had stood her ground, refusing to relent on issues that, for her, were nonnegotiable. Early on, I had opposed her on principle alone, secure in the precision of my own opinions. The horrific arguments that ensued had nearly torn us apart. I was not about to make that mistake again.

"No," I said flatly. "I'll go. Not you. You stay here. I'll move out."

Hannah seemed taken aback, as if forced to contemplate an option not previously imagined. "You?" she exclaimed with a look of concern. "Where will you go?"

"I don't know. Where were you planning on going?"

Neither of us came from close-knit families. Hannah's parents, like mine, had died years ago. After the fire, the few family members left to us refused to even acknowledge our existence, an attitude we had reluctantly supported, thinking it would be unfortunate for our problems to become theirs. The upshot was that, by choice, we were virtual orphans.

Hannah stated defiantly, "I had planned on looking for a job."

"So will I. Where were you going to stay?"

"Probably with a friend."

"I don't have any friends," I admitted quietly, "certainly none I like enough to live with. But don't worry, I'll find a place. I'll be okay."

Hannah tugged on an earlobe as she regarded me.

"Look," I said, nodding toward the second bedroom, "your studio is here. You're settled in. It will be easier for me to move out. Besides, you can still get a job if you choose."

"Oh, so now you approve?" Even from the first days of our marriage, Hannah had never worked. I had always insisted that a husband's duty was to provide for his wife. Relying on a spouse's income had seemed unmanly, demeaning.

"Circumstances change," I declared. "Anyway, you won't have to work unless you want to since I'll soon be paying the rent. Besides, we both know your vision is a problem."

"You think I won't be able to find work. I can function as well as you can, thank you."

"Easy. All I'm saying is I know this neighborhood. You don't. Out on the street, it's not like you'd imagine. We don't have the same genteel neighbors we had in Manchester." I pointed toward the morning brightness beyond the kitchen window. "Out there, people will cut you for a pair of shoes. If they find you bleeding in the gutter, they'll pick your pockets and laugh as they walk away."

"I don't believe the risks are as great as you say. Sure, there may be a few bad individuals, but people are fundamentally good."

"Not around here, they're not. Trust me, I've seen it. One night, I watched three young punks rough up a bum. They hurt him just for kicks. I've watched gangs go at one another with two-by-fours spiked with ten-penny nails. You're nowhere near being prepared to deal with that kind of carnage."

"And I suppose you are?"

"Better than you, that's for sure. If you're determined that we're going to live apart, then I'm the one who's going to move out. Besides, after I'm back on my feet, I'll know where to find you."

I tried to fashion an encouraging smile but widely missed the mark, judging by Hannah's reaction. She seemed deeply troubled. Perhaps for the first time, the subtler ramifications of her decision were becoming apparent. I wanted to say, "Is this truly necessary? Is it essential that we go through with this?" But I knew what her answer would be. She was not about to relent.

I stepped around the table and took hold of my wife's hands. "I can do this. This isn't the end of us. It may even be for the best. I don't know. I guess we'll find out. But I do know that I love you, and I will come back to you. I promise."

When she did not resist, I took her in my arms and kissed her. Her body pressed against me, and I felt myself start to respond. The lapels of my robe gaped open.

"No," Hannah said, forcefully pushing me away, smoothing her hands down the front of her plaid shirt. "Not now."

"That means someday soon, maybe?"

"That depends."

"On what? Never mind. I get it. If that's the case, I'd best get to it." I drew my robe closed and turned toward the bedroom.

I was about to exit the kitchen when Hannah volunteered, "You'll need the suitcase. We only have the one, remember? Dump my things on the bed. I'll put them away later."

I looked down at the battered valise on the floor by the door. "Thanks for the offer, but no."

"Aren't you taking your things?"

"Nope. I'm going to make a completely fresh start," I declared with a show of bravado. "That way, you'll know I'm serious." I turned away again. "It will be a completely new beginning." *Besides, if things work out the way I hope, I won't be gone all that long.* I kept that comment to myself, not wanting to seem overly optimistic. Besides, my penitence might take longer than expected. Who could know?

"Wait!" Hannah exclaimed. "I have an idea."

I halted and turned expectantly.

"You mentioned looking for work."

My heart sank. "That's right. Priority one."

"What about your friend Ike? What's his last name?"

"Roosevelt?"

"Right, Ike Roosevelt. He owes you. He wouldn't be in the construction business if you hadn't helped him. Maybe he has something you could do."

Isaiah Tyrell Roosevelt was the blackest man I have ever known. He stood six feet three inches tall and weighed 235 pounds, all muscle. He had started his career swinging a hammer. I first encountered

Ike when our framing carpenter failed to show up for work. In a bind, I had recruited Ike to finish building the home I had designed.

In bright sunlight, Ike had the appearance of an obsidian monolith. His laugh was rolling thunder. It hadn't taken long for us to become close friends. Later, I had loaned him enough to launch his own construction company. In gratitude, he had sent clients my way whenever he could. Through hard work and perseverance, his firm had become a going concern. After the fire, our relationship had soured.

"Ike won't help me, I'm afraid."

"How do you know?"

"Because I've already been in touch. His crews are convinced I'm a jinx. If he hires me, they'll quit."

"He told you that?"

"He also told me to stay away. He said he was grateful for how I helped him, but there was nothing he could do, and he hoped never to see me again. Far as Ike is concerned, we're quits."

"He said that?"

"Close enough to his exact words."

"Why didn't you share this before?"

"Why do you think? If one of your best friends tells you to take a hike, it's not something to brag about."

"But I'm your wife. See what I mean about shutting me out?"

"Right, and now you're telling me to take a hike, but it's okay." I held up both hands to show her I meant no offense. "I have no intention of losing you like I did Ike. We will work this out. You'll see."

Before Hannah could respond, I disappeared into the bathroom to take a quick shower. As I was getting dressed, I thought about what lay ahead. It then occurred to me there was a name for people who found themselves in my predicament—homeless.

CHAPTER 4

Late in the afternoon on the day I moved out, I stood in a small clearing on the western side of Monroe Creek, watching a trickle of water meander along the channel six feet below. The creek's opposite bank rose sharply to a tall bluff from which the citizens of Logan Heights could gaze down upon the stain of Branford Gardens.

Dusk was approaching. Tiny wavelets reflected the violet hues of sunset. I imagined the stream in the wet season, swollen with run-off from streets and rooftops. After a rainless summer, only dry rocks bleached slate gray by the sun lined the nearly empty watercourse—a few shallow pools glimmered like fragments of a broken mirror.

Poplars, ash, and dogwood trees guarded the creek's banks in uneven thickets. Dead branches and leaves lay rotting on the ground. The duff was half a foot thick in some places, having lain undisturbed for decades or longer. Away from the creek, clusters of trees gave way to tangles of weeds.

Monroe Creek bounded the far edge of the vacant lot across from what was now Hannah's apartment. The creek served as the hypotenuse of a right-angle triangle, with Lois Avenue and Beach Street forming the northern and western edges, respectively. All told, the weed-infested lot measured three acres in size, though from an architectural point of view, the vertices were essentially worthless. Yet, if properly developed, the plot had enormous potential. I again imagined structures that would complement the lot's geometry.

When I realized I was daydreaming, I mentally kicked myself. Those days were gone. Wasting time on useless fantasies was more than foolish. Soon, it would be too dark to see. I would be out in the open without a protected place to spend the night. I might not freeze to death, but the chill in the air promised that I would pass the night battling to stay warm rather than logging some much-needed sleep.

Picking my steps carefully, I advanced to the midpoint of the nearly invisible footpath that paralleled the creek, mindful to avoid roots and snags that tried to trip me. Along the way, I recognized a variety of plants. Musk thistles competed with clumps of saw grass for sun-favored patches of ground. In the fading sunlight, multiflora rose clashed with purple loosestrife, though their petals appeared washed out and gray.

I turned toward the center of the lot and began pressing deeper into the urban jungle, feeling my way with my feet as I went. I planned to build a nest. I would fashion a blanket of weeds, using layers of foliage as a covering. The surrounding growth would block the wind. I pictured myself curled up in a leafy cocoon and tried not to worry about the bugs and critters that might become my bedmates.

Admittedly, it was a terrible idea, but with night closing in, my options were few. Besides, my strategy wasn't entirely without merit. By stationing myself across the street from my wife's front door, I could keep an eye out for trouble. Burglaries and worse were common in Branford Gardens. Hannah would make an easy target for anyone who learned I had moved out.

I thrust my hand into my pocket. The four-bladed folding knife was still there, a small but precious treasure. As a weapon of defense, it lacked authority. A stiletto or fixed-blade hunting knife would have afforded superior protection, but a pocketknife was better than nothing. With one long and one short blade, plus a hooked can opener, and a thin screwdriver that could double as a pick or leather punch, the handy tool offered proof that my day hadn't been a complete waste.

While shortcutting through an alley in my quest to find gainful employment, I chanced upon a roll of electrical tape lying discarded near a dumpster. The find had brought to mind a woman I had previously met, a denizen of the streets who trundled her life around in a shopping cart. She had constantly complained that the cart's cold metal handle troubled her arthritic fingers.

Upon tracking the woman down, I had convinced her to swap my roll of tape for one of the cheap watches she wore. After popping the watch's crystal to clean its face and polishing the leather strap with a dab of 30-weight from a discarded can of oil, I had been tempted to keep the watch since it now appeared nearly new. However, watch in hand, I had tracked down a derelict who owned three pocketknives, the most rusted of which was now in my possession, though it, too, had cleaned up nicely.

As I inched forward, my foot impacted what I thought was a chunk of concrete. As I went to step over it, I nearly pitched head-long into a deep pit. If not for a stand of Japanese stiltgrass I grabbed reflexively, I would've broken my neck.

Squatting down, I discovered that I stood atop a concrete wall. Below me, a deserted basement opened like a giant black craw wait-ing to swallow anything that stumbled into it. Like jumbled tooth-picks, collapsed beams and fallen timbers filled most of the space.

How had I failed to notice the anomaly while gazing out of my kitchen window? Hannah's kitchen window, to be precise. As I puzzled out the structure's design, the reason became apparent. A large portion of the empty space lay concealed beneath what, at one time, must have been the building's main floor. Accumulated soil and debris had created a covering layer several inches thick. As with the rest of the lot, weeds had taken root, shrouding the ruins under a tangle of verdant camouflage.

I grinned from ear to ear, pleased with my immense good for-tune. I now had a place to spend the night. Hastily, I looked around to see if anyone nearby had noticed. The sidewalks bore the usual foot traffic, returning laborers hastened along by the approaching dinner hour. Down the street, a group of kids played kick the can. A block farther on, four men loitered at a bus stop, sharing a joint and berating life in general. Otherwise, the areas surrounding the vacant lot seemed devoid of human activity.

I searched to see if I could find a way down. Then, I noticed two thick timbers positioned side by side, creating a ramp. Some one-by-fours, nailed down irregularly, served as steps for the precarious ladder. I wasn't the first vagrant to envision turning the abandoned basement into a subterranean shelter. Then it occurred to me that the previous occupant might return. How would they feel about sharing their hideaway? I was too exhausted to care. I needed rest. My joints ached, especially my knees and ankles, having walked uncounted miles searching for work. Blisters stung both heels, and the little food I had procured had long been consumed.

The slanted timbers seemed stout enough to support my 185 pounds. Still, I proceeded cautiously, firmly gripping the concrete lip and transferring only a little weight at a time.

As I eased my way down, I remembered that after boasting I would start with nothing, I had found myself on the sidewalk with precisely that, nothing—no friends, money, tools, clean clothes, food, phone, utensils, transportation, urban survival skills. Not even a plan of attack. With nowhere to go, I had set off, confident in the knowledge that if I were to walk in expanding circles, I would eventually chance upon an opportunity, and I was right.

After hours spent pestering shopkeepers and offering to do whatever was needed, the urge to empty my bladder had taken me to a filling station. The attendant, hoping to silence my whining, had relented and produced a key. The men's restroom, I soon discovered, was filthy.

Swallowing what little pride was left to me, I'd volunteered to clean up the mess for ten bucks. After some serious haggling, I agreed to do the men's and women's restrooms for five. The wage wasn't much, but it afforded me a little nourishment from Emile's Market. A loaf of bread and a brick of cheese had gotten me through the day. Though filling, the edibles were now a memory, and the gnawing hunger had returned.

When I stepped away from the makeshift ladder's bottom rung, something cold and wet oozed up through the hole in my shoe. Enough of a glow from the city's lights filtered through an opening above my head, and I could see I was standing in a shallow puddle. Groundwater had seeped up through the concrete. I stepped aside and looked around. Objects more than a foot away were swaddled in darkness. Perhaps my next trade item should be a pocket flashlight or a candle, which reminded me of my intention to scrounge another box of matches.

I called out softly, "Anyone down here?"

Happily, no one answered.

Arms extended, I eased forward, ducking beneath and stepping over fallen joists and rafters. Within a few feet, the way became impassable, forcing me to wrestle a large plank aside to open a hole while worrying that the interlocked structure might collapse on my head. And what about spiders, snakes, or rats? The closest medical care was twenty minutes away by bus, not that I could afford the fare. If bitten or otherwise wounded, Providence and good fortune would have to serve as my physicians—not an encouraging prospect.

With exceeding caution, I slipped through the hole I had created. The clutter thinned out beneath the remnants of the floor above, which I discovered by sense of touch alone. The intact floor overhead shrouded everything in a curtain of blackness. Virtually blind, I shuffled forward until I encountered a wall. Then, I tracked my way toward the corner farthest from the ramp. My hand groped empty shelves. Little else was recognizable.

A sharp pain evoked a yelp when I banged my shin against a raised platform. Bending down and exploring with my hands, I sensed that someone had constructed what seemed to be a sleeping pallet in the corner. Perhaps Providence and good fortune were reliable companions after all. A sheet of plywood rested atop a rickety assemblage of studs and four-by-fours. Not quite level and festooned with splinters, the bed was at least dry and sheltered from the elements. I thought about gathering weeds to serve as a blanket but then cast the idea aside since it would entail negotiating the maze again.

Instead, I lay down, shifting my body cautiously and hoping the platform would support my weight. As I curled into a fetal position,

I detected an odor that sparked a sense of alarm. The distinctive tang of soot and ashes mingled with the musk of decay.

In panic, I sat up and looked around, quickly realizing that what I had smelled was the lingering aftermath of the fire that had filled the basement with charred debris.

A rush of terror drove me to my feet. Blindly surging toward the ramp, I tripped over a chunk of rubble. Tragic images flooded my mind. My hands began to shake. Sprawled face down, my only thought was to flee.

With increasing panic, I started to rise. As I got to my knees, I suddenly recalled my promise to Hanna, my brave assertion that I would change—that I would make a new beginning.

Failure was unacceptable, especially on my first day.

I deliberately slowed my breathing and willed the searing visions to leave my mind. My stomach roiled. I nearly vomited. Silencing the screams echoing in my ears proved most difficult, but after a while, I could stand.

Shaken, I returned to the sleeping pallet and lay down again. A shiver ran through me. My refuge no longer felt secure. A sense of vulnerability had invaded the basement. Exposed and defenseless, I struggled to close my eyes.

Childhood images sprang forth as I hunted for a distraction from my terrors. I saw my father, strong and supportive, but aloof; my mother, kind and protective, but oblivious to other people's sensibilities. The deeper I descended, the more sharply defined the memories became. Patterns emerged from my early years. I pursued trails of cause and effect and relived choices that had defined the paths I would follow. Above all, I sought to understand how I had sunk to such a wretched state of existence.

Try as I might, I could piece together no explanation for the misery I was now forced to endure, except perhaps for the one transgression, the momentary lapse that even now I had trouble admitting to myself.

Could the world be that cruel? I wondered. Would God condemn a man for a single mistake?

No doubt I deserved my fate, but why should the fire's victims suffer for my lapse? I refused to accept that random chance had played any part in the equation. That innocents could suffer and die for my failures seemed a violation of all notions of justice and fair play.

With the lingering question "Why?" nagging me and the answers floating just out of reach, I eventually fell asleep.

The following day, I sat on Hannah's front porch and faced the eastern horizon. A line of clouds drifted above the bluffs, threatening rain. Bits of sunrise slid through gaps in Logan Heights' serrated skyline. A single shaft of illumination touched the vacant lot where I had spent the night. A rainbow, born from a thin layer of ground fog, winked out of existence as shifting clouds sealed the breach. I blinked in amazement, startled by such fleeting beauty.

Almost certainly, Hannah was still asleep; both the kitchen and studio windows were dark. Or she had awakened even earlier than I had and had gone out to search for work. Though possible, that scenario seemed unlikely.

Upon arising, a sense of loneliness had taken root in my soul. I missed sitting and talking as we had when we first married. Apparently, sleeping apart leads you to appreciate the way things used to be. I especially wanted to know how her day had gone and learn about her experiences. Some conversations, which initially seemed so casual, become dearer in retrospect. Physical intimacy is much the same.

The cold concrete step upon which I sat seemed determined to leach all the warmth out of my backside, but I was too stiff and sore to stand while I planned my day. Soft chairs and comfortable beds are for homebodies, not for vagrants huddled in cinderblock caves.

I flexed my back and stretched, only to be rewarded by a cramp beneath my shoulder blade. I added soft bedding to a rapidly expanding wish list.

After settling in, the previous night had passed without calamity. Upon awakening, I was more than a little pleased to find that I wasn't buried beneath mounds of rubble, frozen stiff, or the hapless victim of a murderous psychopath. I felt pretty good, except for a horrendous thirst and so many aches and pains that for a moment, I tried to recall if I'd been run over by a train.

Most impressive of all was the satisfaction that had lifted my spirits. Not only had I survived, but my first day as a nomad had proven that I could adapt and, therefore, could expect to endure whatever lay ahead.

I fished in my pocket for the gold locket and chain I had discovered inside a tortoiseshell box. The box had been unearthed when I had shifted the beam aside in the dark. A third the size of a brick, the ornate jewelry box was the sort of keepsake a young woman of means might value.

Curious as to the origins of the treasure box, I noted the rainbow colors that darted across its surface as I studied its workmanship. Careful not to damage the fragile mechanism, I had picked the simple lock with my new pocketknife. Inside, I had found several treasures: a rhinestone-studded comb, a ring inset with a small blue gem, what appeared to be a house key, and the locket and chain I now held in my hand.

The comb and ring would become handy trade items. The key was probably worthless, the door it opened having been no doubt destroyed by fire. The box I would keep to contain my own treasures, if any happened to come my way. But the locket and chain were something special.

I pressed the locket's tiny latch to open its clamshell halves again and reveal the face of a strikingly handsome woman in her late teens or early twenties. Her formal hairstyle, combined with the monochrome image's faded sepia tones, suggested that the miniature portrait was quite old.

Abandoned and forgotten after the fire, the box must have lain amid the rubble for decades. But why hadn't the heat damaged its contents? Perhaps it had escaped the blaze above by being sequestered in the basement. Whatever the reason, the photograph in the locket was intact. More than that, the image had captured my imagination.

I appreciate a pretty face the same as the next man, but my attraction to the photograph wasn't physical. Instead, I felt drawn to understand the woman's character and would have gladly discussed my fascination with my wife had recent events unfolded differently.

The young woman's aristocratic brow, strong cheekbones, and finely curved lips spoke of good breeding, perhaps regal. Displayed only from the shoulders up, I tried to imagine how she had stationed herself—back straight, hands in her lap. Her complexion seemed unblemished, and only the sadness in her eyes betrayed what I sensed was an air of gentle serenity.

Rather than directly facing the camera, her head was slightly turned, as if attending to sorrows only she could see. Her air of patient acceptance made her appear more experienced than her years. What hardships had she known? How had she come to possess such equanimity? More than that, I wondered if she had gained the answers to those same questions that haunted me. Serenity is often reserved for those who have weathered the struggles of a full life.

Admittedly, I was enthralled. Sitting there on the apartment building's front steps, I experienced a pang of regret. I would never have an opportunity to get to know the lovely young woman.

A flicker of movement jerked me out of my reverie. I looked to the south.

Thirty yards away, a man was rapidly striding in my direction, though he seemed unaware of my presence. Head down and shoulders hunched against the cold, he advanced purposefully, his gaze fixed upon an imaginary spot three feet ahead. Rather than warming his hands in the pockets of his tan windbreaker, he held them at chest level where his fingers traced repetitive patterns.

I snapped the locket shut, scooped up the dangling chain, and put both in my pocket.

His trimmed mustache and beard were dark brown like the man's neatly parted hair. My impression was that he had grown the facial hair to add years to his youthful appearance. Also, I noticed his lips were moving. His intense expression suggested he was engaged in a hot debate with himself.

Great, I thought, *another crazy headed in my direction*. Heaven knows, I had crossed paths with a remarkable number of psychiatrically challenged people since moving to Branford Gardens. Yet this man seemed out of place, except perhaps for his cross-trainers. Even dudes who can't afford their rent will splurge on a pair of cool tennies.

The man's tan slacks and pale blue dress shirt, with its button-down collar, seemed appropriate for a midlevel executives' luncheon, not for Branford Gardens. Even his sneakers appeared to be oddly out of place. Too new, I decided. There were no broken-down heels or holes in the toes; the laces weren't frayed.

Mace came to mind. I wondered how he was doing.

As the man drew near where I sat, I recognized that he held a rosary as he conducted his religious rites with practiced proficiency. After uttering a final Hail Mary, he raised the artifact to his lips and kissed the crucifix. When he went to deposit the rosary in the side pocket of his windbreaker, he missed. It fell to the pavement, unnoticed.

Alternating blue and white beads on a silver chain caught the violet hues of the morning. The chain and crucifix looked silver, and the beads were perhaps lapis lazuli and ivory. Anyway, the thing had to be expensive, and I was sorely tempted to remain inert until the man had disappeared from view. Holding my breath, I imagined what I might buy with the money a pawn shop would offer.

A conscience is a strange beast. Like a gross in-law, it always shows up when it can do the most harm. Troubled by my avarice and ashamed, I said, "Hey, man, you dropped your beads."

Startled, the man missed a step and nearly stumbled but recovered athletically. He turned to face me, eyes wide. Then his eyes narrowed, as if troubled by having failed to sense my presence.

"Excuse me?" he said.

I pointed. "It fell out of your pocket."

"Oh, heavens!" the man exclaimed as he hastily returned to retrieve his property. He carefully examined each bead in detail, his fingers testing for scrapes and imperfections. After inspecting the rosary, he said quietly, "It was a gift from a family friend when I was very young."

After returning the rosary to his coat pocket, ensuring it was secure, he looked to where I sat. "Thank you. Some things are far more valuable than the money it takes to replace them."

"How true," I agreed with an affirmative nod. "You live around here?"

"It's the clothes, right? I've been getting that a lot lately. People assume I'm from somewhere else. I just rented an apartment over on Octavia. I guess I haven't mastered the art of blending in. My name is Samuel, Samuel O'Bryan." He stepped forward to extend his hand.

I leaned down to return the handshake. His fingers were cold as ice, but his skin was free of calluses and his grip firm, not the hand of a day laborer.

"Justin Moore."

"Nice to meet you, Justin. Thanks again."

"Anytime," I said with modest bluster, as if such displays of honesty were an everyday occurrence. In truth, I was having trouble shedding my disquiet for having passed up the windfall that could have been mine.

Samuel's gaze traveled down Beach Street toward Westridge Boulevard. Sadness and disgust sullied his countenance. "I was born not far from here, you know. Dad moved our family when I was three. I have a few memories, but the neighborhood has changed a lot. It's not what I expected to find when I decided to return." He pivoted to face me. "What about you? You live here?" His attention shifted to the building behind me.

"Second floor." I hooked a thumb toward the apartment where I assumed Hannah was still asleep. It was a small lie, hardly worthy of the embarrassment I experienced. Yet a minor distortion of the truth seemed preferable to admitting that my new abode was the pit across the street.

"Justin, do you like sports? Basketball? I ask because, on Wednesday mornings, some guys I know get together at St. Anthony's. Maybe you'd care to join us for a quick game?"

"It's been a long time since I dribbled a ball. Even then, I wasn't very good. I'll pass, thanks."

"They let me play, and I'm lousy. You might enjoy yourself. They're good guys—if you're not too busy." He regarded the concrete porch with its drab railing.

"No thanks." A thought suddenly struck me. "You mentioned your apartment is over on Octavia, and you're headed to St. Anthony's. Aren't you taking the long way round?"

Samuel gestured toward the trees and tangled foliage along the banks of Monroe Creek. "The autumn colors remind me of the Iowa farm where I grew up. Being close to nature helps me prepare my mind for my devotions."

"That explains the rosary. You're a religious man."

"I prefer to think of myself as spiritual."

"There's a difference?"

"Oh, absolutely—form versus substance."

"Okay. So," I said hastily, hoping to avoid discussing religion, "what is it you do here in Branford Gardens?"

"I'm the new priest at St. Anthony's." Samuel's grin revealed an even row of very white teeth.

An hour later, I found myself in Father Samuel O'Bryan's office, doing my best to appear at ease, though it felt odd addressing a man several years my junior as Father.

Surrounded by weathered brick buildings, St. Anthony's Catholic Church stood out as an architectural anomaly, a neo-Gothic throwback to an age when stone carvings were intended to remind parishioners of the terrors of hell. Gargoyles, demons, and denizens glowered down from the eaves, hideous snarls warning of God's impending judgment of the unfaithful. Massive blocks of granite formed the church's base. Ribbed vaults, fluted columns, and flying buttresses soared upward, a masonry exoskeleton supporting a jumble of ornate frescoes.

The cramped office in which I now sat seemed no less medieval. I might have imagined myself in a monk's cell, except for the apparent luxuries like the gold pen and pencil set mounted on Haveli black marble from India, the top-of-the-line laptop on the maple desk, and the high-back executive chair done in red Corinthian leather, from which Father Samuel regarded me expectantly.

I had agreed to accompany the priest to his office because he had offered to help me find work. As he had explained, a member of St. Anthony's parish, one Yuri Something or Other, had tweaked his back, and his employer was threatening to replace him unless a temp could be found to finish the carpentry project he had started. Somehow, the good father had cajoled me into revealing I had once worked in the construction trades—the man had a knack for putting people at ease. He had suggested that I apply for Yuri's position without knowing anything else about me, which he was now about to do on my behalf. The position was temporary, not permanent, a point the priest had stressed repeatedly. Yuri would want his job back once he had recovered.

When I nodded in the affirmative, the priest tapped a number into his state-of-the-art cell phone.

I tried not to listen while Father Samuel negotiated with the party on the other end of the line, not that cell phones have lines. Instead, I scanned titles on his bookshelf and diplomas on his wall: a bachelor's degree in psychology from Tarver Bible College in Topeka, Kansas, and a master of divinity from Tarver Seminary. There was also a certificate for being honorably discharged from the navy and a fair number of scholastic commendations.

Noting dates, I realized the navy tour had come before his college years. Altogether, it seemed a lot of living for a man who, according to my calculations, was still on the youthful side of thirty.

Reminded of college, the image of a sea of green grass sprang up before my eyes. Father Samuel's diplomas brought to mind the seven years I had spent at the Stonefield Institute of Technology—four to earn a bachelor of architecture and three more for my master's.

I pictured the institute's broad lawns that extended out behind the dorms, a great place to study on spring days. I recalled how Hannah and I had crammed for semester finals, lounging on an old patchwork quilt, both doing our best to keep our minds on our studies. I also pictured graduation day and how Hannah, my newly pledged fiancée, had adjusted my mortarboard and smoothed the shoulders of my gown before bestowing a good luck kiss on my lips. She had seemed so proud, but so was I, truth be told.

The prospects for our future had seemed so bright, despite being deeply in debt with student loans. By mutual consent, we had agreed that I should work construction and forego taking a position as a junior partner with one of the architectural firms that had come a-courting. That way, we figured, we could save enough in a year to get married, which was how things had worked out.

After two years of grueling labor in the trades and having finally set enough aside, I launched Heartland Designs. Finally, I could do what I loved: create magnificent buildings, which had been my dream for as long as I could remember.

But that dream was now in ashes. Never again would I work as an architect. The future Hannah and I had planned was gone, incinerated along with Liberty Tower One.

Gouts of orange flame sprang up from the embers of my memories. Screams, faint at first, rose in a crescendo of terror. I felt my grip on reality slipping away. Desperately, I fought to drive the apparitions from my sight. I balled my fists and, through clenched teeth, hissed, "Not this time."

"Are you sure? Sounds like a sweet opportunity."

The question startled me. Disoriented, I looked at the priest, eyeing me with concern from behind his desk. His right hand covered the mouthpiece of his cell phone. "You okay?" he said.

"Sorry—somewhere else. What did you say?"

"I asked if you could start today."

"Start what?"

"Harwood Manor—the construction project?"

It took a moment for his words to sink in. He was offering me a job. "Sure," I blurted out. "Why not?"

"Great."

The priest returned to his phone conversation, leaving me to puzzle out how my life was about to change again. Still dealing with the horrors, I strove to focus on the present and let the past dissipate like wisps of smoke. For the moment, it seemed to work.

The thought of being employed again made me uneasy. If the opportunity panned out, it could mark a new beginning. If so, Hannah would be overjoyed. Yet there was still one hurdle to clear.

I waited until Father Samuel ended his call, and before he could speak, I interjected, "You don't recognize me, do you?"

He hesitated as if thumbing through his mental archives. "No. Should I?"

"You mentioned that you'd just moved back to your old neighborhood. About a year ago, something happened. There was a fire—people died. For a time, the authorities claimed it was my fault. A lot of folks are convinced I should've gone to jail. Most of the rest don't want to be around me. Vouching for me might not be such a good idea. I thought you should know if you wanted to call that person back." I thrust my chin toward his cell phone. "I had to mention it. You would've found out eventually."

"Does this fire have anything to do with your being able to saw wood or hammer nails?"

"It might, depending on the attitude of the person you were talking to."

The leather padding of the priest's chair creaked as he leaned back and stroked his beard. "In that regard, I think we're okay. The person I was speaking to, by the way, is Greta Lonergan, nursing supervisor at Harwood Manor. From what Yuri has told me, she's strict about people obeying the rules and knows how to pinch a penny, but apparently, she's also a pragmatist, judging from our conversation. Perhaps you heard me tell her that if she hires you, the church will tap into its hardship fund, eliminating Slowiki's need to file a workman's comp claim."

"In truth, I wasn't paying attention. Why are you doing this? You just admitted you don't know me."

"I know you're honest"—Father Samuel fished the rosary out of his coat pocket and held it up—"for which I am most grateful. I also know you need money." He allowed his gaze to take note of the sad state of my shabby clothing. "And I know by your demeanor that you've seen better times. No doubt you'd like to see them again. The Church is about repentance and forgiveness. Forgiveness is what I offer. The repentance part is up to you, but that's a topic for another day. Look, do you want this job or not?"

"What, specifically, would I be doing?"

"Well, yes, I imagine that would be important to know. Harwood Manor is a skilled nursing facility and an old folks' home. From what I understand, Yuri has designed an exit ramp for their solarium, and they need to get it built. It has something to do with a state inspection that's coming up."

Doubts began creeping in. "I haven't done carpentry in years. I don't know if I still can."

"Take the job, find out after you get there. What have you got to lose?"

"There's that." After weighing the pros and cons, I slapped my palm down on the arm of my chair with more resolve than I felt. "All right, I'll do it. How do I get to Harwood Manor?"

"Not so fast. First, we need to fit you out in some decent work clothes. The ladies' auxiliary runs a thrift shop in the basement. There's a good chance they'll have what you need."

"I don't take charity. I'll make do with what I have on."

"It won't be charity. Take what you need now and pay for it out of your first paycheck. Until then, consider it a loan."

Father Samuel stood and moved around from behind his desk to lay a hand on my shoulder.

"Come on. Let's see what the ladies have in your size."

Reluctantly, I rose to follow him, but when we reached the door, he stopped and turned to face me. Digging in his hip pocket to retrieve his wallet, he took out a $100 bill, which he handed over. "You'll need bus fare. Harwood Manor is on the eastern edge of Logan Heights, about five miles from here."

Consumed by misgivings, I eyed the money. "That's a lot of bus rides."

"A man needs to eat. Pay me back out of your second paycheck." He deftly tucked the money into my shirt pocket before I could refuse. The priest then stepped out into the hallway.

I extracted the $100 bill, refolded it carefully, and slid it into my pants pocket beside the gold locket—two treasures in one day. Feeling extraordinarily self-conscious yet grateful, I followed Samuel toward the stairwell that led to the basement.

Buses are one of the things that wealthy people hardly ever think about, like spending five minutes agonizing over which brand of cheap razor blades to buy. Unless you're poor, it's not an issue. The privations that derive from being poor become especially acute if you're accustomed to having had money. Things like transportation and groceries become significant concerns. Only in the last year had I learned to read a bus schedule. Owning my own car was one of so many things I had once taken for granted.

The particulars of transportation occupied my mind as I gazed out the windows of the number 10 crosstown bus that traveled the length of Westridge Boulevard, from New Waterford to the far edge of Logan Heights. Some changes happen rapidly, while others are more gradual, like the measured metamorphosis of the shops we passed, shifting from secondhand marts, bars, and pawn shops into jewelry stores, salons, and upscale boutiques.

It made me wonder about the people who lived in those neighborhoods.

Looking closely, I noticed that even though dark clouds dotted the morning sky, the business day was gathering steam. Ladies in pantsuits and carrying briefcases, or others in knee-length dresses with shopping bags looped over one arm, traveled the sidewalks. Men in coats and ties hustled with resolute strides, important people with places to be and reasons to be there. Absent were the loiterers, the urban infantry with their shell-shocked expressions. The citizens we passed moved with purpose, undeterred by poverty's burdens. They seemed satisfied and, if not happy, at least self-sufficient. But then, wealth is a concern only for those who don't have any.

A woman studying a window display reminded me of Hannah and how much I missed being with her. Intimacy—like money, I suppose—is one of those things you can't appreciate until forced to do without. It wasn't the sex; it was the companionship I missed. Physical attraction had drawn us together—our first years had been all fusion and fireworks. It was the sharing, the uninhibited communication, that had cemented our partnership. As we had grown to know each other, the tendrils of our souls had intertwined, blending us into one being.

After leaving St. Anthony's, I had desperately wanted to rush home to share the good news. The incineration of Liberty Tower One and its aftermath had damaged our marriage so badly that I had spent the preceding night in an urban cave. Any glimmer of hope, any spark in the darkness, was to be celebrated, but Father Samuel had insisted that there wasn't time. Ms. Lonergan, as she preferred to be called, needed her ramp finished immediately. The project would be awarded to someone else if there were any delays. The joyful sharing with my wife would have to wait, which might not be a bad thing when I thought about it.

There was no guarantee I could do the job. Booze, brawls, and a destitute lifestyle had taken their toll. I flexed my arm, feeling the muscles of my biceps and shoulders. After leaving the trades to found Heartland Designs, I had worked out faithfully a couple times a week. But the fire had ended those routines too. Now, in place of firm contours, there was sinew, bone, and not much else.

Swinging a hammer is hard work, and determination will carry you only so far. At some point, endurance becomes a crucial factor. I wondered how long I could last. Probably not long at all. Well, in that case, I told myself as the bus doors swooshed open and I stepped out onto the pavement, determination would have to serve. There was too much at stake to surrender to the pain and fatigue I knew was coming.

Father Samuel had been right; I did hope for better times. I wanted to be done with the misery of having nothing. More than that, I wanted my marriage restored. I wanted my wife back.

Four blocks ahead lay my destination. Steeling myself, I began walking. When I stuffed my hands into the pockets of my new secondhand jeans, my fingers found the gold locket and chain. I remembered how the image had spoken to me. I opened the keepsake again, but this time, I recognized what I had merely sensed before. Beyond the sadness and serenity, I noted a look of deep resolve.

That's your secret? I asked in silence. *It's how you endured, by force of will. Well, if it worked for you, it will work for me.*

Another thought struck me, and I laughed at my whimsy.

Moore, I asked myself, *what are you doing, strolling along, commiserating with a woman who's undoubtedly been dead for decades?*

Oh, how I missed Hannah.

CHAPTER 5

Stacks of lumber confronted me as I faced the solarium at the rear of Harwood Manor. The boards had been haphazardly sorted into piles of one-by-eights, two-by-sixes, four-by-fours, and other sizes. Boxes of eight-penny nails and three-inch wood screws sat on a pallet beside the wood, along with aluminum fasteners, brackets, and joiners. Off to one side lay a row of concrete footings that would support the uprights, plus half a dozen cans of latex primer and exterior semigloss paint. Both the primer and the paint were forest service green. To me, it looked as if someone had dumped a giant three-dimensional jigsaw puzzle onto the ground, and now that I was an employee of Harwood Manor, it was my job to put it together.

The Manor, three stories tall, resembled a colonial great house built on an L-shaped foundation. I'd been given a brief tour. On the side of the building opposite where I stood, the main entrance, bracketed by fluted columns, faced the street from the middle of the *L*'s long arm. To my left, the perpendicular base of the *L* housed the administrative offices, the residents' dining room, and the facility's kitchen, all connected by an access corridor. The employee break room lay just past the kitchen, closest to the rear entrance, placing it as far away from the action as possible, yet still inside the Manor.

The upper floors housed residential apartments. Unlike Liberty Tower One, each floor consisted of two parallel rows of apartments separated by a central hallway. A strategically placed nurses' station served each floor. Three additional residential units were built at the ground level. I soon learned these were highly coveted because of their ease of access and because they were near the lounge where the ambulatory residents liked to congregate. Also, the great room where special events took place was downstairs.

The 24×30-foot solarium, to which I was supposed to attach an emergency exit ramp, stuck off from the top of the *L* like an after-thought, converting the building's footprint into a lopsided *U*.

Ms. Lonergan, the woman who actually ran the facility, despite the administrator's posturing when we had been introduced, had provided me with a set of rough sketches, the crude diagrams Yuri had drawn up. They called for an interrupted ramp with two land-ings. Yuri's folded design seemed an efficient use of space. Properly built, the ramp should serve the necessary safety functions, unlike the stairs that were being replaced.

I tried not to think about a full-scale evacuation and why it might be necessary, but if something horrible happened, safely get-ting everyone out had to run smoothly and without delay. On that point, Ms. Lonergan and I were in complete agreement.

As I studied the makeshift diagrams, my analytical abilities, long dormant, began to stir. I soon realized I was facing two problems.

The first problem was that there was a lot of lumber. I felt fatigued just thinking about turning the scattered piles into a ser-viceable ramp—no wonder the handyman had tweaked his back. Manhandling 6×8-foot sheets of plywood into stacks must have been incredibly daunting. During my interview, Ms. Lonergan repeatedly stressed that I would be working alone because of budget constraints.

The second problem was more serious. There wasn't enough lumber. Yuri had skimped on stringers, cross braces, and upright sup-ports to save time and money. The ramp would collapse if a panic ensued during an evacuation and everyone used it at once. According to my calculations, the supporting elements would never handle the weight as specified by Yuri's diagrams.

Something had to be done. The question was what.

Pressuring Ms. Lonergan to buy more supplies was not an option. She had made her position clear. I was expected to make do with what was available. Otherwise, I might as well get back on the bus and head for home.

In addition, I had promised Father Samuel that Yuri would have a job when he recovered. If I were to reveal the flaws in his designs, his temporary layoff would undoubtedly become permanent.

On the other hand, the administration could conclude I was pulling a fast one, crying wolf to hit them up for more money. Or they could accuse me of making everything up just to steal Yuri's employment. That would never do.

Then it occurred to me that I could simply walk away. I could feign some excuse and bow out like Yuri had; except I needed the work. Quitting was unthinkable, but so was being part of another catastrophic project. That left me with only one alternative. I had to figure out how to shore up the ramp without letting my new employer know.

I looked around, hoping to chance upon an extra supply of building materials.

The maintenance shed where Yuri kept his tools stood twenty yards away, near the employees' parking lot. I had already inspected his marginally adequate collection of carpentry tools. Some were so old that it made me wonder if they might have once belonged to one of the senior residents of Harwood Manor. Sadly, no extra lumber was to be found, not in the shed nor any other place I looked.

"Mr. Moore," shrilled a voice behind me, "I'm not paying you to stand around gawking. Get to work." Hands on hips, Greta Lonergan stood framed by the open portal of what was to become the solarium's new double-door exit. A short, wiry woman, she came nowhere close to filling the space.

"Right away," I said. "Just making sure I know where everything is, and it's all here. Wouldn't want to get started and find something missing."

"Everything you need is in front of you. Mr. Slowiki is very thorough, I assure you. He's been with this facility for nearly two decades, and we're looking forward to his return. In the meantime, I strongly suggest you follow his blueprints." Her she-wolf grin seemed more warning than smile.

"Yes, ma'am."

I dug around in the abraded leather pouch strapped to my waist. Pulling out a fifty-foot tape measure, I began marking off the ramp's corners. There was no reason I couldn't stake out the boundaries and position the concrete footings while I wrestled with the problem of what to do about the insufficient bracing.

After laying out the ramp's footprint, my next most critical task was to set the double doors that would seal the hole in the solarium's outer wall. The space where the exit doors were to be hung gaped dangerously three feet above the ground, literally an open invitation to disaster.

As I set hinges into one of the double doors, a female voice, marinated in a thick Southern drawl, startled me from behind.

"Would y'all mind if Gracie here watches you work?"

Focused on my task, I jerked the chisel as I brought down the mallet, gouging the mortise. With a muttered curse, I inspected the damage. Thankfully, the hinge plate would cover the flaw. I looked up to see a chubby nurse's aide grinning sheepishly.

"Sorry 'bout that." The aide parked a wheelchair near the card table where I had tossed my thrift-store windbreaker. "Grace here won't be no trouble. All she do is sit, like she done since she got here." The aide stepped around and bent down to adjust the crocheted lap blanket that guarded the old woman's legs against the cold, securely tucking its edges beneath her frail thighs.

The late afternoon breeze had turned chilly. With an open breach in the solarium's windowed walls, the ambient temperature inside was as bracing as the air outside, perfect for doing carpentry but a little brisk for sitting around.

I regarded the old woman, who stared into space, oblivious to her surroundings. "How long has she been like that?" The woman's pure white hair seemed undiminished by the thinning processes of age. At one time, it might have been worn quite stylishly. Now, drawn back and clipped at her temples, strands fell in straight lengths to her shoulders where the ends sought their natural curl. Her hands hung inertly off the ends of the wheelchair's armrests. Networks of veins connected knuckles with wrists beneath her pale white skin, sullied by only a few age spots. Her fingers were those of an artist, a musician perhaps, except now they dangled woodenly.

"Don't rightly know. She been with us four months now. Before that…" The aide shrugged.

"Will she be warm enough?"

"She be fine, least wise she never complains. You don't mind her watching, do you?"

"I suppose not. She's not going anywhere, is she?"

"Not likely." The aide laughed and turned to leave but looked back from the doorway. "I come get her in an hour or so."

"What time is it? Would you happen to know?" I called out, but the aide had disappeared from view. "What about you?" I asked the old woman. "You know what time it is?"

No response, not even the flicker of an eyelid.

"No matter. Nothing wrong with quiet. Besides, I need to get these doors hung. Wouldn't be right to leave a big hole for somebody to fall through, would it?"

I continued broadcasting a steady stream of lighthearted banter as I resumed my work. It felt good having someone to talk to, though I could not know if any portion of our morbidly lopsided conversation registered. I could just as easily have been talking to the double doors.

Babbling about nothing in particular kept my mind off the ramp's design flaws. For most of the afternoon, I had racked my brain, seeking a solution to my problem. Every plan I had cobbled together ended up with me getting laid off.

Yet my musings identified two critical concerns. First, I would need to show steady progress to keep from being summarily fired. Second, to keep the ramp from collapsing, I would have to build it to proper specifications.

With no better solution in view, I considered the path I had decided to follow. I would strengthen the foundation with adequate bracing, using whatever materials were needed, even if that meant I would run out of lumber before the job was finished.

As plans go, mine fell woefully short, but all other options were similarly worthless. The course of action I had chosen to follow did have two advantages. If I ran out of lumber before completing the project, the worst thing that could happen would be that Ms. Lonergan would label me incompetent and refuse to pay me. Even so, she would be obliged to finish the ramp, and by then, it would be strong enough to withstand a human stampede. Also, forging ahead would allow me time to think of something else that didn't end with me getting fired.

Standing upright, the solid-core door teetered precariously on the sill as I snugged it up against the jamb. Double- and triple-checking measurements seemed a good idea before chiseling hinge sockets into the dark oak. With no outside landing to catch it, if the door fell, it would leave a mark for sure and perhaps render it unusable. Wrestling the door's bulk into place and keeping it balanced was tricky. With me being able to maneuver from one side only, if the door were to tip and gather momentum, it would crash to the ground and possibly take me with it.

The squeak of rubber-soled shoes against the solarium's black-and-white vinyl distracted me. I nearly lost my grip. Recovering barely in time, I looked around. Ms. Lonergan was striding in my direction with an air of authority undiminished by her small stature.

"What do you think?" I said, stabilizing the door. "They'll look especially nice from the outside, where the white paneling will set them off." For maximum effect, I thought about closing the first door, which was already hung, though obviously, I couldn't while still holding the second door upright. "Antique brass locks and knobs were a nice touch. They'll go well against the dark wood when set in."

"I'm sure they'll be fine." Ms. Lonergan halted three feet away, her hazel eyes taking in details of my workspace: the protective tarp I had laid down, the cardboard squares I'd placed under the legs of the sawhorses. I guessed that she never missed a trick. Yet she ignored the wheelchair and its occupant, who, as far as I could tell, hadn't shifted her position one inch. Grace might as well have been a hunk of sculpted marble, or downright invisible, for that matter.

"What can I do for you?" I said to Ms. Lonergan. With deliberate caution, I teased the door away from the jamb and hefted it back onto the sawhorses. If the nursing supervisor approved of the progress I'd made, she offered not a clue.

"It's five o'clock, and you are still working."

"Yeah, so?"

"It's time to quit."

"Today is Wednesday. As I recall, your state inspection is on Tuesday of next week. That's five days, including the weekend. This ramp won't build itself."

"I have no intention of paying overtime. Tomorrow, you can take up where you left off. You'll just have to work more efficiently, that's all."

"I'd like to continue, if you don't mind. It won't take long to chisel in the hinges—twenty minutes max. Then this big gap in your wall will be sealed, and the room will be safer."

"That's not an issue. As before, we'll lock the solarium after you leave. No one will be in here."

"Isn't this a fire exit, and that's why I'm building a ramp? Besides, it's only twenty minutes I'm asking for."

"Mr. Moore, I am not accustomed to having my employees argue with me."

"Of course. I apologize. I meant no disrespect. How about this? What if I clock out now and then come back and hang the door on my own time? Would that be acceptable? It won't cost you a dime, and tomorrow, I'll be that much farther ahead."

For a moment, I wondered if the nursing supervisor might find some excuse to scuttle my suggestion. Instead, she shrugged. "If you're willing to do that, fine." She turned briskly and left the room, her shoes giving off little mousy squeaks that followed her down the corridor.

"Great!" I exclaimed to Grace. "Now I'm working for free. Brilliant." I approached the card table to retrieve my jacket.

Starving earlier in the afternoon, I had purchased two candy bars from a vending machine in the employees' break room. After eating one, I had stashed the other in my windbreaker pocket. As I bent down to reclaim the candy bar, I looked to where Grace was parked within arm's reach. "What do you think about the doors? Do you like the look so far? I do."

Surprisingly, when I slid my hand into my jacket pocket, my snack was gone. I searched my memory and distinctly recalled having tucked the candy away for safekeeping. I remembered because two bucks had seemed an exorbitant price for two small chocolate sticks.

Perhaps my snack had fallen out of my pocket. I got down on my hands and knees. Other than construction debris, the floor was clear. The candy bar was nowhere to be found. I straightened up and gave Grace a stern look.

Startled by a glimmer of recognition, I peered closely as if seeing the old woman for the first time. To my surprise, she seemed vaguely familiar. There was a look in her sea-gray eyes I couldn't quite place. Despite my scrutiny, she sat quite still as if entirely oblivious to my inspection.

"Ah, well," I sighed. "No real harm done." I turned toward the solarium exit and the break room beyond, irritated at the prospect of spending another dollar. Perhaps I should do without, except my muscles were starting to cramp. A burning tension had set in at the base of my neck. I needed real nutrition, but vending machine pastries and sweets would have to suffice.

At the doorway, I paused. Looking back, I made sure the brakes on Grace's wheelchair were securely set. After all, she was my responsibility since I was the only one around. I decided that if the nurse's aide hadn't returned to collect her by the time I finished hanging the doors, I would see that the old woman safely made it to her room. That way, my conscience would be clear.

Still troubled by the notion that our paths had crossed before, but satisfied that my charge would be safe till I returned, I started down the wide corridor. Along the way, I kept my eyes peeled. As I passed the residents' lounge, I peeked inside. To my great disappointment, not a single candy bar could be seen lurking anywhere. Instead, an aseptic hospital smell filled the hallway and nearly ruined my appetite. Astringent odors were probably just one of many annoyances the regular employees learned to overlook.

The break room was deserted. Clearly, quitting time at Harwood Manor meant precisely that: the nine-to-fivers quit and went home.

I clocked out and headed back to work.

CHAPTER 6

Gray clouds hovered in a hazy sky. Dusk was settling on Branford Gardens, leaching the color out of storefronts and tenement houses.

The crosstown bus pulled away from the curb. A plume of exhaust fumes enveloped me where I stood on the sidewalk, bone-tired, hungry, sore in places I had forgotten existed, and surprisingly content. I had put in five solid hours, six if you count the unpaid overtime. Not bad for a day that had begun with me crawling out of a pit.

Three other rush hour stragglers exited the bus, rush hour being a misnomer in a neighborhood where less than half the adult population was gainfully employed. After muttering, "See ya later," two guys headed east on Westridge, the other guy headed west.

I dragged myself south on Beach Street. Another man, face shrouded under the hood of a charcoal gray sweatshirt, materialized ahead of me, weaving unsteadily in my direction. In the dimness, we nearly collided. His grunt as he passed could have meant either "What's up, dude?" or "Get the hell out of the way, jerk."

A block ahead, I saw the empty lot where I had already decided to spend another night. I still had most of the hundred dollars Father Samuel had loaned me, enough to afford a room in a flophouse and satisfy my need to curl up in a real bed. However, I had determined to put the money to better use, except I had already succumbed to temptation. On my way home, as a consolation to my aching bones,

I had picked up a cheap, thrift store pillow and a surplus army blanket, both securely tucked under my arm.

I had elected to return to my cave mainly because a twenty-four-hour separation would never convince Hannah that I had repented. Usually, I tend to be an optimist, though not so much since the incineration of Liberty Tower One. Hannah, on the other hand, is pragmatic. As such, she is generally skeptical of things that seem too good to be true. Our travail had merely strengthened her way of thinking. I would have to prove myself, and that would take time.

I planned to see my wife and ensure she was okay but refrain from revealing my good fortune. After the ramp was finished and I had been paid, I would produce a check for $1,400, the amount I expected to earn—a fortune given our current finances. If that didn't prove my sincerity, nothing would.

My strategy presumed that I would finish the ramp, which meant solving the dilemma of the insufficient bracing. I needed a truckload of boards, but lumber doesn't grow on trees.

Well, it does.

With a conspiratorial eye, I regarded the leafy silhouettes that lined Monroe Creek but quickly abandoned the notion of felling trees, milling planks, and hauling boards five miles across town. The task would take more time and energy than I had available. Besides, the authorities would probably object. I needed finished lumber, the kind you don't find lying around.

As I approached the intersection where Myrtle dead-ended into Beach Street, I noticed that Hannah's apartment lights were on. I have never been good at keeping secrets from my wife. She's always been keen at guessing my plans for birthdays and anniversaries. Since losing her sight, she'd become even more perceptive.

While thinking about seeing Hannah, I suddenly became concerned that my recent activities at Harwood Manor might be found out. Torn between anticipation and apprehension, I paused on the concrete stoop. Eventually, my need to check on my wife won out. I climbed the stairs to the second floor. After stashing the pillow and blanket in a dark corner of the landing, I knocked on my wife's front door.

"Do you think God cares or even knows what happens to us?" I stood at the kitchen sink, scanning the weed-infested lot for signs of movement. Soon, I would go to my basement hideout through that tangled jungle. I recalled the discarded syringe and used condom I had uncovered that morning while climbing out of my pit, proof that the lot was being used for adult recreation.

Hannah said, "That's a strange question coming from you. A night and a day batching it, and you're getting religion?" She sat in her customary place at the kitchen table. Her leather sculpting apron hung on the back of the chair beside her. She'd been wearing it when I had begged to come in.

The few dishes from our meager dinner were slotted in the drainer beside the sink. I had gathered them up and washed them, my contribution to our meal. The night had become too thick to see anything more than pools of light beneath the streetlamps. I turned away from the window and faced Hannah.

From the outset, our reunion had unfolded cautiously, both of us fearful of pressing each other's hot buttons. After granting my request to be allowed to shower and change my underwear, Hannah had gone the extra mile and volunteered to feed me.

Mostly, we ate in silence. We didn't need words to guess what the other was thinking. Hannah had refrained from commenting on my new clothes, though she was very curious. Instead, she seemed determined not to notice, as if showing interest might open up new levels of intimacy. She could be stubborn when it suited her.

Casually, I volunteered, "I've been mulling over something this guy I met said."

"One of your drinking buddies?"

"Hey, not a drop."

"Then why are you hung over?"

"I'm not. I swear. Why would you think that?"

"Because you look like you're coming down from a three-day binge."

"It's rough out there on the street, earning a living. Seriously, not a drop."

"Remember, I warned you. You won't get another chance. Screw this up, and we're done."

"I'm keeping that in mind. So, what do you think?"

"About?"

"Does God watch us? Does He keep tabs on what we do, handing out celestial brownie points or demerits? Does He hear our prayers?"

"You are getting religious."

"No, I'm not—least I don't think so. This guy I met is convinced that God answers every prayer."

"Who are we talking about? This guy you met?"

"His name is Father Samuel O'Bryan. He's a new priest at St. Anthony's."

"The big church on Century Boulevard?"

"That's the one. Would you let me finish?"

"How did you meet this priest?"

"That's what I'm trying to tell you. If you'd allow me—"

"By all means." Hannah sat back in her chair. As she cocked her head, waiting, a lock of blonde hair settled at her throat.

Distracted by her beauty, I found it hard to concentrate.

"Well?" she said evenly. "Go on."

"Sorry." A flush arose in my cheeks. I took a deep breath to clear my thoughts. "Do you remember what I told you the other night, that I saw what I was becoming? Well, it's true. And I've been trying to understand what happened."

"What does that have to do with God answering prayers?"

"I'm getting to that. I remember walking home feeling ashamed after the fire had burned itself out. No harm done, but—"

"What fire?"

"The trash fire I helped put out—you thought you smelled smoke."

"Oh, right."

"Anyway, I was feeling ashamed."

"Why were you ashamed? You helped put out the fire."

"I was ashamed because I'm the one who started the fire."

Hannah became suddenly alert. "You started a fire?" Her green eyes speared me with a look of disbelief.

"Nothing major. It was a trash fire. Relax. I can explain later. What's important is what happened next. I was on my way home, feeling apprehensive—not because of the fire. Anyway, I stopped in the middle of the block and remembered looking up. There was this big rip in the awning overhead, but other than this one star, there was nothing above me, just blackness. So, I prayed, 'God, I need your help. I can't do this alone.'

"I remember that prayer because it was the first I ever truly meant. I couldn't hold it in. I also remember that everything seemed disconnected. It's hard to describe the emptiness I felt at that moment. And then thirty-six hours later, this priest shows up, and I've got a new wardrobe. So how do you explain that?"

"Let me get this straight. I'm lost. You were out with your friend getting drunk, and you had this epiphany, or whatever you call it, and then you started a fire, and then you prayed, and this priest comes along and gives you new clothes."

"He didn't give them to me. I'll have to… Well, let's say they're on loan."

"This priest loaned you the clothes you're wearing?"

"Yeah, sort of."

"Justin, what the hell is going on? You're holding back. I hate when you keep things from me. No, forget I asked. I'm not sure I want to know. What you say may be important to you, but it has nothing to do with fixing our marriage."

"It has everything to do with fixing our marriage."

"How? I mean, so what if you had a vision? How does that change a thing?"

"It's in the mind where changes begin. You can't become what you can't envision."

"That's poetic, but instead of spending time pursuing meta-physical distractions, how about getting out and looking for work?

Do something that will put food on the table. That's how you get right in the head. You need to regain your sense of purpose. Anything else is a waste of time."

"Actually, I—no. You're right. I knew there was a reason I had to see you."

"Don't patronize me. And I am right. Spend time finding a job, not all tangled up inside your head. Speaking of which, I have a headache. Now I'm the one who needs some aspirin." Hannah rose and left the room.

When I heard her enter the bathroom and the door close, I swiftly crossed the floor to retrieve the empty jam jar where we kept our rent money. After unscrewing the lid, I gathered $65 out of my pocket and stuffed it into the jar. I then replaced the lid and returned our glass piggy bank to its place beside the peanut butter.

When Hannah reappeared, I was in the living room waiting for her. "I need to go," I said. "Both of us are tired, and tomorrow, well, it is what it is. I'll see you later." I stepped forward to kiss my wife on the forehead.

She responded by touching my cheek. "I do love you." I could tell she meant it. She seemed on the verge of tears. "Take care of yourself."

"I love you too."

On my way downstairs, I realized that my wife had failed to mention, and I had failed to ask, how her day had gone and what she had done with her time, which made me wonder what, if anything, she was hiding. I almost turned back, but sometimes, filling in the gaps requires too much effort.

I lay on the wooden platform in my cave. Rough surfaces irritated whichever pressure points made contact, adding to the aches that kept me awake. Shifting positions didn't help. I tried lying on the army blanket, but the night's chill soon forced me to cover up again. Even folded double, its wool fabric failed to prevent the cold from seeping deep into my bones.

Feeling my way in the darkness had again been a slow, hesitant process, made only marginally easier for having navigated the route once before. At one point, I scraped my ankle on a tilted plank.

In keeping myself from falling, I reached out and grabbed a tilted beam causing a splinter to lodge in my palm. It would fester if not removed, but its extraction would have to wait till daylight. Upon considering the matter, I decided that a pocket flashlight would be a justifiable expense, though I hated the thought of spending more money. As it was, $31.87 would have to last a week unless I borrowed more funds from Father Samuel or reclaimed some of what I had left for Hannah, which I was determined not to do.

With a sigh, I curled into a ball and closed my eyes. Rather than focus on physical complaints and needing a distraction, I began mentally checking off the day's highlights.

Perhaps mentioning my prayer to Hannah had been a mistake. As a couple, we had attended church in the first years of our marriage but had fallen off as the pressures of launching a new business had multiplied. As a result, discussing spiritual matters had become uncomfortable. In any event, my prayer and my encounter with Father Samuel had been genuine.

As I considered various priorities, finishing the ramp seemed to be the key to restoring my marriage. Seeing the job through would earn enough to make a fresh start, perhaps as a handyman or main-tenance man like Yuri.

Hannah was right, though. Work instills a sense of purpose. For the first time in months, I could see myself doing something worth-while. Eventually, perhaps, we could build a new life or even think about having children before it was too late. A man can dream.

But as far as I could tell, I'd need another miracle to finish the ramp. I decided to pray again—as an experiment.

I shut my eyes and kept them shut. "God, if you're there—" *No, I told myself, that can't be right. I know He exists. It's just that I'm not sure if He's listening.* I decided to keep it simple. "Sir, I need lumber, a big pile, if it's not too much trouble."

My eyes snapped open, and I sat up. Although unable to see three feet before me, I could sense the jumbled heap surrounding me. Indeed, there had to be a few salvageable boards that I could cut to size.

I squinted into the darkness. "No way, Sir. You didn't…?" The implications were staggering.

"If it's not too much bother, I could also use a truck."

Buoyed by a whisper of hope, I laughed for the first time in I don't remember how long.

The supports for the ramp's top landing stood upright on concrete footings. Cross braces kept the foundation square. *Not a bad morning's work*, I thought, *considering that a sleepless night had done nothing to relieve my aches and pains.*

Arising at daybreak, I had inventoried the basement's contents and searched through the surrounding weeds. Most of the boards I had unearthed were charred and fire-singed. Still, even with the damaged areas trimmed away, a fair number of planks would be serviceable. The ramp's support structures would be out of sight beneath its decking. Whatever boards I might bring in didn't need to be pretty, just sturdy.

I returned my attention to the job at hand. A 2×4 stud of sufficient length lay across the sawhorses. Using a sliding T-bevel square, I marked off the proper angle, rechecked my measurements, and reached for the rip saw. A power saw would've made my task infinitely easier and faster, but Ms. Lonergan had complained about the noise and had requested that I make do with hand tools whenever possible.

With the problem of where to find extra lumber solved, transportation had become my next critical concern. The Illinois Transit Authority would no doubt frown upon a commuter hauling lengths of timber onto their buses. I needed a truck, but barring an honest-to-God miracle—no pun intended—it seemed I was out of luck.

A burning ache spread from the base of my neck, across my shoulder, and down the back of my arm. It reminded me of how thankful I'd been to transition from carpentry to designing buildings.

Beyond the solarium's inner doors, I noted a gaggle of old folks leaving the elevator and shuffling toward the first-floor lounge, a clear sign that lunch would soon be served. Many of the residents leaned on walkers or teetered on canes for support. A few rode in wheelchairs. I wondered if Grace might be among their number or if someone would feed her in her room, coaxing her to open wide for every spoonful.

My question was answered when a matronly kitchen worker steered a food cart into the elevator. Seeing lunch trays neatly stacked in the cart's slots gave me an idea.

Every Harwood employee, me included, was required to take a half-hour lunch break. It was a rule. I'd rather have continued working since I was progressively falling behind. Still, no one had specified when I had to clock out. As far as I could tell, no one would care if I took my break after the bedridden residents had been fed. That way, by waiting, I could steal their leftovers.

With a nefarious scheme taking shape inside my head, I paused to consider the risks of pilfering food. One thing seemed certain. If challenged, I would need a valid excuse for having invaded the residential areas. I thought about bringing a tool pouch and claiming I had been summoned for emergency repairs, but such a blatant falsehood could easily be exposed.

Calling upon an "old friend" would provide a more reasonable alibi, especially if that "old friend" was mute and couldn't rat me out.

After studying the plan and looking for flaws, I decided it might work. It was worth a shot since my hunger was becoming a serious concern. The biggest challenge would be waiting for the proper moment rather than jumping the gun because I was starving.

I had to remember to wear my jacket—to stash whatever food items I snagged. Besides, is boosting leftovers really stealing?

CHAPTER 7

The nurse who emerged from the med room was not the person to whom I had introduced myself the night before when I returned Grace to her studio apartment. This woman was younger and better-looking. Azure blue eyes, auburn hair, and a cute face caught my attention. Immediately, I felt a pang of guilt when Hannah's image came to mind.

That's not why you're here, I reminded myself.

Dealing with an unfamiliar face, even a cute one, surprised me. I was briefly tempted to turn around and purchase my lunch from the break room's vending machines. I had assumed that the woman from the previous night would be on duty and that she would recognize me. As it was, I would now have to justify my being there to a stranger.

Seeing the food cart stationed partway down the corridor, not far from Grace's door, quelled my reluctance. Steeling myself, I approached the nurse who stood in front of a large, red, multidrawer cart with wheels, like a mechanic's tool chest.

As I approached the nurses' station, I noticed that rather than having been walled off behind a counter, the work area felt open and accessible. A large round table dominated the center. At one edge, a row of modular cubicles faced outward. I assumed the cubicles with built-in desks were for charting, dictating, and such. A side wall opened into a utility room plainly labeled Staff Use Only.

Sensing my presence, the nurse glanced up from the chart she had read. Freckles dotted the bridge of her nose. The corners of her mouth curved upward slightly, implying a naturally pleasant disposition. Her patterned blouse and pale blue scrubs did little to conceal her figure, which I tried desperately to ignore.

"May I help you?" A slight brogue suggested second-generation Irish. According to her name tag, her given name was Erin.

"Sorry to interrupt."

"Not a problem. What do you need?"

"I'm not sure what the rules are around here, but I was wondering, would it be all right if I paid Grace a visit?"

"Grace McFarland? Sure, I don't see why not. I expect they've finished feeding her by now." The nurse returned her attention to the chart in her hands.

I hesitated. Something seemed amiss.

The nurse looked up. "Was there something else?"

"No, just—aw, never mind."

"What?"

"Nothing. I'm not sure what I expected."

"Ah. You think I should quiz you, demand to know why you're visiting a woman in Grace's condition."

"Well, yeah. I'm a stranger. You don't know my intentions. What if I was up to no good?"

"You're no stranger. I've been watching you work." She indicated the window behind the nurses' station. "And if your intentions were evil, you wouldn't have rescued Grace last night. Beulah confessed in this morning's report that she had gone home early, leaving her patient stranded."

"Beulah?"

"My aide—heavyset woman, thick Southern drawl, major dimples."

"Guess I didn't catch her name. Why were you watching me?" Suddenly, I felt self-conscious rather than flattered.

"Curiosity, mostly—wanted to see what the racket was all about. You're more agile than Yuri and seem to know what you're doing."

She leaned closer and lowered her voice.

"It's a shame the man hurt his back, but we'd never pass inspection with him on the job. There's no way a slouch like Yuri could finish on time. I'm Erin, by the way. Erin Fairchild." She extended her hand.

I returned her handshake. "Justin. Justin Moore. Pleasure to meet you."

"Likewise. Grace is in 207, but you know that. She'll be happy to see you."

"You're joking, right?"

"Not at all. Grace has a way of showing if she's pleased or upset. Surely you noticed."

"Not really."

"No? Then why do you want to see her?"

Uh-oh.

I blurted out, "To say thank you." As excuses go, it was as lame as any, but it was the best I could do without time to prepare. Sometimes, I really suck when it comes to thinking on my feet. Erin was starting to suspect a ruse, so I hastily added, "It was nice having someone to talk to, even if the talking was one-sided." I mentally crossed my fingers. "I hoped she might understand, like you said. I figured it couldn't do any harm, telling her I enjoyed her being there."

"Indeed. If you feel that way, I could have Beulah bring her down to the solarium again this afternoon."

"Okay. Yeah, sure—just so long as we're not breaking any rules. I wouldn't want to get anybody in trouble."

"Are you kidding? Yesterday, you paid more attention to Grace than anyone in the last four months, except for the staff. She'll be there every day if you'll allow it."

Mentally, I cringed but was careful to conceal my lack of enthusiasm. Instead, I said with a magnanimous display of generosity, "Why not? If you think it'll do her good, though I would still like to stop by her room."

"By all means."

"Good." With a quiet sigh of relief, I headed down the corridor but then turned back, puzzled. "McFarland? You said her last name is McFarland? How do I know that name?"

Erin looked up again, her cheerful expression the same as before. She seemed unperturbed at being interrupted for the third time. "Probably because people talk."

How true, I thought to myself and nodded in agreement.

The nurse continued, "The McFarland clan derives from a different era. They used to be well connected—upper crust socially—influence that goes along with having lots of money, but that was years ago.

"During Prohibition, Grace's father-in-law bought a parcel of land that his son, Grace's husband, later inherited. The story goes that her husband set out to build a grand mansion for himself before Branford Gardens became skid row. One day, Grace's husband disappeared. Nobody knows what happened to him. Rumors have it he was mixed up with a crime syndicate or something of the sort.

"A week or so after her husband vanished, Grace came home one afternoon to find her only son shot dead in their living room, a mob hit according to the police. A couple days later, the son's wife splits, apparently afraid for her own life. Without so much as a good-bye, the woman takes off and leaves Grace to look after her twelve-year-old grandson.

"After the daughter-in-law skips town, Grace is on her own, having just lost both her husband and her son. Rather than stick around, she gathered up her grandson, for whom she was now the sole provider, and moved to London, England, I think. From what I've heard, even from the beginning, she's refused to talk about any of this, not that I blame her. And now she can't because of her stroke. That's all I know. What puzzles me is why she decided to return to the States."

"If she can't speak, how do you know these things?"

"You would not believe how much of a gossip mill an ECF can be."

"A what?"

"Extended care facility—Harwood Manor, that's us. Some of our residents are old enough to have known the McFarlands personally."

"Sounds like Grace has lived a really sad life."

"Not as sad as the one she has now."

"I suppose you're right. Well, thanks. See you later."

"I hope so," Erin said under her breath, but loudly enough so I could hear as I turned toward Grace's room.

At Harwood Manor, most residential living quarters were the same size. A few one- and two-bedroom suites were available, but these were reserved for couples. Grace, like the majority of residents, occupied a studio apartment, which included a sleeping alcove, a walk-in closet, a multipurpose area, and a kitchenette.

I knocked on Grace's open door and peeked inside. She was alone. The night before, I hadn't looked around. This time, I noticed curios and mementos on tabletops, shelves, and counters—barnacles that attach to a long life. A plush light brown carpet matched the beige drapes and the off-white walls.

Grace sat in her wheelchair, facing away from the sliding glass door that opened onto a narrow terrace. Her hair was combed as before, and the same crocheted lap blanket covered her legs. She still showed no awareness, even when I crossed the threshold and advanced in her direction.

"Hi, Grace. You don't mind if I hang out for a few minutes, do you?" I moved closer but remained standing. "Didn't think so.

"So how you doing? You like it here at the Manor, do you? It seems like a nice place, but as far as places like this go, I don't know much about that stuff. You've got a friendly nurse out there. Is she kind? Does she treat you well? I imagine she does. Seems like the sort who cares about her patients."

I studied Grace's facial expressions for any sign that my words were sinking in. The wrinkles in her forehead and the creases in her cheeks remained static. Behind the trappings of age, I noticed a hint of beauty and was again seized by the odd impression that I had encountered this old woman before. I racked my memory but could not place how or where we might have met.

"You look familiar," I told her. "I know you from somewhere— it's starting to bug me. I wish you could help me out." I studied her features even more intently.

When I looked into Grace's eyes, seeking to spark my memory, I could tell there was intelligence behind her unfocused stare. "You are in there, aren't you? You may be unable to talk, but you understand what I'm saying."

My heart went out to the elderly woman.

"It's got to be tough, knowing what's going on—not being able to respond."

I waited. Nothing.

"Look, if any part of what I'm saying is getting through, show me something. Blink, grit your teeth, wiggle your ears—anything."

Again, there was no reaction.

"Or maybe not."

I straightened up and looked around. Someone had furnished Grace's apartment with items of quality, not to mention the keepsakes and mementos that also looked expensive. They certainly weren't the cheap souvenirs tourists collect on summer vacations.

Then it occurred to me. There was no rogues' gallery and no photograph or portrait of an actual person. "How unusual is that? How do you live a life that's totally free of human attachments?" I wondered aloud. The photo of Hannah I carried in my wallet came to mind. "Or perhaps you'd rather not be reminded? Is that it?" I turned to face the wheelchair. "Were your in-laws that bad, being criminals and all?"

Admittedly, Grace McFarland had lived a sad life, but to turn her back on everyone—or was it that those family members who now oversaw her care had turned their backs on her?

The more I thought about it, the less judgmental I became. Moved by sympathy, I said, "Well, I suppose everyone has burdens to bear, right? Some more than others. Besides, is being lost inside yourself any worse than losing yourself in a bottle?"

Suddenly remembering why I was there, I moved to the door and cocked my head to listen. The corridor seemed quiet. Poking my head out slightly, I peered in both directions. It appeared that I was in luck. The food cart was parked merely a few feet away, and no one was in sight.

With great stealth, I eased forward and began rummaging through the leftovers, avoiding the partially eaten selections. To my delight, I found an unpeeled banana, two pudding cups with their seals still intact, and a tuna fish sandwich wrapped in cellophane.

I was reaching for the sandwich when a noise from down the hall alerted me. I looked up just in time to see Beulah emerge from a resident's doorway. She was facing away, so I scurried unseen back to Grace's room.

"That was close," I told the old woman as I looked for a place to stash my booty. If Beulah were to pass by and glance in, it wouldn't do to get caught food-handed, so to speak. The low table beside Grace's wheelchair seemed the perfect place, the assumption being that any items sitting on the table would be hers.

"Keep an eye on these for me, will you?" I set the banana and pudding cups down, close enough that an animated person could touch them. Pleased with my deception, I went back to listening at the door.

Peeking out again, I watched Beulah gather a set of fresh linens out of a storage closet. She then entered another resident's room to make the bed. With the nurse's aide otherwise occupied, I retraced my steps and grabbed the sandwich off the food cart, along with an unopened pint of milk.

Feeling like a street hustler scrounging my daily bread, I returned to Grace's room. After stuffing the milk and sandwich into my jacket pockets, I leaned down to fetch the banana. That's when I noticed that one of the pudding cups was missing.

"You old fox!" I exclaimed. "First my candy bar, now the pudding."

For a moment, I considered frisking the old woman, but how would it look if someone were to catch me with my hand beneath an octogenarian's lap blanket?

"Very well," I said, "it's yours. Enjoy. But I'm on to you. You may have fooled the staff, but now I know better."

I wanted to hold Grace's feet to the fire and make her admit her deception, but I had to return to work.

"Trust me, this conversation isn't finished."

As I stepped out into the corridor, I marveled at the scope of human trickery. With a casual stride, I returned to the solarium, keeping my arms close to my sides to prevent my bulging pockets from drawing attention. *What other secrets*, I wondered, *has Grace McFarland stored up over the years, and why was she pretending to be a human statue?*

CHAPTER 8

Having returned to the outdoor area where I was building the ramp, I looked back up at Harwood Manor and marked what I thought was Grace McFarland's room. A wrinkled face appeared behind the sliding glass door and furtively peered out across the second-floor balcony. I wondered if someone might have repositioned Grace's wheelchair, but the face disappeared. I kept my head down while I worked and monitored her room out of the corner of my eye.

The job was progressing slowly. The pain radiating from my shoulder to my arm had become more than an annoyance. For a time, I had tried hammering nails with my left hand but had given up after smashing my thumb. Some carpenters are ambidextrous by nature. I'm not. As a consequence, I had lost my momentum.

Ms. Lonergan had stopped by. With arms akimbo, she had inspected the job site like a vulture waiting for its next meal to keel over. In no uncertain terms, she had stressed what failing a state inspection would mean for the facility. If Harwood lost its license, people would be thrown out of work, residents would be evicted, and it would be my fault. Her scolding had ladled an additional helping of guilt onto my plate.

Despite the impending deadline, the woman had flatly denied my request to put in overtime hours, even when I had again volunteered to work for free. Despite being reminded of the precedent we had set, she refused to relent. I would carry out my assignment between the hours of nine and five, Monday through Friday, and that was final. The woman could be incredibly stubborn.

The face reappeared behind the sliding door. To my amazement, the woman it belonged to stood up, confirming my suspicions.

An hour later, the exterior door across the corridor from the employees' break room opened, and Erin wheeled Grace out onto the service cul-de-sac. When the nurse saw me, she smiled. "Beulah is giving bed baths," she called out across the asphalt. "I thought I'd bring Grace down rather than leave her waiting in her room."

The old woman sat unmoving, staring straight ahead. Extra blankets swaddled her in a woolen cocoon. There seemed little likelihood that she would be cold.

Erin maneuvered her charge to within nine feet of the sawhorses where I was working. Before latching the brakes on the wheelchair, she looked around as if making sure there were no safety hazards nearby. "There you go, Grace," she said, straightening up. "You should be fine here. Enjoy the afternoon, and don't be giving Mr. Moore a hard time."

The nurse stepped closer. "The solarium is too far away. She wouldn't have been able to see anything, nor would you have been able to keep an eye on her. Besides, she could do with some fresh air. It gets stuffy inside. I imagine you've noticed. So how's it going?"

"It's going…not as quickly as I'd like."

"Don't let Ms. Lonergan get to you. Like they say, she has a rough exterior, but her heart is solid granite." Erin chuckled softly. I assumed she had witnessed my encounter with the nursing supervisor from her second-story window. "Daisy's okay, once you get to know her, and she's a damn good administrator."

Daisy? I looked toward the wheelchair. "Every project needs a foreman. Mind if I ask what's Grace's diagnosis?"

"Cerebral infarction caused by atherosclerotic vascular disease."

"In English?"

"She's had a stroke. A small clot cut off blood flow to part of her brain. As a result, she can't remember how to speak." Erin stooped down to pick up a crosscut saw lying near my toolbox. She flexed the blade so it vibrated with a metallic whine. "My brother used to do that. He could even play a tune. He was handy with tools, like you."

"How much do you think she understands?"

"It's hard to tell. She has a way of letting us know how she feels, but she can't follow simple commands. I know some stuff gets in. As to how much…" The nurse shrugged. "With thirty residents to care for, hopefully someday I'll get to know her better."

Without proof that the old woman was faking her disability, exposing her charade could be problematic or potentially harmful. People have reasons to act the way they do. Until I understood Grace's reasons, I figured it would be best if I kept my mouth shut. Besides, her affairs were none of my business.

All that having been said, I was still curious. "She have any family?"

"A grandson, Warren McFarland. He's the one who brought her here to be admitted. That was four months ago, and he hasn't been back since. Not once. Too busy making money, I expect."

"They don't get along, Grace and her grandson?"

"That would be my guess."

"Any other family members?"

"None that I know of. You really have taken an interest, haven't you?"

"I can't shake the feeling that I know her." It was time to change the subject. "Tell me about Yuri. Does he own a truck?"

"An old Ford pickup, I think. Why?"

A potential solution to one of my problems had just fallen into place. I tried to act nonchalant. "Oh, I was just wondering how he hurt his back. Did he haul this lumber in his truck and unload it himself?"

"Yuri? Are you serious? No, that's right. You've never met the man. Two guys from the lumberyard did the unloading. Yuri stood around and watched. It wouldn't surprise me in the least if his back strain becomes a claim for permanent disability."

"Ms. Lonergan said he's been with the facility nearly twenty years."

"Whining and complaining every minute. He's one of those poor souls for whom any excuse will do."

"I gather you don't hold Mr. Slowiki in high regard?"

"I believe people should earn the wage they're paid. Speaking of which…" Erin returned the saw to its place near the toolbox. "It's time for me to do my charting. Thanks for keeping an eye on Grace."

"My pleasure."

For her part, Grace ignored us both.

"By the way," Erin commented as she was leaving, "tomorrow, why don't you join us upstairs for lunch? I'll order up a tray from the kitchen."

"Busted," I said sheepishly and tried not to blush.

"Don't sweat it. I take food home all the time. No sense letting it go to waste."

"I'll bet that makes your husband happy, eating nursing home leftovers."

"I'm not married. Never have been."

"But the ring—"

"Keeps the dirty old men from flirting." She hooked a thumb toward the extended care facility. "Fortunately, most of our residents grew up in an age when fidelity meant something."

"I see."

"Later then." Erin smiled and turned away.

I called after her, "Do you want me to bring Grace back upstairs when I'm finished?"

She paused to look back. "It might not be good for her to be outdoors that long. Why don't I come get her in an hour or so?"

"Not a problem." I regarded the old woman in the wheelchair. "What do you think, Grace? Time to swap secrets?"

The nurse laughed as she strolled away. When she reached the employees' entrance, she glanced back and waved.

The ramp's two landings were finished, one attached to the solarium and the other where the ramp doubled back on itself. With a plumb bob and tape measure, I checked to ensure they were square and precisely aligned.

But there was a problem. I wasn't as far along as I should have been. In my prime, I could've knocked off a similar project in the time I'd already invested. With only two full workdays remaining, Friday and Monday, plus what was left of the afternoon, I wasn't going to finish on schedule. There was too much to be done, not to mention that I still had to haul in the extra lumber I would need.

I considered my predicament and realized I would soon be breaking the rules. That fact had become apparent, but how to defy the imposed restrictions and not get caught? That was the question.

Nearly done in by fatigue and with every joint and muscle in my body aching, I unfastened the utility belt from around my waist and dropped it onto a sawhorse. That's when I noticed that my hands were shaking. For a moment, I seriously considered quitting and walking away.

Stuffing my hands into my pants pockets, I stared at the unfinished ramp. What I needed was a dose of fortitude. Deliberately considering why I was there and why the struggle was worth every ounce of energy I could muster helped.

With my hands in my pockets, my fingers again found the locket and chain. As I visualized the woman's image, I recalled that I had foreseen this moment when exhaustion would compel me to turn tail and run. I also recalled promising myself that patience and determination would see me through.

A jolt of recognition surged through me like an electrical shock. I turned to stare at Grace, having nearly forgotten she was there. I snatched the locket out and popped it open. After considering the effects of aging, I was certain the woman in the locket was Grace McFarland.

How can this be? I thought. She can't be that old. Still, the facial similarities were undeniable: the shape of her eyes, the bow of her lips, the aristocratic contours of nose and cheekbones. It had to be her. There was no doubt about it.

Squatting in front of her wheelchair, I kept my balance by clutching an armrest. As I held the locket at eye level a foot in front of Grace's face, I said, "I knew I'd seen you before. Look at this pho- tograph. This is you, isn't it? You're this woman. Aren't you?"

The vacant expression in Grace's eyes indicated that she was a million miles away.

"Talk to me, damn it. I know you can. I've watched you stand up and walk. The staff may think you're a vegetable. I don't, not someone who steals candy bars and pudding cups. You understand what I'm saying. I know it. Why continue this hoax? What do you hope to gain?"

Unused to squatting, I stood up when my knees began to ache. Looking down, I again positioned the open locket in Grace's line of sight. "Talk to me. Please. I have so many questions I want to ask you. I know this is you. It can't be a coincidence. It's too much of a perfect match. Is it that you want to speak and can't? Perhaps so, but I know you can move. I've seen it. Gesture. Wink. Nod. Show me that I'm getting through. Give me some sign that you understand."

The old woman remained inert except for a few strands of white hair ruffled by the afternoon breeze. She glanced neither right nor left but stared impassively beyond the image in the locket.

"This woman…well, to me, she's something special. I have this crazy idea of how great it would be to know, talk with, and be her friend. Look, if you're afraid I'll reveal your secret, I won't. You can trust me. No one will know, I promise, not unless you decide to talk to them too. It's your call."

The only sounds to reach my ears were the muffled hum from inside the residence and a rumble of traffic a few blocks away.

Then I noticed a tear forming in the corner of Grace's eye. The pulse in her thin neck had quickened as well. My words had gotten in. There had to be something that could get her to respond.

I regarded the locket. The sight of it triggered a spark of inspira- tion. "How about we make a deal? I imagine this is rightfully yours. Talk to me, and I'll give it to you, plus the little box it was in when I found it. They will be yours to keep, along with the ring, the comb, and the key—all your treasures. What do you say?"

For nearly a minute, I waited, but to no avail.

"Fine. Have it your way then, but I know you hear me." In frustration, I threw my hands up. "That's it. I have neither the time nor the inclination to babysit someone who refuses to talk to me. Go ahead. Continue this charade of yours, but you can do it without using me as your audience. I'm taking you back to your room. And I'm going to keep this locket."

I bent down to unlatch the wheels of her chair.

As I headed her wheelchair toward the employees' entrance, I thought I heard a faint whisper, nearly inaudible. The implications took a moment to register. Grace had spoken.

I halted and stepped around to face her. Kneeling again, I confronted her face-to-face. Tears were trailing down both cheeks, but rather than stare into space, she looked me straight in the eye.

"What did you say?" I asked gently.

In a soft voice, hoarse from long disuse, she said, "That woman was my mother."

"Is she all right?" said a voice coming from the direction of the employees' entrance.

Startled, I glanced over my shoulder to see Erin approaching. Even from twenty feet away, I could tell that a look of concern had replaced her usually cheerful expression.

"She'll be fine," I called back reassuringly.

I returned my attention to Grace, who had again donned her mask of detachment. Gone was the anguished look, the shadows of painful memories. All that remained were tears on her cheeks. I dabbed them away with the cuff of my shirtsleeve.

I looked up and called out to Erin, "A gust of wind blew some sawdust into her eyes. I wasn't paying attention. Sorry, I should've been more careful."

To Grace, I whispered, "Don't worry. I won't tell. We'll talk again soon, and you can tell me all about her." I pressed the locket and chain into the palm of her hand and closed her fingers snugly around them.

As Erin drew near, I stood up and turned to face her. "I really am sorry."

"It wasn't on purpose, I'm sure."

A pocket flashlight materialized in the nurse's hand. She bent down to examine her patient.

"Grace, are your eyes bothering you?" She straightened up after gently pulling each lower lid down and inspecting for debris. "She seems okay. We'll watch her and make sure there are no secondary effects. Right now, we need to get her back to her room. She's not looking so good."

"I hope this won't keep her from visiting again. I appreciate her company."

"We'll see. Grace is more fragile than she appears."

"So it would seem. Say, you wouldn't happen to have an extra one of those, would you?" I indicated the flashlight. "Recently, I've had to do some fumbling in the dark."

"Nope, sorry. You might check upstairs. Sometimes the drug reps leave them for the staff." She stepped around to grasp the handles of the wheelchair. "Come on, Grace, let's get you warm."

I felt awful as I watched the wheelchair disappear into the Manor. I couldn't help but think, *You fool. When will you learn to keep your damn mouth shut? Why is it always about what you decide is important? Who knows what psychological trauma you may have caused?*

For the next two hours, I kept seeing the pain in Grace's eyes. As a consequence, my progress was even slower than before. When five o'clock rolled around, I hurried upstairs, anxious to learn how the old woman was doing. Erin had already gone, but another nurse informed me that Grace had suffered some sort of spell. The consensus was that it was a problem with her heart. In any event, her status had been downgraded to no visitors allowed.

When her grandson had been notified of the change in her condition, he had staunchly refused to come in. Instead, he restated his instructions that she be listed DNR—do not resuscitate.

The evening nurse relented and contacted Grace's doctor only after I had threatened to raise a fuss. He had issued orders over the phone and promised to visit her in the morning. At that point, it had seemed there was nothing more I could do other than worry.

Despite my concerns for Grace, I accomplished an important bit of business before leaving: I acquired Yuri Slowiki's home address. The charge nurse had initially refused to share such personal information. She had relented only after I had informed her in strict confidentiality that a discreetly wrapped package had been delivered to the maintenance department. The Manor's handyman, I had suggested, might resent having his supply of male enhancement pharmaceuticals left lying around for anyone to see.

CHAPTER 9

The Hispanic community of Paloma Blanca lay south of Branford Gardens. In daylight, the streets throbbed with an ethnic heartbeat and hummed to the lilt of Midwestern Spanish. A cultural bias toward large families assured that the neighborhood was always full of commotion. At night, however, the drug gangs took over, and the community became a virtual war zone. Despite my concerns due to the lateness of the hour, my visit with Yuri could not wait till the next morning.

I did my best to become invisible as I navigated treacherous streets, my destination being the tenement building where Yuri Slowiki lived. Could Yuri be involved in the drug trade? I wondered. Voicing such speculations could get you into trouble, so I decided to abandon that train of thought and focus instead on what I would say after introducing myself.

Yuri answered his door after my third knock. He looked to be in his mid-fifties. Bushy eyebrows bisected an oval face, dividing a vast expanse of forehead from fleshy cheeks and a double chin. What drew my attention, however, was his massive girth. I was reminded of when Linda, my executive secretary at Heartland Designs, had become pregnant. She had once balanced a teacup on the shelf of her swollen abdomen. Yuri could have balanced a steak dinner.

"Whatever you're selling," Yuri grumbled before I could open my mouth, "we're not—"

About to slam the door in my face, his eyes narrowed. He paused for a second look, and then there it was. His spark of recognition dredged up within me bucketfuls of self-loathing.

"What do you want?" Yuri spat.

I offered my hand. "Mr. Slowiki, my name is—"

"I know who you are," he snapped, ignoring my goodwill gesture.

"I've been covering for you at Harwood Manor." I lowered my arm to my side. "Mind if I come in? It's cold."

"First, tell me what you want."

"It's been a hard day, and I'm really bushed. Besides, I'm freezing. What do you say? Can we talk inside?"

"The family's eating dinner. Get to the point."

"As you wish. I need to use your truck for the weekend." I indicated the three-quarter-ton Ford pickup sitting at the curb. Its rusting door panels, dented fenders, and cracked windshield told that it had seen better days.

"Take a hike." He backed up a step.

"I found the invoice from the lumberyard." The words were barely out of my mouth when the front door slammed shut three inches in front of my face. I stood there shivering on the porch until the portal opened again.

"Yeah? So what?"

"I can prove theft. The Manor paid for twice as much lumber as was delivered. What did you do? Did you sell half the load on the black market? And this isn't the first time you've skimmed off the top, is it?"

"You're crazy, you know that?"

"So I've been told. How about this. At some point, you realized the ramp you designed is unsafe, but it's too late to beef up your blueprints. The materials have already been paid for. So you fake a back strain, hoping somebody else will take the blame. You figured the guy they hired to fill in for you would be too dumb to notice your design flaws. Oh, and by the way, you're moving pretty good for a guy who, two days ago, could barely walk."

"You think you can blackmail me? Listen, bud, I know about you. And I know what you did. I checked you out when the priest called to tell me you were covering my job. I'll tell them you stole the lumber—that every board and every screw was there before you showed up. Who are they going to believe, me or the guy who torched a condominium?"

"Daisy knows all about that. I told her the whole story before she hired me. Besides, I don't own a vehicle. So how did I steal the lumber? Did I throw a bunch of eight-foot boards over my shoulder and saunter off to a flea market? I'm sure they'll buy that. Come on, man. You don't really want an investigation, do you? Get the police involved, and who knows what other shenanigans might turn up?"

"Go to hell."

"Look, I have a solution that works for both of us. All I need is to borrow your truck for a couple of days. I'll pick it up tomorrow evening and bring it back Monday after work. I promise I'll take good care of it, not that anyone would notice a couple more dents."

As concisely as possible, I explained how I planned to complete the ramp using timbers from the rubble in the vacant lot.

I finished by saying, "See, this way I get paid, and you get credit for having designed such a fine ramp."

"And if you get caught?"

"I'll leave you out of it. I swear. Sure, I rented your truck, but I never told you why. They'll believe that. You'll be protected. Look, I'm not interested in taking over your job or exposing your shady dealings. All I want is to finish this project and get my money."

After another round of negotiations, Yuri reluctantly consented.

"Don't worry," I told him, "I can make this work, and then you'll never see my face again. Just leave the keys under the seat. Hey, it's not like somebody's going to boost your ride. I mean, give me a break."

After nailing down the details, I turned to leave but had a second thought. "Pass the word, will you? Let the neighborhood know I'm simpatico, okay? I'd rather not wind up with a shiv in my ribs. Also, leave a note in the truck stating that I have your permission to use it, not that you'd report it stolen. Oh, one more thing. Make sure there's gas in the tank. Don't worry. I'll reimburse you when the project is finished."

The ladies' auxiliary, Father Samuel, Hannah's landlord, the electric company, and now Yuri—the list of people I owed money to was growing progressively longer.

I turned and walked away, head down, shoulders hunched, hoping not to be noticed.

"How's the roast beef?" Erin Fairchild's teasing smile confirmed that she was kidding. She sat diagonally across the round table in the middle of the second-floor nurses' station. As promised, she had ordered a food tray and even stopped by my job site earlier that morning to remind me that I had been invited to lunch. I felt like a hired hand trying to pass himself off as a family member.

"Delicious." I swallowed another chunk of meat. Considering that I'd been slowly starving to death, broiled shoe leather would have tasted like filet mignon. Saving money by skipping meals is a poor idea, especially if your days are spent swinging a claw hammer.

"In nursing school," Erin said, "we would've called the stuff mystery meat since it's impossible to tell where it came from."

"Is that why you brown-bag it?"

"Among other reasons." She popped the lid off a plastic bowl, revealing a tossed salad garnished with tomatoes, olives, and cucumbers. From a smaller container, she poured on oil and vinaigrette dressing. "The main reason is the Manor makes us pay for our meals. Over time, the costs add up."

I regarded my tray, troubled by a sudden insight. I looked at Erin. "Did you buy my lunch?"

She shrugged.

"You did, didn't you? Well, thank you. I suppose I should have guessed."

"You're welcome." Erin smeared a dab of cream cheese on her bagel. "I appreciate what you're doing for the Manor. We can't afford to lose our license. Besides, even mystery meat has to be more palatable than scrounging leftovers."

"There is that." I scooped up a forkful of potatoes and gravy but paused before taking a bite. "Would the state inspectors really shut this place down? I can't believe an exit ramp is that important."

"Normally, no, but we've had two warnings already. The last time, they made it clear that the ramp would be built—or else. State officials don't joke around when it comes to safety matters. I'm sure you can understand their reasoning." A crimson flush colored Erin's cheeks. "I'm sorry, I didn't mean you personally. I was just—"

"It's all right. I know what you meant." I lowered my fork to my plate. "It appears you know my history. Probably everyone in the building knows by now. Look, all I can do is accept things as they are and move on." Brave words, I thought. Hard to bring about. I eyed my lunch and discovered I had lost my appetite. I sat back.

Beulah Roosevelt spoke into the silence. Seated tangentially across from Erin, I had almost forgotten she was there despite her size. "I hear tell we got us some rain coming."

"You sure?" I replied, glad for a change of subject.

"That's what the weatherman say. This weekend gonna be thunder and lightnin'."

My spirits sank. "Great." An early winter storm would put a damper on my plans- no pun intended. Well, so be it. If fate decreed that I was to wrestle planks and boards in the rain, that's what I would do. I'd done it before—when I was younger, in better shape—and owned the proper rain gear.

Patience and determination, I reminded myself. I would've laughed at such Pollyanna platitudes in my early days, but they seemed to shore up my resolve. Patience and determination- I wondered, what do they mean anyway?

One definition of wisdom might entail knowing when to quit, but sometimes you can't quit. Sometimes, all you can do is hang tough. A face came to mind—the image in the locket.

Looking at Erin, I asked, "How is Grace by the way? Can I stop in and say hi?"

"Briefly, perhaps. She's better, but she's not out of the woods yet. She's had episodes of heart failure before, but this was the worst I've seen. Grace doesn't suffer stress well. I should never have left her out in the cold for so long."

"It wasn't your fault. Nobody could have predicted what would happen." I rose from the table.

Erin gave me a questioning look. "Aren't you going to finish your lunch?"

"I would, but I don't like feeling stuffed when working—slows me down."

"Well, then take it with you. No call to waste food, not even institutional food." She rose from the table and transferred the remnants of my meal to a paper plate, which she covered with plastic wrap. After fetching a disposable fork and a paper towel from the back of the nurses' station, she handed the leftovers to me. "A hard-working man needs to keep his strength up."

"Thank you," I said with gratitude. "Mind if I leave it here while I visit your patient?"

"Not a problem."

Beulah hefted her bulk out of her chair and headed down the corridor. "I'll make sure Miss Gracie be decent. Don't want her feeling embarrassed."

I looked at Erin. "Mind if I ask you something? What are weekends like here at the Manor?"

Erin seemed surprised by my question. "Pretty much like every other day, just quieter."

"On weekends, you're off duty, right? You, Ms. Lonergan, and the other senior staff members?"

A look of uncertainty arose in Erin's azure eyes. "Why do you ask?"

"Can you keep a secret?"

"That depends. Try me, and we'll see." She formed a hesitant smile.

I braced myself and took a deep breath. "At the rate I'm going, there's no way I'll finish the ramp on time. I'm going to have to break rules and put in extra hours. It'll be a lot easier if those in charge are gone. You're not going to say anything, are you? I had the impression you'd be sympathetic. You want me to finish, right? Well, this is how it gets done."

"I won't squeal. Besides, Ms. Lonergan is too much by the book. Some rules are meant to be broken."

"Miss Gracie, she be ready for you now," Beulah said, returning to station herself at my elbow.

I looked at Erin. "See you Monday then."

"Monday it is."

I turned toward Grace's room. Behind me, I heard Beulah whisper, "That man, I think you like him."

The bubbling of Grace's oxygen humidifier muted Erin's reply.

Grace lay on her side, face toward the window, knees drawn up into a fetal position. Midday sunlight, diffused by gathering clouds, cast soft shadows across her shoulders and hips. Covered by a sheet and a thin blanket, she seemed frail and more insubstantial than when tucked into her wheelchair. A tube attached to the wall oxygen system snaked beneath her chin and behind her ears to deliver life-giving gas through prongs in her nose.

I remembered my grandmother's last days and how she had refused to submit to her infirmity, even though the family, for the most part, had accepted that time was running out. Yet there had come a point when Grandma had finally given up. Over a few days, I had watched her devolve from an active, vibrant woman to a living corpse, waiting to exhale her last breath. And that was how Grace appeared to me as I stood in the doorway, wondering what to say.

I entered the room to be greeted by a wall of heat. Someone, probably Beulah, had set the thermostat well above seventy.

Stepping around the foot of the bed, I faced Grace with my back to the sliding glass door. Her eyes were open, yet riveted on infinity—the same vacant stare as when we were first introduced. For a moment, I was reminded of those coma victims who regain awareness for a day but then slip back into unresponsiveness.

Then, I recalled the tears rolling down her cheeks. There had to be a functioning mind inside that withered husk. How could I draw her out without causing additional harm? That was my primary concern. I was reminded of the motto on my doctor's wall when I was younger: Primum Non Nocere—First Do No Harm.

In preparation for my visit, I had crafted a short speech to explain the episode in the cul-de-sac. Instead, all I could think was, "I'm sorry. I had no right to treat you like I did. Can you forgive me?"

There was no response, no nod of recognition.

It felt awkward standing there. So, I pulled up a chair and made eye contact. "I'm pretty sure you can hear me. I want you to know I'd still like to be your friend. For reasons I can't explain, I feel as if I know you. The last thing I want is to upset you again. Please understand that what I'm about to say is not meant to be critical. I'm simply expressing what's in my heart.

"You can hide inside yourself, waste whatever time you have left. That's your prerogative, but there's a better way."

I drew my chair closer so I could speak in a confidential voice.

"I believe we can help each other. Like you, I've had my share of problems to deal with. That's an understatement, by the way. But the point is that by sharing, maybe we can sort things out. I doubt that your mother—no, forget I said that. I wasn't going to mention her or the locket. I'm sorry."

As monologues go, mine was a catastrophe in the making. I had planned on cajoling her with compassion. Instead, I had just chastised her for cloaking herself in silence. Then, I had invited her to vicariously share the tragedy that had turned me into an alcoholic bum. And now, I was about to reopen private wounds that had brought on her heart failure. *Keep it up*, I thought, *and you'll push her over the edge*.

"Maybe this wasn't such a good idea." I started to rise.

"You promised I could have the tortoiseshell box."

I froze halfway out of my chair.

Grace was studying me through narrowed eyes.

I lowered myself slowly. "That's right. I did say that, didn't I? I would've brought it today, but I wasn't sure if—"

"I'd still be alive?"

"Be receiving visitors. I'll bring it and its contents by tomorrow."

"I can't tell if you're lying to me."

"I'm not lying. I'll be stopping by early tomorrow. I'll bring the box and all your things then."

Grace frowned. "Tomorrow it is then. Perhaps I'll still be here."

"I should hope so."

"Why? What do you care what happens to me? Who am I to you?"

"I was telling the truth when I said I wanted to be your friend."

"You don't want to know me."

"Oh, but I do. I'm drawn to you like a moth to a flame."

"Usually, that doesn't work out well for the moth."

I laughed. "See, we're already communicating."

"If you say so."

I regarded the old woman with puzzlement. "Why did you open up? Why did you decide to talk to me?"

For a moment, I was afraid she would refuse to answer. Then, as if making a decision, her compressed lips relaxed. "Because you showed me my mother's photograph. You reminded me of things I hadn't thought about in years."

"She must've been someone special?"

"She was. I'd forgotten how much I miss her."

"I'd like to hear more about her."

Alerted by footsteps in the corridor, I raised my index finger to my lips. "Someone's coming."

Beulah's wide frame filled the doorway. "Mr. Moore, it be twelve thirty. You gots to go back to work, and Miss Gracie here, it's time for her bath."

"Sure." I stood and returned my chair to the corner of the room. To Grace, I said, "Remember to keep happy thoughts. No telling what treasures will come your way."

Beulah confirmed my declaration with an ample show of dimples. "That be so true."

On my way past the nurses' station, I gathered up my leftovers from the round table. Down the hall, I saw Erin conversing with a stooped gentleman who had to be in his nineties. She waved, and I waved back. I quickly stepped into the elevator when the doors opened.

Modular sections of ramp lay in organized rows not far from the concrete pit I now thought of as home. The dense weeds at the center of the vacant lot had offered my best hope of concealment. The components I had already shaped filled a third of the clearing I had tramped down like a crop circle.

I blotted my forehead with my sleeve as I regarded my progress. Earlier, I had remembered working on prefab homes. In a moment of inspiration, I had wondered, why not use that same design principle?

By sawing, shaping, and painting the ramp's components in advance, come Monday morning, the final assembly would be a straightforward affair, like piecing together a giant by-the-numbers erector set. My spirits had lifted as the day had progressed, and it had become increasingly likely that the project would finish on schedule.

I flexed my back to release a kink. Hauling materials and hand tools in from the Manor had worn me out.

The smell of decay mingled with the scent of freshly crushed vegetation. I gazed outward to survey the empty lot and noticed Yuri Slowiki's battered truck at the curb where I had parked it. I wasn't especially concerned that anyone would steal such a cantankerous pile of junk. Yet, as pathetic as the vehicle might be, I wished it was mine. Without a truck, my scheme would never have come to fruition.

Overhead, dark clouds threatened a wet afternoon, but my luck had held so far. As long as I kept moving, I hardly noticed the cold. The freezing would come at nightfall, when darkness would force me to suspend my labors. I considered sleeping in Yuri's truck despite the risk of being challenged by a cop on patrol.

I looked up. The lights were on in Hannah's studio. I assumed she was working on her forlorn cherub, sculpting final details by sense of touch and polishing the Carrara marble to a fine luster that would cause the statue to seem to glow from within.

Staying away had tested my resolve.

Working in broad daylight across the street from my wife's window, I knew I risked being seen, but even with binoculars, Hannah's failing eyesight would make recognizing me problematic. Besides, there was no other place to set up shop.

With an upwelling of satisfaction, I set another finished piece aside.

That morning, shortly after daybreak, I had kept my promise to Grace. The night nurse had initially insisted that I leave and return during regular visiting hours, but when her back was turned, I had slipped into Grace's room unseen. The need to avoid discovery had prevented me from communicating openly, but I had returned her possessions, for which Grace was sincerely grateful.

The old woman had perked up upon being reunited with her treasures. She hadn't exactly smiled, but I could tell she was pleased. I thought I understood her attachment to the locket, but why the other items mattered was a question that sparked my curiosity. Perhaps one day she might explain.

I fetched a plank from off the pile of salvageable lumber and placed it on the low platform I had fashioned. After cutting away the charred bits, the remaining length was fire-singed but sturdy enough, despite being exposed to the elements. Using a tape measure and a carpenter's square, I laid out the pattern for a diagonal strut.

As I shoved and tugged the rip saw through the weathered wood, I tried to imagine why someone would give up on life. One reason that might be true in Grace's case was that the struggle becomes increasingly futile as death draws nigh. No matter how valiant the effort, the end is preordained. So, why fight the inevitable?

But to shut everyone out seemed like an inherently poor choice. In the past eleven months, I had come to understand loneliness and how devastating isolation can be. So why would someone shun all human contact? As life winds down, isn't that when people need each other most?

It occurred to me that some terrible trauma must have triggered Grace's emotional lockdown.

The idea seemed plausible, but it would never do to ask her directly and risk another crisis. Perhaps I might learn what had happened by speaking with her grandson, Warren. I immediately dismissed that idea because not only had he abandoned her, but he was very likely part of the problem. I would have to consult someone else, a local who would have known the McFarland family.

A particular face came to mind.

I froze in the middle of a saw thrust. Tomorrow was Sunday. I could attend church, assuming Catholics would welcome a Protestant to their mass. I jotted a mental note to myself to determine when the service started. No doubt Father Samuel would try to convert me.

CHAPTER 10

Father Samuel O'Bryan stood to one side of the narthex, greeting St. Anthony's parishioners as they exited through the double doors. Msgr. Aldrich stood on the opposite side, conversing with a young mother who carried her infant daughter in her arms. The monsignor had preached the morning message and was, therefore, claiming the lion's share of the expressions of goodwill. I had learned his first name was Eric, though everyone called him Archie. A small, sinewy man, he had lost his youthful vigor.

By tarrying in the nave, I had allowed most of the congregation to exit ahead of me, not that a vast crowd had attended the second mass. The sanctuary had, in fact, been less than a third full, which was not surprising given the monsignor's uninspired delivery. Twice, I had noticed Father Samuel reading from a small book cradled in his cupped hands. Once, unable to stifle a yawn, he had earned a scowl of disapproval from his superior. After the service, the two men had marched down the central aisle side by side without looking at one another.

"Glad to see you made it," Father Samuel said.

I gripped the padre's hand. "It's always a blessing hearing heartfelt words of inspiration."

The priest stifled a chuckle. "How's the nursing home business working out? I've been praying for you."

"Extended care facility," I corrected. "They're touchy about such things. By the way, I wanted to thank you. You took a chance on me, and I appreciate it. This opportunity means a lot to me. You can't imagine how much."

"It was an honor to help. So, working with tools and doing carpentry all came back to you?"

"Like I never left, except for the aching joints and stiff muscles. They're worse than I remember. I expect to finish tomorrow."

"God willing."

"Indeed."

Samuel nodded a greeting to an older couple as they shuffled out of the church, arm in arm. "Have a blessed day," he called out, returning his attention to me. "So, what's next? What are your plans?"

As the couple passed, the old man glanced in my direction and whispered to his wife, who turned to look.

I acknowledged them with a smile but received none in return. "I don't know," I answered truthfully. "Up to now, I've been focused on the job at hand."

I wondered if my work clothes might have drawn the couple's notice. At least I could hope that was the case. I'd worn the same duds for three days straight, though I'd made an effort to look presentable. Rising before daybreak, I had spruced up in a filling station lavatory.

Half naked and shivering violently, I'd washed my shirt and trousers in the shallow sink. After wringing them out as best I could, I'd put them on wet and then walked the streets till they dried. At least the stench of stale sweat was gone.

I turned to Father Samuel. "I was wondering, do you have time to talk?"

"I do. I've been hoping to meet with you again. Say, are you hungry? You want to grab some lunch?"

"Only if you're buying. I haven't been paid yet." A flush of color rose in my cheeks. One thing about poverty, as I was learning, is that it plays havoc with social niceties. As much as I hated being indigent, I hated even more the possibility that one day it might not bother me to inform people I was penniless.

"My treat," Father Samuel offered without hesitation. "Come up to my office. I need to shed these vestments." He fingered the flap of his stole.

Everything in Branford Gardens is within walking distance. Groovy's Diner was four blocks south of St. Anthony's. By matching Father Samuel's brisk stride, the jaunt had taken hardly any time.

Doo-wop music rattled out of the tinny speakers set at ceiling level. Here and there, placards extolled the virtues of companies that had gone out of business more than half a century earlier, like the faded poster on the wall behind the cash register, a framed advertisement for a Royal Enfield Indian Chief motorcycle.

Blue vinyl trimmed in silver upholstered the bench seats in every booth. I wondered if anyone still recognized Brenda Lee, Ricky Nelson, or Bob Dylan, though their autographed images were prominently displayed behind the soda fountain.

I devoured another bite of my Reuben sandwich, thick slabs of corned beef smothered in layers of melted Swiss—undoubtedly the finest meal I had enjoyed in months.

In deference to my fierce appetite, Father Samuel had tactfully refrained from making small talk, choosing instead to focus on his tuna on rye with chips and a pickle.

Satiated at last, I sat back.

Framed by his trimmed mustache and beard, Father Samuel's lips curled into a grin. "Good grub, huh. Told you it would be."

"You were right, and thank you."

"My pleasure. So, what is it you wanted to talk about?"

"How much do you remember about your early childhood, Branford Gardens, and how things used to be?"

"Not much. Nothing makes sense to a three-year-old."

"Did your parents ever reminisce about people who used to live here?"

"No."

"They never discussed the old days?"

"I confronted my dad once—asked about our family history and why we had to move. He refused to talk about it."

"Are they still alive, your parents?"

"My father is. I don't know about my mother."

"They divorced?"

"My mother took off when I was five, couldn't adjust to life on an Iowa farm. My father tried to raise me as a single parent. We were close initially, but then he gave up after Mom left. Nothing seemed to matter to him anymore, not even when I announced I'd be joining the clergy."

"He's not a spiritual man?"

"On the contrary, he's a devout Jew. He used to be Roman Catholic but converted to Judaism when he married my mother. Her maiden name was Finkelstein. After she left us, Dad continued in his Jewish ways. Perhaps he thought if he kept the faith, she'd come home. When I committed to the Church, he was forced to face the possibility that he'd made a mistake by abandoning the faith of his youth. I thought he might revert for a time, but I guess he missed Mother too much. Besides, he's convinced all priests are pedophiles."

I feigned surprise. "You mean they're not?"

"Quite the opposite."

"Does that mean they're all girl crazy? Relax, I'm just teasing. You know, I've never understood that whole celibacy bit. What's the point?"

"It's an issue of surrender. Every man must choose whom he will serve, God or himself. It's the fundamental question that confronts every human life. Forsaking sexual relations is one of many commitments a priest makes. It's our way of surrendering everything we have to the Lord. Honestly, it's hard sometimes, but celibacy has its rewards."

"Such as?" I said in disbelief.

"Discovering your life's purpose—devoting yourself to its achievement. What can be more satisfying than that?"

I pictured steamy nights with Hannah, but rather than debate the issue, I recalled a point my father had made: we're all entitled to our misguided judgments. I swept a crumb off the laminated tabletop. "Your father, what did he do for a living?"

Father Samuel folded his napkin and set it aside. "He was a newspaper man. He owned the Westlake Gazette. He was also its editor."

"Here, locally, in Branford Gardens?"

The priest must have recognized my befuddlement. "You've never heard of it because the paper went out of business two years after we moved to Iowa. Mind if I ask where this is going? Why this interest in my family history?"

"I met a woman who used to live in Branford Gardens years ago. She's now a resident at Harwood Manor. Her health is failing, but that's not the issue. The staff believes she's had a stroke, but I think she's walled herself off—to the point she refuses to acknowledge that other people even exist."

"Why would you think so?"

"Because I believe she's hiding from her past. For hours, she sits staring at nothing. Yet, for some reason, I've been able to make contact. I know she's not as detached from reality as she wants people to believe. I'd like to try to help her—if I can."

"What's her name?"

"Grace McFarland. She's eighty-two years old, according to the nurses."

A dark scowl shattered Father Samuel's casual demeanor.

"Is something wrong?" I said.

"McFarland. That's a name I've heard before when I was growing up. It was spoken as a curse."

"From my understanding, her husband and son were somehow linked to organized crime. I was told her son was shot to death in his own home."

"Why is any of this important?"

"Something is causing Grace to shut down. I believe the key lies in her past. I'm sure of it. If I can figure out what that something might be, maybe I can help her."

"Do you think you're qualified?"

"Probably not, but it's damn certain nobody else is trying."

"And you're willing to make this effort because…?"

"I want to be her friend."

"Why her? Why befriend a woman who stares at nothing?"

"She needs someone in her life, someone who cares."

"We all need someone. Why her in particular? What makes her so interesting?"

"If her past is as screwed up as mine, maybe we can help each other. Is that reason enough?"

"Easy. I'm saying that mucking around in other people's psyche can have unintended consequences. Be careful you don't make her condition worse."

"I've considered that, but what could be worse than spending your final years as a human rutabaga?"

"There's the rub. You don't know what's worse. Push the wrong buttons, and there's no telling what horrors you'll unleash. There's a reason the brain seals itself off with false memories and fugue states. If you plan on getting inside her head, tread softly and be damn sure you know where you're going—pardon my French."

I stared out the window while I mulled over what the priest had said. Perhaps he was right. Maybe I was trespassing—do no harm. Except I knew I had to try—a moth to the flame.

I looked at Father Samuel. "As a man of the cloth, mind if I ask you something?"

"More delving into my early years?"

"No, but now that I think about it, did your father's newspaper keep an archive? And if so, does it still exist?"

"Yes, and I don't know. Every newspaper saves its back issues. When the Gazette closed its doors, its assets were sold to various publishers. I have no idea who purchased what, but that's not what you wanted to ask, is it?"

"No. I was wondering, why does God destroy people's lives?"

"Now there's an off-the-wall question if ever I heard one."

"Not really. Grace, me, even your father from what you've just told me—we're all damaged goods. What does God gain? You suggested that every life has a purpose. What if a man discovers his purpose, and it's suddenly ripped from him, so he loses everything? How is God served by that?"

"You're asking how a loving, omnipotent, omnipresent deity can allow bad things to happen to good people. It's an age-old question. Do you want the simple or the complex answer?"

"Simple."

"Fair enough. Man can't know the mind of God."

"That's it?"

Father Samuel nodded once in affirmation.

"Meaning he's too big, and we're too small, and therefore, we need to shut our mouths and accept whatever comes?"

"Basically, that's correct."

"How about the complex version?"

"Sure. People suffer for many reasons—for instance, God's purposes and man's often conflict. When we think we have life figured out, He lets us know we don't. Tribulation forces us to draw closer to our Creator, to depend on Him.

"Also, there's the issue of free will. Free will means exactly what it implies. We can choose to do good or to do evil. Both choices have consequences. Evil causes suffering for which God is not accountable because the anguish derives from the choices we freely make. In other words, the suffering we experience is often our own fault."

"Are you suggesting that people choose to suffer?"

"Not at all. I'm saying that when we make bad choices, it's up to us to deal with the consequences."

"Go on."

"Perhaps the most compelling reason people suffer is that without travail, we will never truly know ourselves. Only in privation are the layers of self-deception stripped away. In the moment of crisis, we learn who we truly are, what we really believe, and to whom we're willing to entrust our lives."

"I think I'll go with the simple answer."

"No, I doubt that. If you could have, you wouldn't have asked for the longer version."

"Touché." I reached across the table to check the time by exposing Father Samuel's wrist. "Wow. I didn't expect to be gone this long.

I need to get back to work. Thanks for lunch. I owe you—again. And thanks for giving me some heady stuff to think about."

"I also enjoyed our conversation. Let's do this again."

"Sounds good, but next time, lunch is on me."

The doorstop screwed easily into the pilot hole I had drilled. It would keep the solarium door from banging into the ramp's railing. Then I stood back and heaved a grateful sigh of relief. The ramp was finished. My scheme had worked perfectly.

Early that morning, well before dawn, I had risen from my pallet and loaded Yuri's truck with the prefabricated components. Assembly had proceeded without a hitch. By noon, the decking and treads had been installed. After that, it was a matter of touching up the paint job and gathering the last scraps of debris.

With unabashed pride, I walk down the ramp, stopping twice to test its stoutness by jumping up and down. There was no give, no play. It would serve the purpose for which it was intended, even during a mass exodus.

More than anything else, I wished Hannah could be there to see what I had built. I had made something with my own hands, something useful and durable.

Moving a few feet away, I turned to admire the completed project. With my hands on my hips, I tried to imagine with whom I could share the moment. I glanced up at the second-story window to Grace's room. Would she appreciate what I had built or shut me out?

I pridefully opened the solarium doors and maneuvered Grace's wheelchair onto the upper landing. "How do you like the view?" I gestured toward the dark green ramp. "Notice the nonslip surfacing and the handrails within easy reach."

There was no verbal reply, but Grace tilted her head slightly, which I interpreted as a nod of approval. Convincing Erin to let her patient visit the job site had taken some doing. The nurse had finally consented when reminded that Grace was the project's de facto forewoman. Concerned for her charge's welfare, Erin had initially indicated she would come with us. As we were leaving, however, she had been called away to attend to a resident who had fallen.

"Here we go." I shut the double doors behind us and started down the ramp. Gravity's tug on the wheelchair was easily resisted, confirming that Yuri had at least gotten the incline right. When we reached the bottom, I squatted beside a chrome wheel, close enough that if Grace chose to respond, she could do so without raising her voice. "So, what do you think?"

"It's nice. Do we have to go back up?"

"It's perfectly safe. I assure you; it's not going to collapse. But that's not what you meant. You don't want to go back inside."

"A bird in a gilded cage is still caged."

"Have you spoken to anybody? Do they know you can talk?"

"Nobody at Harwood knows."

"Are you going to tell them?"

"You promised you wouldn't say anything." Apprehension furrowed Grace's brow.

"I won't, but I think you should. You're missing out."

"On what, listening to a bunch of old geezers whine and moan about their rheumatism and lumbago?"

"On meeting new friends."

"I thought you wanted to be my friend?"

"I do, but you're not limited to having just one."

"Friends assume they have the right to judge you. You won't do that, will you?"

"No," I declared emphatically.

"Because then you'd leave yourself open to judgment in return, yes? I know what happened to you. I may be old and rickety, but I listen when people talk. You'd be surprised what they say when they think you're an empty husk. I don't care about your past, so don't feel like you have to unburden your soul on me."

It was difficult to know whether to feel offended or relieved.

A pensive look came into the old woman's sea-gray eyes. "How did you find my locket?"

"It turned up in a basement I was exploring."

"Ah, The Homestead. That's what Trevor named the house we lived in. Trevor was my husband. The Homestead was to be his grand castle. He wanted the world to know he was king, but his fortress was never finished. He was constantly adding on, making the place ever more magnificent. The man's quest for wealth and status was insatiable." She added with an air of regret, "Megalomania is a trait all McFarland men share."

I suspected she was referring to her grandson, Warren, but I refrained from seeking confirmation. She had honored me by opening a small crack in her shell and allowing me to peek inside. Forcing the crack wider might be unwise, but there was a subject I needed to pursue.

"The woman in the locket, your mother, how old was she when that picture was taken?"

"Seventeen. She had her portrait done the day she got betrothed to a wealthy man she didn't love. Her father, my grandfather, was a self-indulgent lout, a fool who squandered the fortune he had inherited. He regarded my mother's marriage as the only way to save our family from ruin."

"Sounds like an extraordinary woman, willing to sacrifice her happiness like that."

"Her name was Anna—Anna Tate. After getting pregnant, she left her husband in England and moved to this country so I would be born a citizen. She died when I was thirteen. The picture in the locket is the only one I have to remember her by. I thought I'd lost it forever."

"I'd like to hear more about her."

"Someday maybe—assuming I'm still around. For now, take me to my room. I'm tired."

We paused at the middle landing. Grace spoke softly over her shoulder. "It's a nice ramp. Oh, one more thing: tread softly. Erin has a crush on you—case you hadn't noticed." With only the back of her head in view, I sensed she was grinning.

"Thanks," I said, thinking of Hannah. "That's a bit of information I didn't need."

Grace then lapsed into silence, and her vacant stare had returned by the time we entered the solarium.

～ ～ ～ ～

I headed up the stairs to my apartment, anticipating a joyous reunion with my wife. It felt odd being happy while simultaneously being so mentally and physically drained that climbing a flight of stairs was an ordeal. I remembered an occasion when I had come awake after losing a dispute with a pissed-off knucklewalker. I recalled rolling over and retching in the gutter. Even then, I hadn't felt so abused.

At the top of the stairs, I paused to breathe a sigh of relief into the stillness. Supposedly, the body adapts. After five days of hard labor, I expected to be in better shape. True, the shakes were gone and the nausea less severe, but my rehabilitation had a long way to go. Even so, I felt good emotionally.

Upon reaching Hannah's door, I shifted the box of chocolates to my left hand. So what if the gift was an indulgence? Damn the expense. I was in a mood to celebrate, and what better way than by splurging on my wife? Besides, it was a small box and not terribly expensive. I had also wrestled with buying flowers, but my pesky conscience wouldn't permit it.

At the Manor, Ms. Lonergan had inspected my work with an administrator's eye, and the ramp had passed muster. If she had noticed the added lumber, she had refrained from commenting. Instead, she had cut me a check for $1,300, now proudly stashed in my wallet, and since the banks were closed, at my request, she had paid the rest of my wages out of petty cash, some $150.

After returning Yuri's truck with a full gas tank, I had walked to a nearby dollar store to purchase Hannah's celebratory gift. I would've preferred truffles, but caramels with nuts would suffice. Besides, my wife is easy to please when it comes to receiving presents. Between us, intent counts for more than the gift itself.

Outside our apartment building, dusk had turned the city gray. Rush hour traffic had thinned considerably by the time I had stepped down from the crosstown bus, and now the streets were silent, except for an occasional curse or cry of lament.

Squaring my shoulders and putting on a smile, I knocked on the apartment door. A minute later, I knocked again. When my third entreaty went unanswered, I retrieved my key and unlocked the deadbolt. "Hannah, honey, I'm home," I called out as I poked my head inside.

All the lights were off, which meant my wife was asleep in the bedroom or she had gone out. I scolded myself for not having noticed that the windows were dark. Fatigue seemed a reasonable excuse, though I should have been paying attention.

The bedroom was deserted. The apartment looked undisturbed. One thing about my wife is that she's a conscientious housekeeper. Everything had its place. On the other hand, I'm a guy who lets things lie where they land.

When I turned on the kitchen light, I noted a plate of freshly baked sweet rolls on the glass-topped table. They looked delicious, but a protective film of plastic wrap declared that they were not to be touched. It was then I recognized what I had been smelling. A voracious hunger arose within me. Other than a nut bar, I hadn't eaten all day, having declined an invitation to lunch with the second-floor nursing staff.

I set the candy on the table and fetched an empty jam jar from a lower shelf. After filling the jar with water, I took a long drink, hoping to take the edge off my appetite. The trick didn't work. Still starving, I eyed the box of chocolates and the sweet rolls. Giving in to temptation would risk my wife's displeasure, a complication I needed to avoid. Instead, I opened the refrigerator door. A half-empty can of ravioli and the tail end of a stale loaf of bread sat on a wire rack. Otherwise, the shelves were bare. I wondered if my wife had been too frightened or too impaired by her poor eyesight to go grocery shopping. A wave of guilt doused my upbeat mood.

An idea came to me: I would take Hannah out to dinner right after I found her.

I peeled the heel off the stale loaf of bread, switched off the kitchen light, and left the apartment. There was no telling where she might have gone, but sitting around and waiting for her to return home would not do, not with darkness falling on Branford Gardens.

The advantage of living in a compact neighborhood is that every place where a middle-aged woman with failing eyesight might linger can be searched quickly. I soon discovered that most businesses like Big Water Pawn, Carlisle Hardware, and Lorraine's Beauty Parlor were closed for the evening. Others were shuttered permanently, like Imagination Books and the Kindred Spirits Boutique. A couple of haunts were dismissed out of hand, such as the Tempest Bar and Hadron's Adult Movie Theater, which everyone called the Hardon. Those were places where Hannah would never go, and certainly not alone, not at dusk.

But then, perhaps she wasn't alone. Maybe she was visiting a friend. It would have to be someone she had met over the last five days. Before our rift, we hadn't made any friends, not the sort you call on at night.

The thought that she might be seeing another man crossed my mind, but I dismissed the notion immediately. There was no disputing that I could and should have been a better husband, especially over the past eleven months. Hannah, however, had too much class to go philandering behind my back. She would tell me face-to-face if she decided to move on with her life. Her sense of morality would never allow her to soothe her sorrows in a squalid affair.

That left one other possibility—foul play.

The nagging worry that my wife had become the victim of violence quickened my pace. We lived amid a culture of aggression and brutality. Assaults, rapes, and murders were so common, they no longer triggered expressions of communal outrage. The locals accepted society's self-inflicted wounds as the price paid for living elbow to elbow, without respite from the daily grind. All around us, cruel men with evil hearts derived pleasure from inflicting pain, men unencumbered by empathy or conscience. Against such animals, Hannah would be defenseless.

When I turned north on Beach Street from Octavia, having completed my second circuit of the Gardens, I noticed a blue, green, and white squad car a couple hundred yards ahead, cruising slowly in the same direction I was headed. Breaking into a run, I waved my arms. "Stop! Wait!" I yelled, without effect.

Briefly, I considered grabbing a rock out of the gutter and hurling it through the rear windshield, which would've been utterly dumb. Instead, I cranked up my speed until I sprinted as fast as my decrepit anatomy would allow. When the patrol car signaled a turn onto Myrtle Avenue, I angled my pursuit to cut it off. It was then I realized I was nearly home. I raced past our apartment's still-dark windows without slowing.

The driver must have caught sight of my wild approach in his side mirror—a madman yelling like a banshee and barreling forward at full speed. The patrol car stopped abruptly. The driver's door flew open. In one swift motion, the officer sprang out, drew his revolver, and dropped into a shooter's crouch.

When it dawned on me that the muzzle of a large-bore pistol was aimed at the center of my chest, I threw on the brakes and skidded to a halt not more than four feet away. Backpedaling rapidly, I raised both hands in a panicked "please don't kill me" salute.

"Are you crazy?" the officer bellowed. "Never do that." After a moment, he lowered his weapon. I could tell he was as shaken as I was. "What do you want?" he growled, straightening up and holstering his pistol.

"Sergeant Green? Hector?" I slowly dropped my arms to my sides, careful not to make any sudden movements. "Hi. We met about a week ago, remember? The trash fire?"

"Trash fire?" A look of recognition dawned in the officer's walnut brown eyes as he repeatedly stabbed an index finger in my direction. "Right, right. You're that architect fellow. Yeah, what's your name?"

"Moore, Justin Moore."

"Right, Moore. Well, Mr. Moore, what can I do for you, now that you've nearly given me a heart attack?"

"My wife is missing. I was wondering if you might have seen her."

"Your wife, what does she look like?"

"Pretty, beautiful actually…long blonde hair, five foot seven, 120 pounds."

"What was she wearing?"

"I don't know. She was gone when I got home. Possibly a flannel shirt and blue jeans. She likes to feel comfortable unless there's reason to dress up."

"How long has she been gone?"

"I don't know that either. Like I said, she was missing when I got home from work. I've been searching for her for several hours now."

"Work, really? You got a job?"

"Temporary employment doing carpentry. The job ended today. Look, have you seen a woman who seems kind of out of place, maybe a little frightened? I'm worried. She has an eye condition. Even in broad daylight, she has trouble seeing. At night, she's nearly blind."

"What's her name, and how old is she?"

"Her name is Hannah, and she's thirty-two."

"Any physical attributes that would attract notice?"

"How is that relevant?"

"Because I've never met her, but they'll need a description when I call this in. Is she fat, skinny, what?"

Rather than say, "She has a great body," I decided that "She's about average, I suppose" would be more appropriate.

The patrol sergeant reached for the microphone clipped to his shoulder. About to depress the talk button, he looked at me. "If you've been searching for several hours, how do you know she didn't just go home?"

I gestured toward the featureless building on the corner. "That's where we live, on the second floor. If she were there, all the lights would be on."

"Unless she's asleep."

"She's not asleep, okay? Please, my wife is missing. We have to find her."

"Relax. Let's see what dispatch knows."

When Sergeant Green concluded his conversation, he turned to face me again. "Nobody's heard anything, which is good news."

"What about hospitals?" Speaking the words sent a chill down my spine.

"Dispatch handles all the ambulance calls for County General. That's where trauma victims from this area wind up. In the last twelve hours, no woman matching your wife's description has been transported, which is also good news. Look, people do strange and unexpected things all the time. There has to be a perfectly rational explanation. You look exhausted. Why not go home, pour yourself a double, and give it a rest? She'll turn up."

"I don't drink anymore, and Hannah doesn't do strange and unexpected things. This isn't like her."

"Wow. You got a job, and you quit drinking. Maybe I was wrong about you. Tell you what, I'll keep my eyes open. If I find her, I'll bring her home personally. Besides, around here, you don't want to be walking the streets at night."

"That's kind of my point."

"Mr. Moore, go home. Getting yourself mugged isn't going to help your wife."

At that moment, I perceived there was nothing more I could do. Twice, I had visited every shop, diner, and establishment where I imagined her hanging out. I had even visited St. Anthony's. The sanctuary and all the side doors had been locked. There were no other places I could look. If she'd ventured beyond the neighborhood's boundaries, I'd never find her on my own.

I nodded my capitulation.

The patrol sergeant climbed into his squad car and shut the door. He then rolled down his window. "She'll turn up. They always do—99.9 percent of the time. We'll keep in touch. Okay?"

"If you do hear something, you'll have to knock on my door. We don't have a phone." I thrust my chin toward the empty passenger seat. "By the way, where's your partner? Adrian, wasn't it?"

"He didn't measure up." The cop gave an "oh well" shrug and eased the squad car into gear. Patrolling alone, no wonder the man was edgy.

I moved to the sidewalk and headed toward the apartment building. Wearily, I climbed the three steps to the apartment building's front door, which unexpectedly opened as I was about to enter.

Distracted, I nearly collided with Judy Mallow. "Sorry." I stepped aside to allow the woman to pass.

Instead, she drew up short, blocking the doorway. A smile blossomed on her pale face. "Oh, Mr. Moore, good evening, and congratulations, by the way."

"Congratulations? For what?"

"Are you just getting home? Oh, your wife will be so pleased. She was out looking for you earlier, you know."

My heart leapt in my chest. "When? How long ago?"

"Four hours, maybe…just before dinnertime. I was coming home from work, and she was leaving. She seemed excited, but maybe I should let her tell you the good news."

"Good news? What good news? Why was my wife excited? Mrs. Mallow, please, this is important. I need to know. It's okay if you tell me."

"I'd hate to ruin your wife's surprise—"

"Hannah will understand. What did she say?" I could tell the woman was itching to share her tidbit of gossip. "Please."

"Well, if you're sure—"

"I am. Please."

"Isn't it wonderful? She got a job. Today was her first day."

"A job? Doing what?" The notion that my wife had found work so quickly rocked me. We had discussed the possibility, but to follow through…I felt intimidated. My surprise lost a bit of its luster. My wife was employed. I wondered how long it would take to get used to the notion. But then a second thought struck me. My wife was more resourceful than I had imagined.

"She's the new cook at Gresky's Bakery. She could hardly wait to tell you. I thought maybe she had found you already?"

"Found me? Why would you think that?"

"Because I told her I saw you working on the lot across the street this weekend. I wondered if maybe you were still there, doing whatever you were doing. She wanted to share her news. I hope I haven't ruined her surprise." Ms. Mallow's smile melted into a frown of apprehension.

"It will be all right. I promise when she tells me, I'll pretend I didn't know."

"Oh, thank you. She seems like a fine lady. I'd hate to upset her. Well, bridge night—got to go." The thin woman descended to the sidewalk, and then, at a quick pace, she disappeared in the darkness, only to reemerge at the next streetlamp.

I, on the other hand, shut the front door and headed for the vacant lot.

Weeds grabbed at my feet and ankles. I scolded myself for having changed my mind about acquiring a small flashlight, having assumed that I wouldn't need one if Hannah took me back. Wishful thinking is often less painful than admitting the possibility of something terrible happening. I should have followed my instincts rather than succumb to optimism.

After completing a cursory inspection of the weeds surrounding the debris-strewn basement, I spiraled outward through unfamiliar underbrush, periodically calling Hannah's name into the darkness. A root snagged my shoelace and pitched me forward. I scraped my forearm on a rock. After uttering a litany of well-chosen curses, I scrabbled to my feet and shed my coat. When I rolled my shirtsleeve up, my fingers encountered a sticky dampness, and there was pain when I touched the wound. I would have to cleanse the abrasion to avoid infection, but the injury would heal, so I put it out of my mind.

I bent down to brush bits of foliage off my pant legs and groused to no one in particular, "The city needs to clean this mess up. A hazard like this shouldn't exist." But then I wondered if the city had jurisdiction. The lot and the great house had once belonged to the McFarlands. It was the Homestead, as Grace had labeled it, but who owned the property now? I jotted a mental note to ask her the next time I saw her since I intended to revisit her soon—I had a promise to keep. I resumed my circular trek and soon reached the banks of Monroe Creek.

Spongy duff rebounded from my footsteps, like walking on foam rubber slabs. The disturbed debris gave off a moldy, leafy smell. Rather than weave my way through trees that paralleled the watercourse, I eased down the bank until I was near the water's edge. I made my way by holding on to limbs and fragile saplings for support. The crescent moon suspended above Logan Heights did little to illuminate the rocks and snags that waited to do me another injury.

By the time I had trekked the length of the vacant lot, I was beginning to worry for real.

Frustration amplified my sense of helplessness. There was nothing to do except return to the apartment and wait. Then it occurred to me that I should visit the pit and gather up my few possessions, like the army blanket and the lumpy pillow.

I descended the improvised ladder with care, feeling my way with my feet until my shoe touched the concrete slab. Sidestepping areas of groundwater seepage, I crossed to the splintery pallet. My pitiful possessions were undisturbed; I had hidden them beneath a scrap of plywood. Gathering them up, I turned to leave. That's when I noticed a light-colored blur against the darkness of the side wall. Apprehensively, I eased forward, my free hand feeling for tilted planks and other obstacles.

As I drew near, a shape emerged. My blood froze in my veins. All rational thought deserted my mind, driven out by the terrible image of a crumpled human form. I dropped the pillow and the blanket and lurched toward the body, banging my forehead soundly against a charred timber. I never felt the impact or the ooze of blood that trickled down my cheek.

A woman lay on her side, one leg straight, the other bent at the knee. Her right arm was outstretched as if reaching for something, but her left was tucked beneath her. Her head was turned at an impossible angle. I could not see her face. Unruly locks of long blonde hair partially covered her neck and shoulders. There was no movement, no audible breathing—no signs of life. When I reached out to rouse her, slack muscles yielded to my prodding, and her skin felt as cold as the concrete slab. The woman was dead, having apparently tripped and tumbled down from the lip of the basement wall.

Then my mind shut down entirely, unable to grasp a hideous concept so compelling that it ripped the breath from my lungs. All sense of purpose fled from my soul. My wife was dead. Hannah, the source of my existence, was gone.

"Why?" I screamed into the fearsome night. "Why?"

CHAPTER 11

The Tempest Bar stank of rotgut booze, stale cigarette smoke, and human musk—the olfactory residue left by the tide of derelicts and losers that washed in and out nightly. A sports channel blared soccer scores from a TV above the end of the bar, information as useless as the national weather report. Unless you're traveling, who cares if it's raining on the opposite side of the country? And if you are traveling, you're not watching TV.

Just inside the doorway, I paused to allow my eyes to adjust. The noonday sun of mid-November had rendered me nearly blind when I entered the darkness. Winter was coming. The air outside was crisp with a dryness that chaps lips and nostrils.

As the bar's interior became recognizable, I noted that there were three people in the room: Dallas, the daytime bartender, and two patrons. One guy, a little fellow, sat sulking in the corner. He seemed half-sloshed since his chin kept slipping off the heel of his hand as he tried to focus on the TV. The gorilla at the bar reminded me of someone I wanted to forget. Neither man gave even a grunt of acknowledgment when I stepped forward.

"Double scotch," I commanded.

"You got money?" Dallas countered in return.

In an "up yours" gesture, I slapped a ten-dollar bill down on the bar's lacquered mahogany.

Dallas scooped up the money and poured my drink. "I thought you quit?"

"I did." I gathered my glass and my change and turned toward a table as far from the sports noise as possible.

"Sorry to hear about your wife!" Dallas called out. "I was told she had a nice funeral."

A dismissive wave of my hand persuaded the bartender to lapse into silence.

A little over two weeks had passed, and already I couldn't recall the flowers St. Anthony's had provided—no doubt leftovers from a Sunday service. Nor could I remember how many of the faithful Father Samuel had coaxed into attending so the sanctuary wouldn't seem completely empty.

Twice, I had set out to visit my wife's grave. Both times, I had turned back at the entrance to the cemetery, unable to set eyes on her final resting place.

I stared at my drink. The amber liquid taunted me. Yes, I had promised to quit. But like the marriage covenant, death renders all vows null and void. I reached for my glass but then noticed out of the corner of my eye that the big man had risen from his barstool and was lumbering in my direction.

"Hey, I know you," the brute snarled thickly. "You're that wise-ass puke. You and me, we got a score to settle."

"Go away. I'm not in the mood." I set my drink down and placed both palms flat on the table.

"You think you can take me again, punk? You got lucky; caught me when I wasn't looking. This time, I'm going to rip your face off." The man grabbed a handful of air and viciously threw it aside.

"I just told you, I'm not in the mood."

Aware that the big guy probably wouldn't leave me alone, I regarded him more intently. His close-cropped hair and drooping lids made him seem dull-witted. The holes that pockmarked his cov-eralls tagged him as a foundry worker. Unable to dredge up details, I vaguely remembered he was surprisingly quick for his size and wick-edly strong, the type of opponent you box, not wrestle.

"What's your name again?" I asked with feigned indifference.

"Screw you."

"Well, Mr. Screw You, as you can see, I'm minding my own business. Now, why don't you run along and play with your dolls, or ask Mommy for a box of crayons so you can color lots of pretty little pictures."

"Stand up like a man," the monster hissed through clenched teeth. "Take what you got coming."

"Pete, leave him alone," Dallas pleaded from behind the bar. "Show some respect, will you? The man just lost his wife."

"Yeah? Well, she's better off dead. How could any bitch stand to be married to this—"

I launched myself out of my chair and aimed a straight right at the man's throat.

Anticipating my attack, he pivoted sideways and snagged me behind the ear with a roundhouse right that sent me sprawling. Dazed, with a swarm of bees buzzing inside my head, I momentarily lost track of what I was supposed to do next.

A ham-sized fist grabbed the front of my shirt and started pulling me to my feet. Instinctively, I drew my right leg up and kicked straight out, catching the man in the solar plexus with my heel. He let out a woof of pain, and I felt his grip loosen. Twisting laterally, I rolled away before he could recover and kept rolling until I was far enough out of reach to clamber to my feet.

The big man lowered his head and hunched his shoulders, like a bull about to charge. I prepared to slip to the side and use his momentum against him. Instead, after two quick steps, he drew up short and caught me in the ribs with a solid left jab that knocked the air out of my lungs. Rather than counter, I backpedaled several paces and nearly tripped over a chair.

The brute leered at me. "How we doing so far, punk?"

I straightened up and grinned at him. "You call this a fight, pansy? Girl Scouts hit harder than you do."

Enraged, my opponent made the mistake of cocking his left arm to throw a haymaker at my head. I eased to the side and slammed him with a thunderous overhand right. His knees buckled, and he dropped to the floor like a demolished building.

I looked down at the guy. He was out cold. "A mountain of muscle and a glass jaw. Pathetic."

Dallas surged out from behind the bar and grabbed my arm. "That's it. I've had it with you. I was willing to cut you some slack because of your bereavement, but every time you come in here, there's trouble. Get out, and don't come back." He shoved me toward the door. "I mean it. I don't want to see your face in here again."

A gust of cold air embraced me when I exited the bar. My ears still rang, and the world began to spin, making me nauseous. I stumbled across the sidewalk and retched in the gutter. After throwing up a second time, the dizziness started to ease off. I looked up and down Hayes Street and wondered where I should go.

One thing was sure: I would not go back to the apartment. Seeing reminders of Hannah everywhere I looked, catching the lingering scent of her on the bedsheets, recalling how her body had moved, and feeling echoes of her touch had nearly driven me out of my mind.

Abandoned and without purpose, I sat down on the curb and buried my face in my hands. Only one destination was left to me. Over the past several days, its morbid summons had grown increasingly strident, but only now was I finding the courage to respond.

There are occasions when time passes without a trace so that looking back, all that's seen is a gap, a blurry hole in the continuum. I felt a touch on my shoulder and realized I had no idea how long I had been sitting on the curb. I glanced up to find Father Samuel hovering over me, apprehension tugging his eyebrows together.

"Justin? Are you all right?" The priest wore his street attire rather than his church uniform, meaning he was either evangelizing the unsaved or running errands on his own time.

"What's up, Padre?" Still woozy, I climbed unsteadily to my feet.

Eyeing me up and down, Father Samuel pursed his lips. No doubt, I looked a mess. Besides needing a haircut and clean clothes, I hadn't bothered to shave for three days. And since the funeral, I hadn't slept more than twenty minutes at a time. When I did manage to doze off on the couch, I would awaken almost immediately, struggling to free myself from the web of some cloying nightmare.

The priest reached out to steady me when I lost my balance. "You okay?"

"I'm not drunk. I was about to get drunk, but things never work out the way you plan."

"Do you need to see a doctor?"

"There's nothing wrong with me that a doctor can fix."

"When's the last time you ate?"

I shrugged. I honestly couldn't remember. I eyed the priest. "Is this Monday?"

"Tuesday."

"Lost another day. Imagine that."

"Listen, you want to grab a bite? I was on my way to lunch. I'd be honored if you'd join me. My treat."

"What am I, your perpetual beneficence project? Save your pity for someone worth the effort."

"It's not charity. Quite the contrary, you challenge my theology—make me think. Besides, you can buy lunch if you want."

I pictured the $1,300 check still tucked safely in my wallet. With my wife dead, there'd seemed no reason to cash it. The last thing I wanted, however, was to listen to someone spouting off on how to deal with my grief. Some sorrows are too deep to be covered over with words. "Thanks, Padre, but you have better things to worry about." I turned away.

"Where are you going?"

"Does it matter?" I stopped and looked back, suddenly angry. "If I had a specific destination, would it make a difference? Oh, that's right. You need to believe I'm coping. That's the issue. Let's be real. Your calling demands that you have compassion for the afflicted. It's your job, but in the final analysis, do you care? You serve others to feel good about yourself. You measure your personal worth by how much you bleed for humanity. Problem is I don't want your sympathy. Don't you understand? I want to be done feeling sorry for myself. Being reminded of what I've lost isn't going to help. Anyway, what's the use? It doesn't matter. Not anymore. Nothing matters."

I turned and stumbled unsteadily away. Berating a man who had shown me nothing but kindness cut me to the quick. I felt like a proper ass for being so ungrateful, but sometimes, rather than offering comfort, commiseration keeps grief alive and fosters a victim mentality.

Anyway, it truly did not matter. With no purpose and no reason to draw breath, I needed my life to be over.

The decision having been made, I turned west on Lois Avenue. After crossing Polk, I looked ahead toward the middle of the block. Suddenly, a kid no older than eleven burst through the doors of the Cost Right Pharmacy and began sprinting in my direction.

An irate shopkeeper wearing a white smock followed. "Stop! Thief!" the man bellowed, but being overweight and on the sluggish side of middle age, he had no chance of apprehending a slippery street urchin.

As the youthful shoplifter zipped past, he flashed me a grin. I noticed the pair of sunglasses he clutched in his hand, the price tag was still attached.

"Why didn't you stop him?" the man wheezed breathlessly as he rumbled to a halt beside me, having abandoned the chase.

"Do I look like a cop?"

"You could've tripped him."

"And have his parents sue me? No thanks."

"Kids like that don't have parents, leastwise none that give a damn. That's why they steal."

"Right," I agreed indifferently as I moved on. Frankly, I didn't care about the theft of a pair of sunglasses. The ghetto's solution to financial inequality wasn't my concern.

I left the man standing with his hands at his waist, still trying to catch his breath. Two blocks later, I crossed Century Boulevard and entered New Waterford.

Within a couple more blocks, the character of the streets began to change. Citizens moved differently. Affluence is relative. Even poor people take pride in the fact that they're not as destitute as their neighbors. Ownership of even a few essentials fosters the belief that a man can control his destiny, which breeds hope—two attributes I sorely lacked, but not because I was poor.

As a young man, I used to ponder what it would be like to die—the thought of a glorious afterlife and what eternity would be like filled me with anticipation. In later years, especially after the fire, death had become the great unknowable and substantially more sinister.

As I continued south on Lois Avenue, the thought of dying was again on my mind, this time because I had done my homework.

AmRail's milk run operated along a spur line off the Illinois Service, the state's primary railroad. Trains that left Carbondale passed through Centralia, Rantoul, and Effingham before reaching Chicago. Though the locomotives never gathered much speed because of their mass, their considerable momentum was perfect for what I intended.

Suicide is the final option, the ultimate escape available to every tormented soul. The stigma attached to suicide derives from fear, not from an affront to morality. No one wants to be reminded that life can become so intolerable that the only rational alternative is to give up.

I remembered the cardboard box I had clutched in my hands and the devastating prophecy it had embodied. To be used up and cast aside, to become a hollow shell of no value, was worse than death. For me, all that remained was to find the courage to follow through with the choice that was not a choice at all, but merely the final gesture of a life gone wrong.

Ahead, I could see the railroad tracks. Creosote and grease stained the ties. A sheen of oil on a patch of gravel reflected taffeta patterns, and the steel rails along the raised bed glimmered under a late autumn sun. As days go, this one seemed about average, neither too hot nor too cold, a Goldilocks day with only a few clouds to dress up the sky.

I followed the tracks until I found a spot that looked as if it would suffice. From where I stood, I saw that the parallel ribbons of steel curved around a low hillock. That meant an approaching locomotive would have a limited field of view and could not see more than sixty yards ahead. Furthermore, a large oleander had grown up beside the tracks. Devoid of flowers and having shed a third of its leaves, the scraggly shrub would provide some cover. By keeping a low profile, I could stay concealed until the very last minute, when the engineer could not react.

I sat cross-legged between two ties, smooth pebbles cold against my backside. Commuter trains run every two hours. I would not have long to wait.

"Do you realize that every time I bump into you, you're sitting down, cogitating?"

I recognized the voice and looked behind me to find Father Samuel studying me and shaking his head. "Do you suppose that means something?"

"What are you doing here?" I said over my shoulder.

"I followed you. The more important question is, 'What are you doing here?'"

"Didn't I make myself clear? I don't want your help. Go away."

"And miss the big finale? Not a chance."

The priest advanced until he stood beside the tracks, four feet from where I sat, gazing in the same direction I was facing. His hands were clasped behind his back. "In seminary, we were taught how to minister to the sick. As part of our curriculum, we were on call to the hospital. Our job was to tend to the spiritual needs of patients. Several times, I remember being summoned to the emergency department to administer extreme unction. In case you didn't know, being non-Catholic, that's last rites. I encountered some pretty gruesome trauma—auto accidents, a woman mangled in a fall, but I never came across anyone run over by a train. This will be a first. I hope we find pieces of you big enough to bury. Have you given any thought to what kind of funeral you'd like? Closed casket, of course."

"If you're trying to shock me into changing my mind, forget it. You can do what you want with what's left of my carcass. Leave it for the crows for all I care."

The priest turned to face me. The sun at his back caused me to squint when I looked into his face. He paused for a moment before speaking. "Do you remember our conversation regarding free will and how God allows us to choose whether to do good or to do evil? Why do you think He entrusted us with such an awesome responsibility?"

"You know, Padre, I'm not interested in your theology right now. Just leave me be. Go minister to the living."

"It's because when we embrace His purpose for our lives, we become more than our original selves. If you give up now, you'll never experience what you were intended to be."

"Whatever purpose my life might have had died two weeks ago. Look, I don't want to discuss this. I've made my decision. Nothing you can say is going to change my mind."

"Don't be an idiot. Suicide is a mortal sin. Think about where your soul will spend eternity."

"There's no need to shout. Did I yell at you?"

"You're right." The priest raised both hands in a gesture of appeasement. With exaggerated calmness, he said, "Do you want to go to hell?"

"Padre, I'm already there."

Father Samuel cocked his head to gaze down at me. The notion of physically hauling me off the tracks must have entered his mind, though it would be a tussle. He was younger, but I had the advantage when it came to height and reach. Besides, even if he did succeed in dragging me away, he probably knew I would return as soon as he was gone, and he would've been right. Instead, he chose to do something I never would've expected.

Father Samuel stepped to the middle of the tracks and sat facing me, just out of reach. He crossed his legs in the same way I had and then nodded once, a wordless, "So there." With his back to the low hill, he could not see an oncoming train. I could tell by the trepidation in his eyes that he was serious.

My self-appointed conscience cupped his hands in his lap, but they nervously refused to stay there. "You were right about my profession," he said. "Priests are expected to show compassion to the afflicted. I'm paid to do that, but you also asked how much I care. Well, here it is: you die, I die. You need to know you're not alone, and if that means we go together, so be it."

"Look, man, you don't have a dog in this fight. Go tend to the people who need you."

"I am."

I hurled a scowl of disagreement at the priest but then decided to let events run their course. I assumed that he would chicken out. Priest or not, there was no way the man would throw his life away on my behalf. It was another ploy, and it wasn't going to work. My mind was made up.

Sunlight warmed my face as we glowered at each other. For a time, we sat there, reading each other's thoughts, testing the strength of the other man's will.

"There is something I've been meaning to ask you," I said at length.

"What's that?" Beads of perspiration had sprung up on the priest's forehead. I doubted they were the result of the sun warming his back.

I said casually, "I've noticed that you like expensive toys: your shoes, your watch—the odds and ends in your office. Don't priests take a vow of poverty?"

"We do."

"Well?"

"Well, what? I like nice things."

"Tell me, is breaking a vow a sin?"

"Depends on your point of view. I don't covet material possessions. I enjoy the fruits of my labors. I happen to be a fairly shrewd investor. Day trading stocks is a hobby—has been for years. I would've made a hell of a broker if I hadn't joined the clergy. There's a difference between using money and loving money."

"For a priest, that has to be a mighty thin line."

"Have you been talking to the monsignor?"

"Is he on your case?"

"You could say that."

"So, worldly wealth is an issue?"

"All right, yes. I admit it. It's a character flaw, one I'm trying to correct." He glanced at his gold and platinum watch and then drew his shirt sleeve down. He looked away in embarrassment.

"One thing is certain," I offered, "stay seated as you are, and it won't be a problem long." I reached out to touch one of the metal rails. "Feel that? The vibrations?"

The color drained from Father Samuel's face as his fingers made contact with the cold steel.

Gently, I suggested, "You don't really want to do this, do you? You should leave now."

I could see the priest was beginning to panic. His eyes darted to and fro as if seeking help that wasn't there. On the verge of hyperventilating, he gritted his teeth and looked straight at me. "You think you want this? Well, I do, too, but for different reasons."

"So turn around and enjoy the show. It's got to be nerve-wracking, not being able to see what's coming—not knowing when the moment of impact is upon you."

"Shut up." The priest's body was trembling. "I'm not leaving. You are not going to die alone."

After some hurried mental gymnastics, I calculated that from the moment the locomotive burst into view, we would have maybe twenty seconds to live. The last thing I would see would be a dingy, grime-streaked cow catcher.

In the distance, I heard the rumble of a commuter freight rolling inexorably toward us.

"All kidding aside, Father, you need to split now."

"No. Not until you change your mind." The priest's eyes were wide with terror, and his muscles were rigid, frozen by fear.

The rumble grew louder. I could feel the clicking of the train's wheels through my legs and buttocks. I expected my mechanical slayer to pop out from behind the low hill at any moment.

I locked eyes with the priest. "I don't want you here."

"I don't care."

"Go away!" I screamed.

"No."

A gunmetal gray blur exploded behind the priest's left ear, partially obscured by the oleander's branches. We were out of time.

To die alone, with no one to mourn, was one thing, but being held morally accountable for another man's death was a burden my conscience refused to accept. I lurched awkwardly to my feet. The locomotive had rounded the curve and was now heading straight for us. The lens of its huge spotlight transfixed me like a giant cyclopean eye, growing ever larger.

Stepping behind the priest, I grabbed him around the chest and tried to haul him to his feet. He was dead weight in my arms, so petrified by dread that he couldn't move. The train was closer now, merely forty yards away, and there was no indication that the engineer had seen us. Two hundred tons of steel was about to roll right over us, and no one would notice.

I dug my foot into the gravel and heaved, but the smooth pebbles gave no traction.

"Leave me!" Father Samuel wailed. "Save yourself!"

I locked my arms more tightly around him, and with my mouth close to his ear, I said softly, "You die, I die."

Frantically, I planted my foot against an oil-soaked tie—the edge of my sole caught on the lip of an empty knothole. Drawing upon every ounce of strength within me, I thrust with all my might, wrenching both of us up and over the gleaming rail just as the locomotive surged past. The outermost projection of its metal guardrail bruised my heel.

The priest and I tumbled and slid down the shallow incline beside the rails, a flurry of arms and legs tangling together. We wound up sprawled next to one another, surrounded by puffs of dust. I tilted my head up to watch the train rattle by. There was still no sign anyone had witnessed our escapade.

I lay back and looked up at the sky. A feathery cloud that resembled a dachshund loitered overhead. The ground's shaking subsided as the train gradually rolled out of sight. The air smelled of machine oil and diesel, but I also detected a whiff of lavender.

What happens now? I wondered.

Beside me, Father Samuel roused himself. After turning onto his side, he raised up on one elbow. His hands were trembling, but he braved a smile. "Are you hungry? It's your turn to buy lunch."

For reasons I could not fathom, the remark struck me as funny, and I began to laugh. And then I could not stop laughing.

Father Samuel joined in, and soon we were cackling so hard, our sides hurt, and tears were running down our cheeks.

When the levity eased, I lay back and regarded the blue cloud-flecked sky. To my amazement, it actually felt good to be alive.

CHAPTER 12

"I don't need a babysitter," I grumbled in protest. Father Samuel had been fussing like a mother hen ever since I had awakened after spending the night on his brocade sofa. "I'm okay," I said. "Go do church stuff."

With both of us still rattled by our near-death experience, he had demanded that I sleep over at his apartment rather than spend the night alone.

"Are you just saying that? It's not that you want to be alone so that…you know?"

"No. The urge is gone, at least for now. Go do what you need to do."

After measuring my state of mind through narrowed eyes, the priest nodded and turned to examine his reflection in the gilded hall mirror.

From the sofa, I watched him straighten the stole that hung around his neck and down his shoulders. With a critical eye, he plucked a speck of lint off the chest of his chasuble. "You're sure you're okay?" he called out while monitoring my reaction in the glass.

"You think I'm going to wrap a cable from your home exercise gym around my neck and hang myself?" I stifled a yawn.

"What are your plans?"

"I don't know. Probably kick back for a while, if that's all right." In some cultures, when one man saves another man's life, he becomes responsible for that man's future and must provide for his well-being. If not for Father Samuel, I would have died under the wheels of a northbound freight train. On the other hand, if not for me, the cyclopean monster would have crushed him. Technically, we were even, but to my way of thinking, I owed the priest a debt I could never repay. The man had risked his life to save mine. How often does that happen?

"Stay as long as you like. There's food in the kitchen. Help yourself to whatever you find. I shouldn't be gone long. I wouldn't be bailing at all, except I have a wedding to perform." I noticed his hands were trembling as he smoothed the silken fabric of his robe across the front of his chest.

"This early?" I said, rubbing sleep from my eyes. "Who gets married in the morning? It seems uncivilized."

"It's nearly four in the afternoon. I decided not to wake you." He turned to face me and held his arms out to the sides. "How do I look?"

"Like a Catholic priest. Four p.m., really?" No wonder I felt hungover. I glanced around the apartment, noting the gilded crucifix on the wall, the porcelain Virgin Mary on the bookshelf—hand-painted, of course—and the tidy assortment of church publications on the low coffee table. "No TV? How do you relax?"

"I read. I study the Scriptures—pray."

"Sounds boring."

"Watch a lot of TV, do you?"

"Eh, no. Not since moving to this neighborhood."

"So, how do you spend your free time?"

"Point taken."

Father Samuel attempted a grin and then stepped to the door. He stopped with his hand on the knob when I spoke up.

"Are you okay with what happened?" I said.

After a moment of introspection, he looked back. "Honestly, I don't know. Being that terrified…I'm not sure. It's hard to explain."

"Yeah. Me too."

We regarded each other for a time, unable to describe what we had shared. Eventually, the priest cocked his head to look at me. "Tell me the truth. Are you all right? Or do I need to worry?"

"I'm fine, or I will be. At least I no longer feel like ending it all. Go figure."

"God is good."

"Indeed. He is. By the way, about what I said earlier, when we were in front of the Tempest Bar—I'm sorry. I didn't mean it. I was angry, but not at you."

"I know." Father Samuel departed and closed the door behind him, leaving me to wrestle with a knot of tightly tangled emotions that might never get sorted out.

After folding the sheet and blanket Father Samuel had provided, I looked around for something to do. The rows of magazines on the coffee table caught my eye. I rummaged through several stories, but nothing held my interest. The finer points of Catholic theology left me confused and frustrated, like playing a strategy game without knowing all the rules. An article detailing how to minister to the severely depressed prompted me to toss the publication aside. What I didn't need was another round of do-it-yourself psychoanalysis. As I had recently learned, it's not good for a man to spend too much time inside his head.

Despite gnawing hunger pangs, I decided to eat after Father Samuel returned—his dinner, my breakfast. He might be delayed, but I probably wouldn't starve, and it seemed rude to raid another man's larder, even with his permission.

I crossed the soft carpet to inspect a floor-to-ceiling bookshelf. Craning my head to the side, I studied titles and learned my host had eclectic taste in literature. There were more than a few college textbooks, undoubtedly remnants of his seminary days. Various translations of the Bible took up half of one shelf. Also, I found a copy of St. Thomas Aquinas's *Summa Theologica* beside the collected works of Martin Luther. Next came several commentaries written by different Christian scholars.

What surprised me was finding copies of Karl Marx's *on the Jewish Question*, Adolf Hitler's *Mein Kampf,* and *Quotations from Chairman Mao*. I chuckled when I noticed that the priest had placed these tomes beside Lewis Carroll's *Through the Looking Glass*.

The last item on the lowest shelf caught my eye. It was a tall leather-bound album. Its elegant bindings made the adjoining volume that propped it upright seem less flamboyant. No title graced its spine, which I found intriguing.

Upon examination, I removed the album from its place and discovered it was a scrapbook, a pictorial history of the O'Bryan clan. In addition, there was a manila folder inside that contained an assortment of newspaper clippings, all yellowed with age.

I carried the scrapbook to the sofa and sat down to read. My conscience might bridle at pilfering another man's provisions but not at invading his privacy.

I began by studying the images in the scrapbook and saved the folder for last. The first several photos were old black-and-whites, faded with time. In each photo, the men and the women mostly wore semiformal attire—suits and dresses. Judging by their facial features, I figured they had to be distant aunts and uncles, perhaps one set of grandparents.

Next came a series of group pictures where the subjects seemed more at ease. I suspected they belonged to the generation that followed the patriarchs. One face in particular stood out in almost every gathering. The man had Father Samuel's eyes and a narrow chin. He had to be Maxwell O'Bryan, the priest's father. A robust gentleman in his late twenties, his hair was cropped short at the temples, and he repeatedly glowered at the camera with the fervor of a young zealot.

A set of more recent snapshots came next. Taken from different angles, they chronicled life on a modest Iowa farm. A white two-story farmhouse stood facing a red barn with a log corral nearby. Undoubtedly, this was the spread where the priest had spent his formative years after his family had fled Branford Gardens. The contrasts between the farm and the neighborhood I was beginning to regard as home could not have been more striking. In one photograph, acres of surrounding crop land ran flat and featureless, except for a line of deciduous trees that paralleled a shallow creek. It seemed a lonely place to grow up.

I found the photo of a young woman cradling a toddler on the following page. A Star of David hung from a chain around her neck. A nose a bit too large degraded her plain face. It made me wonder what Father Samuel might look like without his beard and mustache. I thumbed through the remaining pages of the album but could find no other images of the woman. If she was indeed Samuel's mother, and judging by the child's age in the photograph, she would be gone within a few months of when the picture was taken.

Something clicked in my mind. I flipped back to the group pictures. Sure enough, there it was. The subjects faced the camera in all but one image, as if posed during ceremonial events. The odd scene stood out because people looked at ease, as would be the case at a reception or cocktail party, a number held drinks in their hands.

The man I had previously identified as Samuel's father stood near the center of the gathering, engrossed in conversation. He seemed captivated by an attractive middle-aged woman who had retained the bloom of youth. To my mind, there was no question that the man was, in fact, Maxwell O'Bryan, and the woman was Grace McFarland.

I then opened the manila folder and began reading. A collection of news articles dealt with daily life in the Gardens. A series of editorials followed them. Many bore Max O'Bryan's byline. Repeatedly, the articles detailed how local criminal elements were preying on innocent citizens. In several, the author decried the misery caused by their nefarious activities—human interest stuff. But then the tenor of the editorials changed. One tirade demanded that the state's attorney general launch a full-scale investigation. Another railed against widespread corruption in city government. The author had chosen not to pull his punches.

Having experienced firsthand the power of the press, I wondered how much public support Max had rallied in favor of bringing down the McFarland syndicate.

Next came a single-column newspaper clipping, the last item in the folder. It told how a prominent banker had been found shot to death. Apparently, Grace McFarland had returned home one afternoon to find her son, Andrew, lying on the Persian rug in their living room, dead from a gunshot wound. Of course, foul play had seemed the obvious explanation, though suicide was considered a remote possibility. Her grandson, Warren, was noted to have been away at boarding school. Lacking an eyewitness, the case was expected to remain unsolved.

And that was it. Whatever events had followed, they weren't chronicled in Father Samuel's scrapbook.

I carefully returned the album to its place on the shelf and sat down again to think. Mulling over what I had learned, one question stood out: *What was the real reason my host had volunteered to serve the Church by returning to Branford Gardens?*

As it turned out, I did not have long to wait for Father Samuel's return. I was still seated on the sofa when the apartment door opened. The priest seemed distressed as he stepped into the room and forcefully slammed the door behind him. It was apparent something was troubling him. Aftershocks, I suspected—echoes of our shared trauma.

"How was the wedding?" I said, noting the scowl that darkened his countenance.

"I made a mess of it, I'm afraid. Couldn't even stay for the reception." His voice trailed off as he disappeared into the bedroom to shed his vestments. After a time, he emerged wearing denim pants and a striped shirt with pale buttons down the front. The preppy outfit seemed an improvement over the country club attire he'd been wearing when we had first met. Still, there was little chance the Gardens' natives would mistake him as one of their own.

Father Samuel entered the kitchen without hesitating and yanked open a cupboard door. He reached in and took out a tall bottle half full of amber liquid. "Want some?" He held the bottle up for my inspection. I recognized the label of a fine Kentucky bourbon.

Belatedly realizing his faux pas, he flushed. "Sorry, forgot you quit. You don't mind if I have some, do you?"

Not waiting for my reply, the priest poured out two fingers' worth, which he promptly downed in one swallow. About to pour a second drink, he glanced at me and returned the cap to the bottle and the bottle to the shelf.

The priest reentered the living room and began pacing in front of the sofa where I sat. "I can't believe I forgot the bride's name." He gestured in frustration. "How would you feel if, during the exchange of vows, the minister looks at your bride and says, 'Do you—eh, what was your name again?' Lord, I should be defrocked. Aw, screw it." Father Samuel returned to the cupboard to help himself to another two-finger salute.

Thinking about marriage unexpectedly reminded me of Hannah on our wedding day. I blanked out whatever comments the priest was making. Instead, I pictured my wife, her face radiant behind a thin veil, the silken train of her gown flowing out behind her. I remembered uttering the words "With this ring..." and feeling the gold band slip onto the third finger of her left hand, knowing she would be forever mine.

A tsunami of grief shattered the inner peace I had so fervently nurtured. For the first time since Hannah's death, I felt my defenses crumble. Pent-up emotions released; silent tears came in unbidden rushes. I tried to stifle my feelings, but the abiding certainty of being utterly and truly alone tore at my heart. I could not quell the anguish, nor did I truly want to. I let go. Waves of grief poured out of me.

A reassuring hand rested on my shoulder. I looked up. The priest stood at my side. He regarded me with deep concern. "It's okay," he said softly. "It's not as bad as you think. Yeah, I screwed up—no question about it, but the monsignor won't fire me. In the worst-case scenario, he'll slip a letter of reprimand into my personnel folder, which is bad enough, to be sure. It means I'll never be pope."

After my emotional meltdown had run its course and I had regained a modicum of composure, I gravitated toward the kitchen. There, I discovered that the priest was a surprisingly good cook. I would have offered to help, except I would've just gotten in the way. Instead, I watched while he single-handedly prepared our meal.

A dash of fennel, a pinch of tarragon, and several other spices I failed to recognize transformed ordinary red snapper fillets into a main course I could savor. Ordinarily, I'm not a fish lover. Being rapaciously hungry and feeling somewhat less depressed undoubtedly goaded my appetite. In any event, I ate heartily, though not with gusto.

The priest, however, picked at his food. I sensed something of greater magnitude than a botched wedding was on his mind. I waited, but he seemed reticent to confront his demons.

"Why'd you return to Branford Gardens?" I said casually when the food on my plate was nearly gone. I hoped that he would benefit from opening up about his past. After all, one good catharsis deserves another.

Like the sudden turning of a road, my question had come unexpectedly, not as a natural progression from the preceding conversation. Taken by surprise, my host's fork hung suspended partway to his mouth.

I added, "A man with your obvious qualifications, there must have been other postings you could have accepted, openings in less blighted neighborhoods. Why here? Why Branford Gardens? Did you know what you'd be getting yourself into?"

"Not entirely." The priest scowled as he set his fork down, his morsel of fish uneaten.

"Are you sorry you came back?"

Father Samuel steepled his fingers. "Yesterday morning, I might have said yes. Now… Well, we evolve, I suppose."

"Near-death experiences can alter your worldview—so I've heard."

"Did it change yours?"

"The jury's still out."

"Precisely."

I ate my last bite of snapper. "Why Branford Gardens? I'd like to know." I guess I had assumed that discussing personal matters might reveal the source of his disquiet, though I didn't expect his troubles to be so near the surface.

"I returned to make amends for my father."

"Amends? For what?"

"What's it to you?"

"You're my friend. Something is troubling you. Why should you have to make amends for your father?"

"Because of his cowardice," the priest spat.

"Cowardice. That sounds serious. Want to talk about it?"

"No."

"You might feel better."

"You think so, do you?"

"It's worth a try."

"Let it drop, okay?"

"Would you?"

The priest heaved a sigh of annoyance, then after a moment, he admitted, "I suppose not. Well, since you're determined, this used to be a good neighborhood, a nice place to live."

Father Samuel's voice sounded stiff and unforgiving.

"Then the crooks moved in. They took over little by little, till crime and corruption were rampant: prostitution, drugs, illegal gambling—all the evils of society. My dad's newspaper could have made a difference. Branford Gardens should never have become this…this ghetto. He should've chosen to stand and fight. But no, he ran away. That's why I grew up on a farm in Iowa; my father was a coward."

"You don't believe this neighborhood became a slum because of him?"

"I do. He should've fought back, but he didn't. Oh, he started to, but then he chickened out. And then look what happened yesterday. Who could have known? When it comes to being afraid, I'm no different than my dad."

"What do you mean?" I sensed we were drawing near to the heart of the issue.

"I just sat there. I was petrified—literally petrified. I couldn't move. I had no idea I could feel that afraid."

"Are you serious?" It seemed incredulous that the man could so completely misinterpret his actions. "What you did, risking your life to save mine, was extraordinary bravery. I owe you a debt I can never repay."

"You don't understand."

"Really? What am I missing?"

"I'm a priest. I preach the resurrection of Jesus Christ. I proclaim that my sins have been forgiven, that death has no hold on me. That's what I believe. That's what I espouse, but I couldn't find my faith when that train was at my back. The only thing before my eyes was empty blackness."

My personal theology was too anemic to console my friend. All I could say was, "It's not like you had time to prepare." Sometimes, it's best to keep your mouth shut and commiserate in silence.

Hurling a glower in my direction, the priest's unspoken retort came through loud and clear: "All my adult life, I've been preparing to face death."

Then it occurred to me that, unlike my host, I had openly sought death. I had yearned to be released from an intolerable existence and had therefore had given no thought to what came next. I found the insight sobering and more than a little worrisome. "So where do we go from here?"

Father Samuel rocked back in his chair. "Good question." He seemed lost in thought for a long interval, and then he looked me in the eye. "There is something I've been meaning to tell you. I've been thinking about your loss, and…I hope you receive this in the spirit it's offered. If it offends you, I apologize in advance."

He hesitated as if collecting minimally incendiary words to convey his thoughts.

"I'd like to believe I somewhat understand your grief. Certainly, I've never lost a wife, but I can sort of imagine being suddenly separated from a loved one and how hard that must be. But the truth is, your loss and all you've been through, the fire, even the fact you almost died—well, it's not about you."

I recoiled as if physically assaulted.

Did he really think I chose to wallow in self-pity, that my anguish reflected an "oh, poor me" mindset? The suggestion demeaned what Hannah and I had shared, not to mention the worth of the lives consumed by the inferno that took Liberty Tower One. Weren't my memories a memorial to their passing? Was not my grief a testimony to how very much they were missed?

Father Samuel leaned forward and gripped my forearm. "Please, bear with me. You need to understand this: what you give to others is more important than how you feel inside. The sooner you realize this truth and get on with your life, the more quickly you will heal. Yes, your tragedies were overwhelming; I realize that. Lots of people give up. It's understandable. But now you've been offered a second chance, and you need to know that the answers you seek will never be found inside yourself. As hard as this may seem, it's important for you to reach out and start serving others. That's how you'll put your life back together. Do you get what I'm trying to say?"

"Is that what you intend to do?"

"It's part of it."

CHAPTER 13

Dusk's indigo curtain descended toward the rooftops and chimneys of Branford Gardens as I walked along Octavia Avenue, away from Father Samuel's apartment, his words still echoing in my ears.

At the corner, I turned north on Beach Street. To my right, Monroe Creek ran like a scar carved into the landscape by an inebriated surgeon. Poplars and dogwoods at the creek's edge became featureless voids in the fading light. Two blocks ahead lay the triangular lot where Hannah had died. I dreaded drawing near to that weed-infested plot of ground. Yet I had promised the priest I would go straight home.

From a block away, I began scanning recessed doorways and the shadowed spaces between buildings, potential hiding places where a mugger might lurk. During dinner, the priest had noted that his parishioners were afraid because of the recent spate of assaults that had plagued the neighborhood.

In every case, the mode of attack had been the same. The perpetrators would lie in wait until their victim opened their front door. Then they would rush forward and strike. After dragging their hapless prey inside, away from the street, they would commit robbery, battery, or worse. One man had died. Another was in critical condition.

Fortunately, the apartment building's concrete stoop was deserted. After opening the front door, I stood utterly still, listening intently and letting my eyes adjust to the inky blackness, the light bulb on the third floor having recently given out.

When I had asked the landlord why the outer door wasn't routinely locked, he had mumbled something about fire department regulations. The allusion to fire had incinerated the retort I had been about to make. I suspect he had grown tired of being called out to admit tenants who had lost their keys. Whatever his reason, an unlocked door meant evildoers could enter the building unimpeded.

A faint creaking noise drifted down from the second-floor landing, like someone shifting their weight on a loose floorboard. As noiselessly as possible, I closed the outer door behind me. Then I froze, convinced I could hear the faint rustle of fabric in the darkness above, perhaps a nylon windbreaker.

The notion of fleeing to seek help seemed gutless and futile. With one officer assigned to patrol Branford Gardens, there was no telling how long it would take to track him down. From experience, the locals had learned that when dealing with crime, you were on your own. Besides, I wasn't about to let some street hoodlum chase me away from my apartment. On tiptoes, I headed up the stairs.

With care, I transferred my weight from the top step to the second-floor landing and balled my fists in preparation for striking out. It seemed unlikely that my stealthy approach had been detected since I had remembered where to place my feet to avoid the squeaky places.

A faint movement at the edge of perception drew my attention toward the middle of the landing. In the near total darkness, I lunged forward, head down, shoulders flexed, like a linebacker driving toward a scrimmage line tackle. The impact jarred my spine, but I was rewarded by a high-pitched squeal. A loud *oomph* resonated across the landing as air was forced from the lungs of the person I had pinned against my apartment wall.

Rather than strong and muscular, my supposed assailant's body was slim and curvaceous. Furthermore, my shoulder had impacted an area of softness, probably a breast. I stepped back but retained a tight grip on one lissome arm. "Who are you? What are you doing here?"

The woman required a moment to catch her breath, for indeed, even in the darkness, I was now convinced my lurker was female.

"I'm Erin—from Harwood," she proclaimed between gasps.

Oops.

I released my grip and withdrew my hand from her arm. After digging the key out of my pocket, I unlocked the apartment door and reached in to flip on the interior light. In the muted glow, I noted that Erin's face was ashen.

"I'm truly sorry about that," I said. "I thought you were a mugger. Come in. I'll get you some water."

As we stepped inside, her breathing was starting to ease, though still somewhat ragged. She waited in the living room while I stepped into the kitchen. Even standing at the sink, I could hear her wheezes.

I have never understood why people offer water in times of physical distress. Besides preventing dehydration and quenching thirst, the fluid has little medicinal value. Still, fetching a glass seemed reasonable, perhaps because even fruitless gestures are preferable to standing around doing nothing, especially if you've caused the other person's misery.

When I returned, I handed Erin a mason jar half full of lukewarm tap water; there was no ice in the refrigerator. She took one sip, scrunched up her face, and looked for a place to set the make-do glass aside.

I held out my hand, and she handed me the mason jar. Returning to the kitchen, I set it down beside the sink.

Erin broached a smile when I reentered the living room. Her distress seemed to have eased considerably.

"Better?" I said.

She nodded.

"No ribs broken?"

She shook her head.

"Look, I'm sorry, but what are you doing here?"

"I was waiting for you."

"Obviously. Why?"

The corners of Erin's azure eyes crinkled when she grinned. "Grace is asking to see you." Erin nestled into Hannah's favorite corner of the couch.

I chose the armchair—appropriately separated. "How long have you been waiting?" I asked.

Erin gave a gesture of unconcern. "Not long—couple hours, maybe." The green and white scrubs she wore beneath her navy blue windbreaker suggested she had come straight from work.

With solemnity, the nurse said, "First, let me express how sorry I am. I heard what happened—losing your wife. A tragedy. Words generally don't count for much, but I am sorry."

"Thank you. I…eh, she was…thanks."

"The entire staff feels the same. All of us at Harwood were saddened by your loss. Even Ms. Lonergan."

I acknowledged her condolences with a nod.

"I don't know if you've heard, but we passed our state inspection thanks to you."

"I'm glad. It was an interesting project. There were some unique challenges."

Under other circumstances, I might have noticed that the nurse was attractive—shoulder-length auburn hair, cute nose and mouth, clear blue eyes—but my grief was too intense. To keep the conversation going, I said, "I'm sorry you had to stand around in the dark. I probably should bite the bullet and fix the socket myself. The landlord doesn't seem inclined."

Erin traced a finger along the seam of the couch's armrest. "It was a bit spooky. Still, waiting in the dark seemed preferable to freezing outside. The nights are getting cold. It'll probably start snowing any day now." She cocked her head. "Do you ski?"

"It's been years, and it wasn't skiing, precisely. It was more like rolling around in the snow. You said Grace asked to see me?"

"Yes. She's talking. Can you believe it? Stroke patients hardly ever recover their speech, not like her, not all of a sudden, and especially not after months of being completely mute. Even her doctor was astonished."

"That's terrific, but why me? Why does she want to see me?"

"She wouldn't say."

I teasingly suggested, "She probably wants to bawl me out for letting sawdust blow into her eyes."

"I doubt that. Considering the role you played in her recovery, I would imagine she's grateful rather than upset."

"What role?"

"The attention you gave her, your concern—including her in your project. I'm not sure how, but it made a difference."

About to protest that I had been focused on my concerns rather than Grace's, it occurred to me that Providence had played its part. I'm sure Father Samuel would have declared that my relationship with Grace had merely evolved according to God's master plan, and he undoubtedly would have been right. The pebble at the water's edge changes the river's flow ever so slightly, and a new channel opens up. The image in the locket had captivated my imagination and, hence, all that had followed. A man could go nuts trying to figure it out—another riddle without a clear solution.

Thinking about riddles caused me to wonder again what sort of trauma drives a woman into a self-imposed exile. Perhaps I was about to find out. "Grace is an enigma," I said somewhat ambiguously. "I'll stop by tomorrow."

Erin grinned. "She'll be pleased."

"Speaking of Grace, how's her heart condition?"

The grin faded. "I'd like to say she's better, but...well, let me know what you think after you've seen her."

"I'm no doctor."

"True, but then I don't believe her problems are physical. She seems...no. You should draw your own conclusions. Find me after you two talk, okay? Look, I'm sorry, but would you mind if I used your restroom? I've had to go for a while now."

I pointed. "In there."

As Erin rose from the couch, I recalled that Hannah's lotions and toiletries were still in plain sight. *What will she think of me*, I wondered, *hanging on to a dead woman's personal items?* It was an irrational thought, but so far no one had explained how the grieving process is supposed to work. How does a widower properly mourn? All I knew was that my heart was broken, and I was barely hanging on. After all, how all together can a man be if he's willing to commit suicide?

I looked around, overcome by a renewed sense of despair. Father Samuel was right. I really did need to get away from myself and back into the world again.

The bathroom door opened. Erin emerged, but rather than return to the couch or move to leave, she stood momentarily, her gaze traveling here and there as if taking stock of my secondhand furnishings. When she glanced through the open door to the second bedroom, she gave a startled shriek.

Light from the streetlamps must have silhouetted the forlorn angel on Hannah's workbench. Wings outstretched, in the dimness, the carving no doubt had resembled a netherworld denizen.

"It's a marble statue, completely inanimate." I rose from the armchair and laid a hand on Erin's shoulder. I promptly withdrew my touch after reaching around to switch on the light.

"It's beautiful!" she exclaimed. "So alive. You created this?"

"Hannah, my wife—"

"Really? Look at the detail, the expression on its face."

I followed as she approached to inspect the cherub up close— another invasion of my wife's personal space.

Erin drew a finger along the edge of one wing, gently sensing the marble. I had watched Hannah perform the same gesture innumerable times.

In a muted voice, Erin said, "I wish I had known her. This is amazing. What about you? Do you have any special talents other than carpentry?"

"Not really." Not unless getting drunk and picking fights count as hobbies, but I wasn't about to mention those activities.

Erin spoke quietly as she admired the little angel. "Personally, I like to garden. I like watching things grow and how the earth smells when I'm tilling the ground." Her comments brought the empty lot across the street and its multitude of aromas to mind. Then I remembered finding Hannah.

Feeling uneasy, I decided it was time to draw Erin's visit to a close. Rather than rudely invite her to leave, I hoped she could take a hint. I asked, "How did you get here? I don't remember seeing any unfamiliar cars out front."

"By bus." She turned to face me. Light from the window drew an auburn halo around her head. "I own a car, but city traffic makes me crazy. Besides, I figured the walk from the station would do me good. Standing on your feet all day—it's not the same as exercise."

I indicated the darkness outside the window. "It's not safe after the sun goes down. I'll walk you to the station."

A hint of feminist defiance troubled her face. Her look told me that she could take care of herself. I did not doubt that under normal circumstances, she was correct. However, a single woman walking alone in the Gardens at night was different.

Erin must have sensed my resolve. "Good," she said. "We'll have more time to talk. I have a favor to ask. I recently bought a small house with a yard so I can do my gardening. I'm in the process of remodeling, and I need someone to open one room into another. I wondered if you might be willing since you're handy with tools. I'm thinking I need to knock a hole in one wall and set in a pair of double doors like you did in the solarium. I'll pay you, of course, whatever you think is a fair wage. Interested?"

"I might be." I did need another job. I took her arm, deftly steered her toward the exit, and then led the way downstairs.

Rather than take the shortcut through the weeds, we followed the sidewalks that skirted the vacant lot. Along the way, we discussed her project, which I estimated would require two to three full days, possibly four.

When we reached the bus station, and I was satisfied she was out of harm's way, I accepted her offer. Two considerations decided the matter. First, I needed to find out if I really wanted to be a handyman. Her project seemed the perfect opportunity to make a decision.

Second, I remembered Father Samuel's counsel that I should start giving of myself in service to others.

As I left the terminal, Erin waved and called out cheerily, "See you tomorrow at the Manor."

Walking back to my apartment, I remembered the battered cardboard box. It had stripped away my defenses and set me stumbling along the path of self-knowledge. I recalled how genuine yet how pathetic that box had seemed, no longer able to serve the purpose for which it had been created. I remembered Hannah. She had become my reason for living, and now she was gone.

A dreadful emptiness came rushing at me like a murderous freight train.

CHAPTER 14

Partway down the corridor, the door to Grace's room stood ajar. I turned away from the nurses' station, having received Beulah's permission to proceed with my visit. With a thick Texas drawl and a conspiratorial grin, she had announced that Ms. Fairchild would be disappointed to have missed me, having been summoned to dress the wounds of an elderly gentleman who had stumbled over his own cane. Beulah had made it abundantly clear that I was to speak with her nurse later. I had assured the portly aide that I would.

Upon entering Grace's room, I realized that the scene that greeted me was not what I had envisioned. The old woman stood by the window. The autumn dress she wore seemed a couple of sizes too large. Loose folds underscored her recent poor health. The flowing cotton fabric bore a bold floral pattern in blue, pink, and yellow, which was not the latest fashion but not seriously outdated either.

Grace must have taken note of my footsteps in the corridor. Without turning, she said, "Glad you decided to come."

"I had to witness the miracle for myself."

"Miracle? Is that what they're saying?"

"Essentially."

"But we know better." Perhaps she chuckled; from behind, it was hard to tell.

I pictured the old woman sitting in a wheelchair, swaddled in layers of blankets. Standing upright, she seemed smaller, more petite, and perhaps even more vulnerable. Flows of wispy white hair, neatly combed, trailed to the nape of her neck. Barrettes at the temples kept wayward strands in place.

"I suppose it depends on how you define miracle." I advanced two paces into the room and tossed a candy bar onto her bed. "That's for you. I assume you still like sweets."

Still facing away, Grace chose not to acknowledge my gift. "What some would call miracles," she said, "are nothing more than the collision of random forces, the unexpected fallout created by the mundane choices we make every day. People like attaching the supernatural to whatever they don't understand."

"Are you asking what I think?"

With her elbows at her sides and her forearms angled to the front, I had no idea if her hands were folded or holding something.

Grace nodded in the direction of the window. "That's a nice ramp you built, quite serviceable. It's refreshing to know that some people still value quality workmanship. It's also impressive that you completed your work in such a timely fashion. By the way, perhaps you think you fooled me, but I know how you came by the lumber you used to finish your project, which is why I wanted to see you."

She turned to face me, and I realized she clutched a cell phone. She held it up. "It's not easy pretending to be a living corpse while staying in touch with one's sources on the outside. I had a man check you out. He figured out what you did—"

"Check me out?" I blurted in dismay, feeling violated. "Why, for heaven's sake?"

This time, her cackle was unmistakable. "A single woman, especially a rich widow, needs to know the character of the men who come a-courting."

The jocularity faded from her voice.

"In any event, I sent for you to discuss your theft. The timbers you took from The Homestead did not belong to you. I inherited that property after my husband died and have retained ownership all these years. The boards you stole belong to me, and I want them back. You will dismantle your ramp immediately and return what's mine. If not, I will sue you and Harwood Manor to recover my property."

"Every stick of the lumber I salvaged was useless trash!" I exclaimed, flabbergasted. "Most planks were so fire-damaged or so rotten from lying out in the weather, you could snap them with your hands. It was hard collecting even a few lengths. What possible use could they be to you?"

"That's not your concern. All you need to know is they are mine, and I want them back."

I gaped open-mouthed at the old woman. How could anyone be so heartless? I recalled the brain-numbing fatigue and unremitting aches I had endured, not to mention the blisters—and the scheming. And what would the state inspectors say if the ramp was summarily demolished? Harwood stood to lose its license.

Then I noticed a twinkle in Grace's eye. I was being played.

"Nice one," I confessed sheepishly. "You had me going." This was not a woman to bet against in a game of poker.

Grace smiled. "I did, didn't I? Perhaps you're more gullible than I had imagined. Come, let's take a walk. I have a proposition I think you'll find interesting. Thanks for the chocolate bar, by the way."

Clouds thick with moisture rolled across a slate gray sky, again threatening rain. I watched them gather through the solarium's plate-glass windows. From Chicago south, temperatures had refused to drop below freezing, but that could change without warning.

Winter's beauty has always filled me with wonder. I especially appreciate the frosted patterns on puddles and panes of glass, and snow formations sculpted by the wind. But the onset of winter, when trees lose their leaves and gathering storms shut out the sun, is a gloomy time. At any moment, I expected a lightning bolt to illuminate the horizon.

Grace had settled nobly into a padded armchair fashioned from curved links of bamboo. Her dress hung loosely. The hem covered her knees and lower legs, exposing merely two inches of pallid skin and the varicose veins above her thin ankles.

I sat in a similar chair. A squat, narrow end table, also of bamboo, stood between us. We faced the solarium's windows, our backs to the entrance. The room was deserted except for the two of us, probably because lunch hour was drawing nigh, not that I had timed my visit to scrounge another free meal. Instead, the morning had slipped away while I had tidied up around the apartment.

With pride, I observed the ramp outside the double doors. It seemed ideally suited for the function it served. Its forest service green color blended with its surroundings. Several low shrubs had been planted along the ramp's length for decorative effect. At least Yuri had contributed something besides the use of his truck.

In the elevator on the way down, and while composing herself to face the gathering storm, I had noticed that Grace moved with dignity. In her youth, projecting poise must have become so deeply ingrained that, like breathing, no conscious thought was needed. Unlike the wheelchair-bound husk I had first encountered, the woman seated near me commanded my attention, like the matriarch at a family gathering.

Twice, I had broached the subject of her transformation, only to be rebuffed by silence, leaving me frustrated and even more curious. I crossed my legs. Resting one forearm on the smooth bamboo, I leaned in her direction. "You mentioned a proposal."

"We'll get to that." Grace then hesitated, as if reluctant to proceed. After a moment, she looked directly at me. Her piercing gaze seemed to measure each of my strengths and weaknesses. At length, she said, "There are things you need to know, background material, so that you can appreciate my motives and why I asked to see you." A shiver ran through her.

"Are you sure you should be out here like this? Don't you need a blanket? How about a cup of hot tea, coffee, or something? I could fetch some."

"Please, this isn't easy. I've spent twenty-six years trying to forget the McFarland family and their evil deeds. Now, their entire history is staring me in the face. It seems there is no escape." Her arthritic fingers, at rest on the bamboo, balled into a fist. A moment later, by an exertion of will, they relaxed. "You may know some of what I'm about to tell you. People gossip. I understand that. Even so, I want you to have the information you'll need to put things in perspective."

An elderly man, his spine bent nearly to a right angle, entered the solarium, leaning heavily on his ivory-handled cane. Spotting Grace, he headed in our direction with a lecherous leer that revealed several missing teeth.

Grace must have caught sight of his approach in the window's reflections. Rotating at the waist, she called out in a sharp voice, "Go away, Henry. I'm not interested. This is a private conversation, and you're not invited."

The toothless grin faded, and the old man shuffled off.

"They're like cockroaches," Grace spat out, returning her attention to the gathering storm outside the window. "I've watched them with the other women. If you don't step on them, they keep coming back. The men around here have only one thing on their mind."

I waited while she again composed her thoughts.

"The McFarlands," she continued eventually, "were scoundrels one and all, except for Warren—maybe. There might be hope for him. Only time will tell.

"Trevor, my husband, Warren's grandfather, was not a good man. He loved money to the exclusion of everything else, including me. Not long after we were married, his talent for buying and selling real estate steered him toward a life of crime. It's easy to make money when you don't have to do it honestly. Bribes, kickbacks, extortion, fraud, intimidation—these were the tools of his trade. I can't begin to count the number of people hurt by his illegal activities.

"Trevor's greed attracted the notice of a gang of like-minded crooks. They were skilled at what they did. They kept chipping away by targeting one corrupt politician at a time until they practically owned City Hall.

"When Andrew, our son, came of age, Trevor convinced him that he should become a banker. With his financial skills, their criminal partnership seemed a natural fit. Together, they cooked up phony land deals, laundered money, doctored the books so they could illegally foreclose on solvent properties, and just about every other crooked scheme you could imagine. Never once did they stop to think about the lives they ruined. But then the *Westlake Gazette* began running a series of editorials. Its editor was a real firebrand."

"You knew Max O'Bryan personally, didn't you?"

"I did. He was a decent man. I respected him…but I need to stay on track. This is hard for me. I've never discussed any of this." Strain deepened the wrinkles in her brow and at the corners of her eyes.

"Do you need a moment?"

Grace's white hair swayed when she shook her head. "It's important you hear this."

Squaring her shoulders, she gathered her energy. The resolve apparent in her bearing reminded me of her mother's image. They shared the same fortitude.

When she was ready, Grace said, "Max's editorials made a difference. With a spotlight on their criminal enterprise, Trevor and Andrew knew they had to do something, something that might involve violence.

"But then Trevor suddenly disappeared. I've always suspected his associates considered him a liability. His greed and megalomania put them at risk. Perhaps they had assumed he was about to strike a deal—rat them out to save himself, and that's why they decided to cut their losses.

"Not long afterward, our son, Andrew, was murdered. Again, his criminal associates were suspected, but nothing could be proven. His wife ran off a few days later, deserting their son. Warren, my grandson, was twelve at the time, a vulnerable age. When he returned from boarding school, he didn't deal well with losing his father and grandfather. I wasn't sure if he could ever cope. He was such a sweet boy. Only much later did I realize that he might follow in his father's footsteps.

"Several weeks after Andrew's murder, fire took The Homestead—burned it to the ground, except for the timbers and rubble that fell into the basement. This you already know. I was too traumatized to deal with cleaning up the property, so everything stayed as the fire had left it."

Chaos theory predicts that significant changes happen all at once. For Grace, that certainly had been the case. My heart went out to her.

The old woman confided, "What followed is something of a blur. It all happened so fast, and I wasn't functioning well. Widowed, with the house gone, and a grandson to raise, I took Warren and moved to England to be with my mother's family. It seemed the best alternative at the time. Warren grew up abroad and went to college at Cambridge but returned to the States to enter graduate school. And now, he's making a proper mess of his finances while he's waiting for me to die. He hasn't exactly turned to crime yet, but he might, especially if he inherits his grandfather's fortune. But I have other plans, which is why you're here."

"Me? How am I involved?"

"I want to deed The Homestead over to you while I'm still of sound mind and physically able. The land will be yours to do with as you see fit. You will have a clear title. The mortgage was paid off ages ago."

I was astounded. "You're offering to give me the property where my wife died?"

"There's more. I want you to turn The Homestead into a community park. If you can do this, there will be a reward. If you clean up the property and deed it to Chillwind County, you'll inherit the remainder of my estate, worth approximately five times what you might otherwise sell the land for, but the choice is yours."

"Is this for real? Are you pulling my leg again?"

"I assure you, this is no joke. While working on the park, any reasonable expenses you incur, including whatever tools, equipment, or help you need, plus a stipend for your services, will be paid by my attorney, Mr. Ingersoll. He will also pay whatever taxes come due, including any gift or inheritance taxes that might apply. He'll explain the details.

"You can work at your own pace. There will be no deadlines, so long as you make steady progress. But be advised, once you start the renovations, if you change your mind and decide to sell the land or do anything else with it, you'll be obliged to repay whatever monies have been dispersed. Of course, if you sell the land, you can keep whatever profits you receive.

"One thing more. You can't talk about any of this, not with anyone, not until all the legal documents have been duly notarized and recorded. No one must know, except Mr. Ingersoll."

"Why me? Why not Warren? Shouldn't he be the one to do this for you?"

"No," Grace snapped. "Inheriting so much wealth would destroy Warren, as it had his father and grandfather before him. My fortune would never be enough. He would always want more. No, he must earn what comes to him. Unfortunately, as it is, his financial affairs are in poor condition. He's barely hanging on, but at least he has his integrity. You, on the other hand, will put my money to good use. I know this."

To my way of thinking, I was possibly the worst choice for such a venture. I looked at the old woman. "Are you sure you're in your right mind?"

"Be quiet. I know what I'm doing. I've had you investigated seven ways from Sunday, and don't be claiming you're damaged goods. I'm not interested in rehashing your tale of woe." She pointed at the ramp outside the window. "There stands proof of your work ethic."

Preemptively put in my place, I mulled over her proposal. "Why now? You've had nearly three decades to clean up your husband's messes. What's changed?"

"I'm dying, to put it bluntly. Living abroad, it was easy to shut out the past and close my mind to Trevor's legacy. That is, until the day I sat down to write out my will. Then, I was forced to envision what would become of Warren. This is why I returned to the States:

to deal with the McFarland legacy. Warren's character won't survive being saddled with such a sizable fortune."

"You're sure of this?"

"I raised the boy. I know him as well as my husband and son."

I began to wonder just how much money we were talking about. I guesstimated that the price of real estate was no longer current. If the land fetched between one and two million dollars, five times that…*whoa.*

"And frankly," Grace added, "the idea that another McFarland might build a home on that property makes me want to vomit. Look, the people of Branford Gardens deserve restitution. This is the only way I know how. Can you do this for me? Can you help an old woman make amends? Remember, time is of the essence. I'll need your answer soon, while I'm still drawing breath." The pleading look in the old woman's eyes was as intense as I had ever encountered.

"Honestly? I don't know if I can." I tried to fathom all that would be required. So many questions remained unasked. Thinking of the challenges, the responsibility—the emotional impact of working near where Hannah died.

Was it my imagination, or was a freight train rumbling in my direction?

Some days never turn out like you expect.

"You were right," I said to Erin, who had waited to take her lunch break and was now seated across the table in the employees' lounge at Harwood Manor. Her home-prepared meal looked far more palatable than the corn nuts I had snagged from the vending machines. "Grace is troubled. Her physical problems might be the least of her concerns."

"She opened up to you? This is good. Why does she seem so… haunted?"

Haunted seemed an apt description—beset by demons from years past. "I can't say."

"Can't or won't? You know something, I can tell."

"Sorry, but she made me promise." I flicked a corn nut into my mouth.

Erin stabbed her fork into a cherry tomato but paused to make her point. "I'm her nurse. I should know these things. If some issue is causing her psychological harm, it has to be addressed. She won't open up to me." An edge of resentment hardened her voice.

"I wish I could fill you in, believe me." In my former life, I had observed that openly discussing thorny issues was wiser than relying solely on my own counsel, especially when a decision had to be made. Grace's offer was a thorny issue, but I was sworn to secrecy.

"But you can't say." Erin sighed. "I understand. A promise is a promise, and I respect you for keeping your mouth shut. But tell me this, is there anything I can do?"

"Talk with her whenever the opportunity arises. Be her friend. Let her know how much you care. Maybe she'll share what's truly on her mind."

"So she didn't tell you everything?"

"I had the feeling she was holding back."

At an adjoining table, an older nurse and a male attendant, the equivalent of a hospital orderly, exchanged lighthearted banter.

I rose from the table and crossed to the vending machines. A single bag of salted corn nuts wasn't going to cut it. After scanning the limited fair, I deposited the requisite coins and entered the code for a package of graham cracker cookies with cream centers. They seemed to be the best value for the price. After all, the money I had earned building the ramp wouldn't last forever, which brought me face-to-face with Grace's offer.

If the old woman was telling the truth, there was a lot of coin at stake—a whole lot. I was tempted to return to her room and accept her terms out of hand, but questions remained: How many permits are needed to create a park? How much labor is involved? And what devils lurk in the details? No project ever goes as intended. There are always hurdles to overcome.

Most importantly, how would Warren respond? Given his lineage, it seemed unlikely that he would take kindly to being shut out of his grandmother's will. I decided that the prudent course of action would be to learn more about the man.

I returned to the table. After opening the cellophane package, I held the cookies out to Erin. "Want one?"

She wrinkled her nose. "So, when can you start?" She said, dabbing the corners of her mouth with her napkin.

"Excuse me?"

"My double doors—you thought you could start fairly soon."

"Remodeling, right. How about tomorrow? Tomorrow is Saturday, right?" Instinctively, I consulted my wrist and again longed for the watch I had pawned. Perhaps I should spend a little of my treasured hoard.

A smile illuminated the nurse's face. "Tomorrow would be perfect. What time?"

"Eight," I suggested, "or is that too early? You do have tools, I'm assuming?"

"Whatever you need, I'm sure. With two brothers and me being the only girl in the family, my father insisted that I learn to fix whatever needed fixing. Over the years, I've collected a decent assortment; if I don't have what you need, I'll get it. And eight o'clock works fine for me. I'm an early riser."

"I'll need a map."

Erin tugged a clean paper napkin out of the chrome dispenser at the center of the table. After fetching a pen from the breast pocket of her scrubs, she began drawing out directions and labeling everything. Her penmanship, I saw, was more than legible, almost flowing. When she handed me the napkin, she smiled again.

As I studied the diagram, I made sure that she had included her phone number, just in case. "Should be easy enough to find. So, tell me, what do you do for fun?"

"I grow flowers, as you'll see when you come over."

"That's it?"

"What with work and renovating my home, there's not much time for other activities. I read. I crochet—mostly homebody stuff to pass the time."

"Is there a boyfriend?"

"There was, but—" A frown darted across Erin's face. She looked away.

"You said you crochet. By any chance, did you make Grace's lap blanket?"

"I did, actually."

"The colors you chose suit her—teal, orange, and rust, as I recall." An architect needs an eye for color. I had learned to appreciate tints that blended well together. Then it occurred to me that Erin had crocheted the lap blanket while Grace was in her self-induced isolation. That meant she had acted purely out of kindness, without hope of receiving anything in return, not even a thank-you. "That was a kind thing to do."

"I thought it would help her to realize she's not alone." The nurse gathered her plastic containers and packed them in her beaded lunch sack. "I guess we'll see you tomorrow."

"Eight a.m."

Erin waited while I shagged a pack of potato chips for the road. When I deposited my trash in the receptacle near the door, its lid swiveled to and fro. We left the break room together.

I considered accompanying Erin to the second floor and revisiting Grace, but there were people I needed to interview first. One was Father Samuel, whose priestly vows would assure confidentiality. I craved his advice.

The second was Grace's attorney, Ruxton Aloysius Ingersoll. I had looked him up in the phone book at the nurses' station. I hoped he would provide two pieces of information: Was Grace telling the truth about her estate and her owning the land? And was she mentally competent? In other words, was she nuts, or was the offer valid?

After dialing St. Anthony's Church from the payphone in Harwood Manor's lobby, a volunteer informed me that Father Samuel was meeting with the monsignor. She didn't know how long he would be tied up. When I explained that I didn't own a cell phone and would be unreachable if the padre were to return my call, she reluctantly agreed to interrupt their meeting. Rather than take my call, the priest sent word back that I should stop by his apartment later that night. The fact that he was unavailable, I later learned, was fortuitous.

Rux Ingersoll's office was thirty minutes away by bus, toward downtown Chicago. Had I gone straight to St. Anthony's and then later tried to see Rux, I would have found his law offices buttoned up for the weekend.

Leather and mahogany furnishings dominated the suite of rooms leased by Ingersoll, Lake, and Johansson. Rux, obviously, was the senior partner. Well past fifty, he seemed somewhat self-effacing, not the stereotypical predator I had imagined, despite being rodent-like in appearance. Beneath a shock of unruly gray hair, his small eyes darted as if struggling to see past his pointed snout. Rather than have his receptionist escort me to his office, he personally came to the waiting room.

The difference in our heights was at least seven inches, with him being the shorter man, which forced him to look up to see my face. With a sweep of his hand, he gestured down a well-lit corridor. "This way, Mr. Moore, if you please."

The attorney gestured again when we reached his office. "Come in. I've been expecting you. Would you like coffee, a soda—a stronger beverage perhaps?" I noticed a wet bar inset into a side wall. A bank of north-facing windows ran the length of the wall behind the attorney's desk. I took special note of an impressive view of Chicago's distant skyline through the windows. No doubt a perk reserved for the firm's senior partner.

"Thank you, no." I had consumed an entire bottle of water on the bus—salty corn nuts. "How did you—"

"Know you'd contact us? Mrs. McFarland told me. She called not long after you concluded your visit."

"Then you know why I'm here." I plopped down into one of two claw-foot chairs facing the desk and the windows beyond.

When Rux sank into his high-backed chair, only his head and the crests of his shoulders were visible above the desktop. "You want to know if you can trust her. Let me assure you, everything she told you is true. The woman doesn't lie, nor does she live in a fantasy world."

"So you're aware she offered to hand me the deed to a property worth more than a million dollars—an outright gift, mine to do with as I wish."

"To do with as you wish, yes. That is correct, though we would prefer you turn the land into a park. There are no strings attached, however."

"And if I do clean it up and deed the property to the county—"

"Markets fluctuate, but as of yesterday's close, you will inherit $8,328,365.42." The attorney recited the estate's worth from memory, which I found telling. Rux continued, "Of course, when Mrs. McFarland finally does pass away, that amount could be more or less, depending on circumstances beyond our control. Over the years, though, her investments have tended to hold their value. The bad news is that there will be estate taxes to pay. I'm afraid they will be unavoidable. When the dust settles, you should receive a little over five million dollars."

"That's still a lot of money."

"To be sure."

"So you approve of this plan of hers?"

"Wholeheartedly!" Rux exclaimed. "The park was my idea. Given her concerns regarding her grandson's vulnerabilities, it seemed an appropriate use of the land. Yep, I came up with the idea for a park. You, however, she found on her own. Apparently, you reached her in ways I have yet to understand, but at her request, this firm did a thorough background check. We know everything about you, including your shoe size and the fact that you cheated on a freshman history exam your first year at the Stonefield Institute of Technology. You were lucky they didn't expel you, but rather let you retake the test."

"I never cheated again."

"We know. It would seem their faith was justified, as evidenced by the fact that you went on to earn your master's degree in architectural design. I believe your professional training was an important factor in Mrs. McFarland's decision. We also know what happened to Heartland Designs and how you used both your corporate and personal assets to make restitution after Liberty Tower One burned down. She was most impressed by that bit of news."

"It seemed the right thing to do."

"No argument here."

"How do I know this isn't some elaborate hoax? You two aren't trying to pull a fast one on me?"

"See for yourself." Rux slid open the top drawer of his desk, reached in, and retrieved a thick manila folder from which he extracted two documents. Standing up and leaning far forward, he passed them across the desk. One was a warranty deed, the other a brokerage account statement. Both looked genuine, and both confirmed what I had been told.

After studying the two documents again, I returned them to the attorney. "This is real? All I have to do is to convert that godforsaken lot into a park?"

"That's the sum of it. Once you start, you can take as long as you wish to complete the renovations, but you must decide quickly. We need to know urgently whether or not you intend to accept her proposal."

"Why is that? What's the rush?"

"It's a legal concern. If Mrs. McFarland dies before you take title to the land, her grandson will undoubtedly challenge her mental capacity. Warren will claim he should inherit everything. He'll allege that you manipulated a deranged woman into rewriting her will. While she's alive, we can easily refute that argument with a simple competency hearing."

"Are you sure she'll pass, considering how long everyone believed she was out to lunch? How rational a stunt was that?"

"You spoke with her not more than four hours ago. What's your opinion?"

"She seems lucid enough now, but that's why I'm here, to make sure."

"My associates and I will testify as to our conversations with Mrs. McFarland during the time she seemed to be in a vegetative state, but was instead allowing events to unfold as she intended."

"I see. The wily old fox defense, huh? Tell me, if I decide to keep the land, what happens to the balance of her estate?"

"All assets will be placed in trust for two years, assuming you retain ownership. That will be sufficient time for you to change your mind and create the park. After that, if you still own the land, several charities will gladly receive various portions, assuming Warren fails to prevail in the lawsuit, which he almost certainly will mount."

"Is that all? Is there anything else I should know?"

"There are details to iron out after you've decided, but essentially, that's the package."

"What happens next?" Through the window, I watched the first snowflakes of winter glide lazily to the ground. It promised to be a cold bus ride home.

"You need to decide, and soon. I can't stress this enough. Let me know when you do. Everything is prepared for your signature."

The attorney accompanied me to the waiting room.

As I was about to leave, he offered benignly, "If you do wind up inheriting such a tidy sum, and you feel the need for legal and financial advice, I gladly offer my services. Our fees are reasonable, and the welfare of our clients always comes first."

"You know, I believe you," I confessed. "You'll have my decision within a week."

"Good. Here's my business card. My home number is on the back. Call me when you're ready to sign, day or night."

I tucked the gold-embossed card safely into my wallet and walked to the bus stop, once more thinking that the world I knew had been turned upside down. Feeling more than a little overwhelmed, it seemed appropriate to say a quick prayer: *Lord, comfort me in my grief, and help me make the right decision. Amen.*

∾ ∾ ∾ ∾

It takes twenty-three mouse clicks to divest yourself of a thousand shares of Trans-G Systems, print out a hardcopy of the transaction, sign off from your brokerage account, and shut down your computer. I know this because I counted each click while I watched Father Samuel deal with a minor financial crisis.

As the logout image faded from the flat-screen display, the priest looked up and said, "Thanks for being patient. I would've closed out my position this afternoon, when the markets first turned against me, except for the monsignor's lousy sense of timing. He cost me nearly two grand."

Father Samuel sat at his computer desk tucked into the corner of his bedroom. Having been invited, I stood behind him, observing over his shoulder. Our shared near-death experience had blunted a few of his expectations regarding privacy. Like the apartment's other furnishings, the desk and portable computer were top quality. Every pen, every slip of paper, and every other item on the desktop seemed to have its place, which spoke of a character trait I had observed before: the priest's compulsive neatness.

"I was told you were with Msgr. Aldrich when I asked to see you."

"More than a week ago, I recommended an outreach program that would dramatically benefit our community, one the church would be well advised to sponsor. And he picked this afternoon to continue our discussion. Ah, well…" Father Samuel rose from his swivel chair and headed for the kitchen.

I followed.

"Want some ice cream?" the priest said as we left the bedroom. "I assume you've eaten?"

"I did." The stale tuna fish sandwich and bag of chips I had snarfed down on the way over came to mind. I had purchased the meager fare at Emil's, the mom-and-pop grocery on the corner of Tyler and Noreen, a block from the priest's apartment. "As for the ice cream, I'll pass." I had no great desire to regain the weight I had shed, albeit involuntarily, in the aftermath of the Liberty Tower One disaster. "Coffee would be nice, though."

The priest filled a mug with coffee, and after nuking it in the microwave, handed it over. We then migrated into the living room, where we took our ease. The priest chose one end of the brocade sofa. I chose the other.

Sitting back, Father Samuel said, "Tell me what you think. See if this makes sense to you. There's a nationwide service that brings mobile medical care to disadvantaged neighborhoods. It's a doctor and a nurse in a specially built eighteen-wheeler. They roll in, set up shop, and treat whichever patients show up. Federal grants cover part of the cost. All they need is for an organization to sponsor them— provide a place to park, schedule appointments, help with security, that sort of thing. They take care of the rest. I thought they could set up shop in the church parking lot four hours a night, twice a week. That way, they could do outpatient clinic stuff—prenatal care, immunizations, and the like."

"Sounds like a fine idea." The nearest medical facility, as I recalled, was twenty minutes away by bus. Most citizens couldn't afford even emergency care, much less routine checkups. "How did the monsignor respond?"

"By fussing about liability issues, a possible disruption of evening mass, and the fact that playing doctor isn't a proper church function. He said the bishop would never approve, though I suspect he might. Bottom line, Aldrich shot me down cold."

"That's a shame. Seems like an excellent plan."

"Maybe I can wear him down over time, but I doubt it. The man is a genuine dinosaur. And if you ever repeat any of this, I'll—"

"Lie?"

"Claim a lack of recollection." He smiled through his mustache and beard. "Anyway, enough about me. What's on your mind? You doing okay? You're not...you know?"

"Thinking about ending it all? Nope, quite the opposite. There's a decision I have to make, and I'd appreciate your advice."

"I'm flattered."

"You're a man of faith. I value your judgment."

"If faith is your criterion, I'm not sure I'm your best resource. Mine's a little shaken."

"There's a fair amount of money at stake, and time is of the essence. I need to decide soon what I'm going to do."

At the mention of money, the priest perked up.

Without referencing Grace by name, I drew a thumbnail sketch of her proposal and what I understood of Rux Ingersoll's involvement.

"How much did you say?" the padre interjected when I introduced the topic of inheritance.

"Five million. A little more, maybe—net after taxes."

"Five! And you're asking me for advice. Are you insane? What's to think about?"

"It's precisely because the estate is so large that I want your opinion."

"Is this a joke? Are you playing on my weakness for nice things?"

"I wouldn't do that."

"This is for real?"

"Apparently. I read documents at the attorney's office that validate what I've been told. Look, I design buildings, not parks. I have no idea what ordinances apply or how landscaping a park differs from what I know. How many kinds of parks are there anyway? And what about social demographics? Who will use the park? Old? Young? What would work best for this community?"

"How hard can it be, assuming this is legit? You bulldoze the ground and plant some grass, trees, and shrubs, and you're done. Then, spend your fortune. Who is this person, by the way, who, out of a clear blue sky, offers to make you rich?"

"Grace McFarland."

"Aha. The plot thickens—no wonder you're apprehensive. I would be, too. Don't trust her. Her whole clan is crooked to the core."

"That suggests that you know her grandson, Warren. I was hoping you could tell me about him."

"Never met the man, but if he's a McFarland, how honest can he be?"

"I thought we're supposed to forgive our enemies."

"Forgive does not mean trust."

"So you're advising that I should tell Grace no?"

"I didn't say that, not if this Ingersoll fellow is on the up-and-up. Maybe there's something there, but I would think long and hard before joining any venture involving a McFarland."

I leaned back and laced my fingers behind my head. "She knew your father."

The priest's expression became even more distrustful. "How do you know this?"

"She told me." Rather than confess to snooping, I chose not to mention the news photo in the leather-bound album on the bookshelf. "She said he was a decent man and that she respected him a great deal."

"She said that?"

"Her very words, and I believe her."

"Why?"

"Because I think she deeply regrets her family's criminal activities. I think a profound sense of guilt is why she wants to turn her land into a park. It's the only way left to her to make amends. You should talk to her—might change the way you feel."

I could tell the priest was unconvinced. Rather than express an opinion, he said, "You mentioned her grandson, Warren. How will he react, do you think? What will he do, being shut out of her estate?"

"Mr. Ingersoll is convinced he'll sue—try to have the will set aside."

"And you? What do you believe will happen? Remember, the McFarlands are no strangers to violence. After all, they tried to kill my father, which is why he ran. You might end up with $5 million and a contract on your life."

"Warren wouldn't. You don't really think—"

"Yeah, I do. That's who they are."

As I considered the possibility, the notion seemed less and less absurd, and the more I turned it over in my mind, the more unsettled I became. "In that case, could you do me a favor?"

Father Samuel eyed me sideways.

"Nothing dangerous," I offered reassuringly. "Certainly nothing that involves throwing yourself in front of a train. Ask around, discreetly. See what you can learn about the man and his activities, especially who his friends and associates might be. If you're right, and there is a risk, it would be nice to know in advance."

"I'm new to this community, remember? I'm not that well connected."

"True, but I can't go poking about, probing into his affairs. He might get wind of his grandmother's plans. Besides, who'd ever suspect a priest of concealing an ulterior motive, especially when distributing a family fortune?"

I thought about offering to pay Father Samuel for his services but decided that, given his appetite for money, it would be like buying an alcoholic a drink. More than that, I had nothing to pay him with. If I turned down Grace's proposal, which was still possible, I would need every cent of whatever earnings were left to me to survive.

"Will you do it?" I asked.

"On one condition."

"What might that be?"

"Introduce me to your friend. If you do decide to turn down her offer, that is. A contribution to St. Anthony's could go a long way toward easing her conscience. Maybe then the monsignor would reconsider bringing medical care to the community."

"I might introduce you anyway, since you two have so much in common. And one more thing, treat this like a confession, will you? Not a word to anyone."

"Agreed. But as for meeting your friend, I was kidding."

"I wasn't. Let me know when you're ready."

We chatted a while longer, and I said goodbye. On the walk home, I remembered Erin's remodeling project and that I had committed to start in the morning, which was good, in a way. I could ponder my decision while I worked.

CHAPTER 15

E rin Fairchild greeted me warmly when I knocked on her front door. Her home stood near the center of Logan Heights, five blocks north of the boutiques and specialty shops that lined Westridge Boulevard. The house's wood siding was stained dark redwood, nearly maroon. White trim along the eaves and around the windows added a bit of charm and gave the structure the feel of a cozy New England cottage.

A festival of colors confronted me when I stepped through the front door—lots of reds, pinks, yellows, and greens. Zinnias sprouted up in ocher pots everywhere, from the carved mantle above the fireplace in the living room to the light oak table in the dining area to the eggshell-colored corners of the master bedroom where I was to undertake her remodeling project.

If a green thumb confers the ability to coax plants to flourish and grow, Erin's hand must've been green to the wrist. Vibrant, healthy-looking blossoms exploded from virtually every plant, creating the impression that I had ventured into a well-tended garden.

"Sorry about the jungle." Erin indicated the pots as we entered the master bedroom at the rear of the house. "I couldn't very well leave my prizes outside to freeze."

"They're beautiful. You must love zinnias?"

"I do, but they're something of a headache. I discovered a secret a few years back: people who love gardening will pay handsomely for prized specimens, so I started a modest Internet business. I grow zinnias and harvest the seeds. I now ship them all over the world. In fact, by grafting and cross-pollinating the best plants, I've developed several new varieties. One reason I bought this house was because of its basement. I intend to add grow lights and bins so I can plant flowers year-round. You see, zinnias need a lot of light. Eventually, there'll be a greenhouse in the backyard. Maybe you could help with that? The construction part?"

"Let's get your double doors hung first. I assume this is where they go?" I indicated the wall away from the window which looked out upon a fenced-in space approximately forty yards on each side. A thin layer of snow covered the well-manicured lawn.

"You are correct, sir. Maybe you noticed from the hallway that there's a smaller bedroom next door. It's where I package seeds for shipping, keep track of orders, and do other business stuff. I feel claustrophobic when I'm working there. I figured opening up this wall would let light from the window shine in and chase away the gloom."

"It should." I stepped forward to inspect the portion of the wall that was to be removed. "This is a weight-bearing partition. The header and jams will have to be reinforced to bear the load. Also, depending on how your wires are routed, the electrical feeds and sockets may need to be revised. Even so, it should be doable." I glanced around. "Where are your tools?"

"In the garage. I'll show you what I have."

"Do you happen to have any ceiling jacks? We'll need at least four. We wouldn't want the roof to collapse when we cut through the studs. If you don't have them, we can rent them."

"Sure, whatever you need. First though, are you hungry? Did you have breakfast? It's not healthy for a man to begin work on an empty stomach. That's what my brothers always said, though as teenagers, they ate constantly, whether working or not."

I regarded the nurse who had seated herself on the edge of the king-sized bed while I studied the wall. Her tailored beige slacks and mist green blouse seemed too chic for a home workday. They were the first outfit, other than scrubs, I had seen her wear, and if they were intended to hide her feminine curves, they didn't.

"Thanks, but I ate on the way over." The stale slice of pizza I had grabbed on my way out the door had done little to quell my appetite, but I had promised myself I would focus on carpentry, not my employer.

"No problem. If you get hungry later, let me know. Or feel free to raid the refrigerator."

"Thanks. By the way, did you talk to Grace after I left?"

"Briefly. Not about anything important. I got to thinking, though, about what you said, that something serious might be troubling her, and it occurred to me how little she socializes since her recovery. When we try including her in group activities, she refuses. She doesn't have any friends other than you. I can't think of anyone else she confides in."

Again, this made me wonder why I was unique in Grace's eyes, regardless of what the attorney had said.

The nurse rocked forward. She kept her gaze fixed on the low shag carpet. "What do you suppose keeps her from warming up to people, now that she's out of her shell?"

"I've wondered that myself. I feel like we're missing something. By the way, just because I'm her chosen one, so to speak, doesn't mean I know what's going on inside her head. Tell me, did her grandson, Warren, call or come by after I left?"

"Not on my shift. I can't imagine why he would, not after being AWOL for four months."

"I was just curious. Is it possible he's heard about her…eh, reanimation?" I had been about to use the word *plans*.

"Oh, he knows. I informed him personally—right after she started talking. He seemed pleased, like he cared, but apparently not enough to visit her."

Through the window, I regarded the frosty dusting of snow outside. It reminded me of Christmas. "I remember my grandmother, Angelica. Angelica James—we called her Granny Angel. She died when

I was eight. I can't imagine that we would have warehoused her in an old folks' home if she'd lived. Beg your pardon, extended care facility."

"You'd be surprised how often that happens. Some families have legitimate reasons, sure, but too often they dump their elderly on our doorstep because it's convenient."

With a start, I recalled I had a job to do, and it was time to get on with getting on.

I looked at Erin, whose upbeat mood had also faded. My fault, I assumed. More brightly, I asked, "Do you have a notebook and a pencil I could borrow? We're going to need lumber and some other stuff. I'll start a list. Then we can check out your tools and see what needs to be filled in. Also, we should pick up a tarp and plastic sheeting. Wouldn't want your zinnias covered in sawdust."

The nurse perked up at the mention of getting to work. "How about a clipboard and printer paper?"

"That'll do."

Erin stood and stepped to the door. When she left the bedroom to enter her office, I wondered if she intended to help. And if so, would she be sawing and hammering in the outfit she had on, or did she plan on changing? I hoped that she would slip into something substantially less sexy.

The nurse returned with a clipboard and a mechanical pencil clipped to a dozen sheets of paper. She handed them over. "Mind if I ask you something? Tell me if it's too personal, and I'll shut up."

I shrugged, but my mental defenses automatically came online.

"Do you like children?"

"I do. A lot, actually."

"But you never had any?"

"No." I had been about to flippantly add, "None that I know about," but that tired old joke was no longer funny, and besides, I had no intention of suggesting I'd been a philanderer in my youth.

"Hannah, your wife, did she want children?"

"She did, but…" I shrugged again.

"How long were you two married?"

"I'm not impotent, if that's what you're asking."

"Sorry." Erin blushed and turned away. "I should learn to mind my own business. Come on, I'll show you what's in the garage."

"Wait." I rested a hand on her shoulder.

She turned to face me.

"My wife did want a family, but it was never the right time. In college, we were poor as church mice; all we could think about was graduation. When I started working the trades, we saved every penny to build a future. Then, after I founded Heartland Designs, all our energies were devoted to making the business successful. The moments slipped by. And then, after losing Liberty Tower One, everything changed."

"That must have been a challenging time."

"You have no idea."

Erin solemnly studied my face. "Mind if I ask something else?"

In for a penny, in for a pound, I thought. "Go ahead."

"Do you regret not having a family?"

"No. Given the way things turned out, absolutely not. But on the other hand, yes, I do. I wish circumstances had been different. Hannah and I talked about raising kids, but it wasn't in the cards."

"I appreciate your honesty. That couldn't have been easy, but I won't apologize for being so forward. You strike me as a man with some fine qualities, and I hope to get to know you better if you'll permit it."

"Erin, I need you to know that I'm not ready for a new relationship. Why don't we open your wall and not worry about what comes next?"

"As you wish." The nurse turned away and walked toward the front of the house.

I remained standing where I was. "You know what bothers me most?" I said.

She halted to look back.

"It's knowing the what and the how, but not the why. That's the hardest part, not having a reason."

"Sometimes things just are. There are no reasons. But I think I understand how you feel. I was engaged once and almost got married, but a week before the wedding, he changed his mind, and to this day, I don't know why. I've always believed it was me, that I was somehow…insufficient."

I blurted out, "A man would be crazy not to desire you."

A smile bloomed on Erin's face. "Really?"

"Yeah, really, but enough of this. Let's have a look at your tools. We need to get this show on the road."

The ugly view from my kitchen window reminded me that I had a decision to make. The weed-choked lot across the street challenged me to make up my mind. Lingering droplets of melted snow on the leaves glistened with reflected light from the streetlamps, like pinpoints of hope in a sea of despair. I tried to imagine how a park might be laid out and what features would best serve the community. Unable to develop any brilliant ideas, I wondered what advice Hannah would have given.

Without question, Monroe Creek presented a problem.

Earlier that afternoon, I had dispatched Erin to the lumberyard to either rent or buy a reciprocating saw. Remarkably, it was one of the few tools absent from her collection. While she was gone, I had used her phone to call Rux Ingersoll at home. I had been mulling over Grace's project, trying to sort out what needed to be done, but gaps in my understanding were interfering with my analysis.

While talking with the attorney, one piece of news had come as a semi-welcome surprise: the lot was not triangular, as I had imagined. It was rectangular and, therefore, nearly twice as large. The eastern boundary stretched to the base of the bluffs that rose to Logan Heights, which meant Monroe Creek bisected the lot diagonally, and any plans for developing the land would necessarily have to accommodate that feature.

A knock on the front door yanked me back from my ruminations—another visitor. I wondered, *Who might this be?* Erin having been my first and only one thus far, perhaps it was the landlord, except the rent had been paid through the end of the month. All my debts were current, including the utility company and the ladies' auxiliary at St. Anthony's. But had I repaid Yuri Slowiki for the gas? I seemed to recollect filling the truck's tank, but if not, perhaps he'd come to collect.

Upon opening the door, I encountered a man approximately my height and near my age, but at least fifty pounds heavier. Balding on top, a ring of salt-and-pepper hair circled the back of his head from one ear to the other, a style sometimes referred to as a Friar Tuck haircut. Dark shadows underscored his fleshy eyes. However, his aristocratic nose and high cheekbones seemed familiar, though I felt pretty sure we had never met.

"Can I help you?" I braced a foot against the bottom of the door to keep it from being forced open should he decide to enter uninvited.

"I hope I'm not disturbing you. I would have called first but couldn't find your number."

"No phone. What can I do for you?"

"I'd like to talk to you about my grandmother. You've been visiting her, I believe. I could come back later if this is a bad time."

"Who are you?"

"Warren McFarland."

"Grace McFarland is your grandmother?"

"Yes, and I was hoping you could bring me up to speed on how she's getting on."

"Me? Why not ask her yourself?"

"That's the point. I can't. When I'm around, she gets distraught. My simply being in the same room causes her distress. Her doctor has advised me to stay away. Look, this is awkward. I know what you must think of me. Is there any chance we could talk inside?"

I considered frisking him to see if he was armed, but his mood seemed more solicitous than confrontational. I decided to go with my gut. "Sure, come on in." Stepping out of the way, I held the door open.

The tailored drape of Warren's charcoal gray suit, the thin blue and yellow stripes of his narrow tie, and the fact that his shoes looked crafted from hand-stitched Italian leather suggested two things: One was he catered to expensive tastes. The other was that he preferred clothes with a European cut. His attire seemed inappropriate for sojourning in Branford Gardens.

Warren remained standing in the center of the room until I invited him to sit down. I could tell he felt ill at ease, how his fingers followed patterns in the fabric of the chair's armrest and how he had trouble deciding where to cast his gaze.

Slumming can do that, make people feel like fish out of water, but there I was again, prejudging. Perhaps there was another reason for his nervousness. The simplest way to know would be to ask.

The problem was what do you say to a man who may or may not know he's about to be shut out of a five-million-dollar inheritance, more if you factor in the worth of the land? My intuition suggested he was unaware of his impending misfortune, so I feigned ignorance.

"What makes you think I know what's happening with your grandmother?" I plopped down in Hannah's favorite corner of the couch despite the feeling that I was trespassing.

Warren said, "Ms. Lonergan has kept me current, but her explanation for what happened seems inadequate. She believes you, in no small measure, were responsible for whatever this was, which is why I'm here. I need to understand. Any idea why Grandma started talking again all of a sudden? I'm no doctor, but I know stroke patients don't do that. I was hoping you could shed some light on her recovery."

"I'm not sure I understand it myself. Tell me about your relationship with your grandmother. You said being near her causes her distress. Why is that?"

"God, I wish I knew. It started right after she returned to the States. When she came to live with me, she kept referring to unfinished business but would never tell me what it was. Whatever the problem, it caused her a lot of anxiety. The harder I tried to sort it out, the more withdrawn she became. I should have backed off. I know that now, but I couldn't. I love my grandmother. I hated seeing her so glum. I wanted to fix whatever was troubling her, so I pushed harder.

"Then one day, she stopped talking altogether. She just sat there, staring into space. She wouldn't answer me. She wouldn't even look at me. I never really believed it was a stroke, but... Tell me, was it me? Am I the reason she closed herself off? That's why I stayed away. I feel responsible. Heaven knows I don't want to cause her any more grief."

My heart went out to the man. I could tell he was sincere. I wanted to offer whatever consolation I could. "It wasn't you. I may not know why your grandmother withdrew inside herself, perhaps even she's not aware, but I'm certain whatever her issues are, they're hers and hers alone."

"You think so? Do you believe that?"

"Without a doubt."

A tide of relief swept across Warren's face as if a heavy burden of shame had been lifted from his shoulders, which pleased me.

"You should go see her for yourself."

"And risk a relapse?"

At that moment, I realized that until a decision regarding Grace's proposal had been made, it would be best to maintain the status quo. "Perhaps you're right. Even though you're not the cause, you could be a catalyst, like striking a match too close to a keg of gunpowder. Perhaps for now, it would be best to stay away."

Dejection swamped Warren's apparent relief, making me feel like a certified heel. To mitigate the damage, I offered, "Only until her issues become clear. I plan on seeing her tomorrow. Maybe I can get her to open up."

I had initially planned on working on the remodeling project every day, but Erin had informed me that she attended church on Sundays. When I offered to continue working in her absence, she had claimed she enjoyed helping. As a result, we had agreed to take up the job the following Saturday, though it meant leaving a hole in her bedroom wall, which she said she didn't mind.

As I looked at Warren, I realized that a golden opportunity lay within my grasp, a chance to probe the psyche of a potential adversary, depending on how the wheel turned. I said casually, "When I'm visiting your grandmother, it might be helpful to know a bit more about you, to formulate the right questions to ask, assuming she'd be willing to confide in me. Are you married?"

"She didn't tell you?"

"Eh, no, though I assure you, you are very much in her thoughts."

"Well, that's good to know. Actually, I just got engaged. Her name is Jennifer. She is amazing, but I don't think Grandma approves. My fiancée's not genteel enough, Grandmother being British and all."

"Have you two set a date?"

"Not yet. I'm saving up for the wedding, but in this economy…"

I wondered, *Doesn't the bride's father pay for the shindig?* "How do her parents feel about your getting married?"

"They're both deceased."

"I see. So, what do you do for a living?"

"I work for Stradford Health Care. I'm vice president of Operations. It's a regional HMO. I'm the go-to guy when there's a problem with provider relations. I also oversee the utilization review and quality control programs, plus several other minor functions." There was pride in his voice.

"Sounds like an important position." I wanted to ask, "Is it true you're nearly bankrupt?" Instead, I said, "Do you enjoy your work?"

"It can be stressful, but yes."

"How do you spend your free time? Any hobbies or interests?"

"Other than work, you mean? I read a lot. I used to do photography, but not so much anymore."

It was becoming apparent that my skills as an interrogator were sorely lacking. Although interesting from a personal perspective, Warren revealed nothing to help me decide. "Tell you what, leave your number, and I'll call you after I've visited with your grandmother."

He fished a business card out of his inside coat pocket. "Anything you can tell me would be appreciated. I'm a fix-it type by nature. That's why Stradford hired me. My inclination is to jump in and make things right." He rose from the armchair. "I'm curious. Why did Grandma open up to you?"

"I'm not sure. Right place, right time, maybe." I, too, stood up and crossed the room to accept his card. "Let's see how she's doing in the morning. She may not be ready to receive you."

"Whatever you believe is best."

I escorted my visitor to the door.

Well, I told myself after Warren had gone, *that was unanticipated.* Not only had he come across as transparently honest, but I found I liked the man. Nothing in his demeanor had suggested he was a crook like his father and grandfather. All in all, his visit had muddied the waters considerably. Maybe Grace could shed new light on the McFarland family dynamic. I sincerely hoped so.

Some days, things don't end up the way you expect.

By chance, I happened to bump into Ms. Lonergan as I entered Harwood Manor through the employees' entrance. Although, in thinking about it later, I suspected she might have been waiting for me since she had planted herself, arms akimbo, in the middle of the corridor, impossible to avoid.

"I know why you're here," she declared sternly as I drew near. "Warren called."

"I'm not surprised. What did he say?" I halted, facing her.

Her short stature and thin frame suggested fragility, deceptively so. The nursing supervisor would have made a formidable opponent in any contest of wills. Self-assurance oozed from every pore. She smiled without actually smiling. "I gather he regards you as some sort of miracle worker."

"Not because of anything he learned from me."

"Perhaps not, but tell me what game you think you're playing?" Her hazel eyes bore into my soul.

"You know as much about Grace McFarland's recovery as I do, probably more. And I assure you, whatever relationship we're developing, it's not a game."

"I've been a nurse for twenty-three years. I've come across all kinds of people. Naturally, I tend to be suspicious when a younger man latches on to an older woman. I ask myself, what's in it for him? Would you mind explaining why you've been interested in one of my patients?"

I recalled the locket and how its image had captured my interest. "I don't know that I can. I'm hoping to get to know her as a person. Is that bad?"

"That's your only motive?"

"Look, Grace just has to say the word, and I'll be out of her life forever. Talk to her, and tell her your concerns. She seems competent enough to choose her own friends. If she shares your apprehension, she can tell me to get lost."

I suspected the nursing supervisor had already talked with her patient, and she had been the one told to get lost.

"You're not as clever as you think," Ms. Lonergan snapped. "We'll be keeping an eye on you. Don't you doubt that for a second."

"It's reassuring to know you're looking out for your patient. By the way, how's the ramp holding up? Any problems?"

"None so far." The nursing supervisor strode away.

"Have a nice day…Daisy," I called out after her.

The nursing supervisor flinched but continued walking.

I finally tracked Grace down in the farthest corner of the Manor's great room, an oversized space just off the main entrance. Generally reserved for special activities, the great room was large enough to accommodate the facility's seventy-plus residents, only half of whom had chosen to attend a piano recital by a local artist. From the center of a portable stage, a lanky middle-aged man sporting a goatee and handlebar mustache enthusiastically tried to coax an indifferent audience into singing along with his moldy oldies.

My search for her had begun in Grace's room, where a rush of anxiety had overtaken me upon finding the space empty and her bed neatly made. I preferred not to think about it, but there was a real possibility that Grace's heart condition might take her life at any moment.

Peering into the great room from the doorway, I regarded Grace as she sat in her wheelchair, well removed from everyone else. Her stooped shoulders and drooping head spoke of her effort to make herself presentable. Seeing her so manifestly miserable caused me to regret not having called ahead and affording her the opportunity of putting on a brave face.

I slipped through the door and hugged the side wall, moving as soundlessly as possible. Erin had mentioned how difficult it was finding volunteers to entertain the residents. I had no desire to steal the pianist's thunder by drawing attention away from his performance.

Moving carefully, I approached Grace from behind. She sat completely still, except for the shallow rise and fall of her breathing. For a moment, I wondered if she had reverted to her catatonic state, but then, as if sensing my approach, she cocked her head slightly to listen.

"Hi, Grace," I said in a barely audible voice. I eased forward to lay a hand on her arm. Her bones were discernible even through a cotton blouse, wool sweater, and shawl.

"Get me out of here," she hissed, loudly enough to be heard several rows away. "If you don't, I'll let out the most bloodcurdling yell you've ever heard."

"Where do you want to go? Back to your room?"

"No."

"Where then?"

"Outside."

"You don't have enough blankets for that. It's winter, remember?"

"The solarium, then."

"You sure it's okay? The staff won't mind if you leave?"

She opened her mouth as if to scream.

I tightened my grip on her arm. "Don't. I'll take you where you want to go." I unlatched the brakes on the wheelchair and rolled her toward the exit. "I take it you don't like piano recitals?" We left the great room.

"Feel free to go back and listen if you're inclined."

"I'd rather visit with you."

When we entered the solarium, three residents, two women and one man, were seated side by side facing the large plate glass windows kitty-corner across the room. As if mesmerized, they watched plump snowflakes drift inexorably to the ground.

I wheeled Grace to where we had last conversed, away from the trio. After shifting a bamboo chair aside, I parked her facing outward and took the other chair beside her.

"How are you?" I was hoping to get an update on her medical condition. When I'd stopped by the nurses' station, Erin had been too busy to fill me in.

"How do I look?"

"Holy cow, you must feel terrible," I teased with mock solemnity.

The old woman glowered at me, and then for the first time, she actually laughed. "You, too, will discover that time is a deceitful friend. It offers gifts with one hand and steals from you with the other. But you're not here to listen to an old lady philosophize. Have you made your decision?"

"Almost, but several things are still unclear. I need more information."

"Like what, for instance? What's unclear?"

"Warren came to see me."

"Did he now?"

"Ms. Lonergan has been keeping him updated on your recovery."

"I suspected as much, not that it matters. That old bitty loves to stir the pot. I'm convinced that many rumors zipping through the Manor started with her. What did Warren have to say for himself?"

"Mainly, he was concerned about you. He wanted to know how you were getting on. He claimed he's staying away because he upsets you—he doesn't want to cause you any additional distress. Is that true? Is he the cause of your...eh, *dissociative reaction*? I gather that's what they're now calling it?"

"My relationship with my grandson is none of your business." Grace's grip on the wheelchair's armrests tightened until her knuckles blanched.

"True enough, though you first commented on his character. Didn't you indicate that he has criminal tendencies and that inheriting your fortune would push him over the edge?"

"Money corrupts. I've seen how greed twists a man—turns him into something evil."

"Except Warren doesn't strike me as the criminal type. Besides, he is the legitimate heir to the McFarland fortune, not me."

"Your compassion is duly noted, but no matter what you decide, Warren will never inherit my estate. I'll not allow him to be seduced by unearned wealth."

"Yet it's okay for me to get rich by doing practically nothing?"

"Practically nothing?" Grace exploded. "How dare you say that?"

"Designing a park doesn't strike me as an especially daunting task, certainly not worthy of your estate. True, there will be problems to overcome, but solving them won't take a Herculean effort."

"Don't be so sure of that."

"Help me understand why this park is so important to you."

"All you need to know is that it is important, vital. It's how I intend to make restitution. And as to your previous point, having money won't corrupt you like it would Warren. You've already shown that."

"How so? Because I once had money, and now I'm destitute?"

"No, because you chose to do the honorable thing rather than protect your bank account."

"Which raises another concern."

"And what might that be?" Grace resettled herself in her wheelchair.

The winter storm outside had increased in intensity. Snowflakes were now falling steadily to form a curtain of white just beyond the windows.

"I'm not sure I want my former life back, being able to buy whatever I want, go wherever I want, whenever I want."

Grace's eyes narrowed. "Now that does surprise me." She pressed an arthritic finger against her pursed lips as if reassessing a previous conclusion. "I was certain you wanted to escape your current predicament."

"I did. That's what I wanted more than anything else, but now there doesn't seem—what's the point?"

"Because your wife is dead?"

I stared through the window at the ramp I had built. Snow was piling up on the railings. I remembered my excitement upon landing the job and imagining how joyful sharing my good fortune with Hannah would be. Now that she was gone…

With sympathy, Grace said, "Isn't your loss reason enough to create a park?"

"What?" My head swung around, and I gaped at the old woman.

"Donating the land is how I plan on restitution to Branford Gardens' citizens. There's no reason the park couldn't also serve as Hannah's memorial and a memorial to those whose lives have ended prematurely." By that, I assumed she was referring to the victims of Liberty Tower One.

Stunned, I rocked back in my chair as the concept exploded in my brain. Designing something beautiful, something people could enjoy, seemed the perfect way to honor those who had been lost. The notion even suggested a name: Remembrance Memorial Park. That's what I would call it until a better name came along.

I reached out and took hold of Grace's hand. Her skin felt cool and nearly as thin and dry as parchment paper. "I'll do it. I'll go see Mr. Ingersoll and sign whatever papers are necessary."

Grace visibly relaxed, indicating how tightly she had held herself against my potential refusal.

I, too, experienced a sense of relief, having made a difficult decision, though one question remained: Why did Grace feel such a strong need to make restitution? Blame for the McFarland misdeeds should legitimately fall on the shoulders of her husband and son. Other than having been there at the time, how did she share in their culpability?

However, my gut told me it was the wrong time and place to inquire.

CHAPTER 16

The hitch I had tied around the eight-foot stud began to unravel. The harder I tugged, the less secure the knot became. Slippery with snow and ice, the rope finally gave way. The heavy plank tumbled back into the debris-filled basement, raising puffy clouds of freshly fallen snow. With a sigh of discouragement, I straightened up and released the now-slack rope. My cold fingers were numb.

Looking down from the lip of the basement wall, I found it impossible to tell what, if any, progress I had made. Two grueling days pushing and shoving timbers around, and the only evidence was a reconfiguration of the three-dimensional puzzle below me.

With temperatures hovering near zero and a steady wind blowing down from the north, the air was so cold that my breath hung in front of my face. Rux Ingersoll had suggested I wait till spring to begin clearing up the lot. Maybe I should have listened, but sitting in my apartment doing nothing had seemed less tolerable than slowly freezing to death.

The transfer of ownership of The Homestead had taken less than a week. The documents had been signed, notarized, and filed with the county recorder's office in near-record time, a testimony to the efficiency of Ingersoll, Lake, and Johansson, Rux's law firm. More importantly, the transaction had been accomplished secretly, meaning Warren McFarland was still unaware of his grandmother's plans. How long he would remain in the dark, I had no idea.

I eased back from the edge of the cinderblock wall and shoved my hands into the pockets of my new winter coat. As I looked around, the realization that I now owned the land upon which I stood was gradually sinking in. The lot was mine to do with as I saw fit—my days as a pauper were officially over.

As the lot's proud owner, I had posted No Trespassing signs at all four corners and along the path that paralleled Monroe Creek. Protests and threats had sprung up from both druggies and ordinary citizens accustomed to using the lot without restrictions. Several of my signs had already gone missing. Enforcing my edict might prove more challenging than expected, especially come spring. Perhaps a fence would be necessary until the weed removal and topographic remodeling were completed. Stringing a chain-link fence around a five-acre plot of ground is no mean feat, especially in winter. The fence, therefore, would have to wait.

As a self-imposed condition for taking ownership, I had promised myself I would do as much of the work as possible by hand. That way, when the project was concluded, I could look back with satisfaction, knowing I had honored Hannah by the sweat of my brow. Beads of perspiration, now frozen to my forehead, testified that I had made a good start.

A thought came to me as I contemplated climbing into the basement to reattach the rope. There was no reason my prejudice against using heavy equipment should preclude hiring an assistant. As a rule, two people working together can accomplish substantially more than one person alone.

A face came to mind, a gaunt, hollow-eyed face bisected by a salt-and-pepper moustache. I hadn't thought of Mace in weeks, but suddenly, it seemed imperative that I find him. With a little inducement, he might be cajoled into lending a hand. It was a long shot, but it seemed worth a try.

I snaked the rope out of the basement and twisted arm-lengths of frozen hemp into coils. When I finished, my fingers were as stiff as the rope. I slung the coils over my shoulder. Even from my first days doing construction, I had hated wearing gloves. They get in the way.

Besides, I liked the feel of wood, especially if it's freshly sanded. On the other hand, frostbite would put a serious crimp in my ability to finish the project. I resolved to revisit the hardware store and pick up a decent pair of winter gloves.

With the rope looped over my shoulder, I trudged toward the sidewalk and the rebuilt Chevy diesel I had purchased. The money had come from the trust fund Grace had established. Nearly as ugly as Yuri's truck, my three-quarter-ton pickup was in far better condition. After taking title, I had outfitted the vehicle with a new engine, new brakes, and a rebuilt drive train. Mechanically, it ran as well as the latest model fresh off the dealer's showroom floor, but because I had opted to go with refurbished rather than new, my ride was less likely to be stolen.

The metal-sided utility trailer I had also acquired was parked behind the truck but not hitched to it. With lockable doors and security clamps to keep the wheels from rolling, it was the safest place I could imagine to store the tools and implements I would need.

With a truck, a trailer, and a decent assortment of tools, I felt like a proper handyman. Oh, how I wished Hannah could see me now. I fired up the diesel and drove off in search of an assistant.

Throughout the afternoon, I traveled up and down every street in Branford Gardens, questioning members of the urban infantry, anyone unlucky enough to be out of doors in such blustery weather.

During my months of boozing and picking fights, I had rubbed elbows with any number of lowlifes bent on self-destruction. Why I should choose Mace to satisfy my philanthropic urge, I couldn't say—perhaps because he had witnessed my epiphany, the cognitive awakening that had changed my life. Even as I searched, I realized there was less than one chance in a hundred that Mace would remember my face.

Near dusk, I finally located my one-time best pal. I found him in an alley, not a block from where he had watched me build my cardboard tower. He had fashioned a nest between two forest green dumpsters. With a wooden pallet for a floor and a large shipping carton for its roof and walls, a tattered bedspread served as the hovel's door. A foot in front of the bedspread, a low fire sputtered in a shallow metal pan.

Stepping down from the truck, I hollered, "Hey, Mace? You in there?"

The scrawny body lying on the pallet stirred. Drawing nearer, I could see the shape of a man curled into a fetal position beneath an old woolen blanket, his back to the fire and his face toward the rear wall of the Big Water Pawn Shop.

I advanced slowly, mindful not to move in a way that could be interpreted as a threat. "Man, it's cold," I said. "Good day to stay in bed."

"Go away," growled the form on the pallet. "This is my spot, and I ain't got nothing worth stealing, so forget about it." The body rolled over to peer in my direction.

Until light from the wan fire illuminated the man's face, I wasn't sure the gaunt form beneath the blanket was the same fellow with whom I had shared a pint of rotgut nearly three months earlier.

Mace squinted past the burning embers of a busted chair. "Who are you?"

"I'm Justin, Justin Moore. We're pals. You remember me, don't you?"

"I don't know you. Go away. Leave me be."

"Are you thirsty?" I held up the pint of liquor I had purchased, assuming that a liquid inducement would facilitate communication.

Mace eyed the unopened bottle, licked his cracked lips, and then looked at me. "What do you want?"

"We'll get to that. For now, though, how'd you like to party?" The amber liquid refracted the firelight as I rocked it back and forth enticingly.

"Where?"

"I got a place where we can go. It's warm, and there's food to eat."

Fear widened Mace's eyes. He shrank back into his cardboard cave. "I ain't going nowhere."

"It's all right, man. I won't hurt you. I promise. You'll be warm, and you'll be safe."

"Get out of here. Get away. I don't know you."

"I mean you no harm, Mace. Aren't you hungry? Thirsty, maybe?" I held the bottle up again.

"Go away!" he shrilled.

"Are you sure?"

"Yeah, I'm sure. Leave me alone."

"As you wish." I exhaled a disappointed sigh. I couldn't drag the man out of his hovel by the scruff of his neck. It wouldn't look right. Besides, even down-and-out bums get to choose their destiny.

I bent down to hand him the bottle. "This is for you—a gift."

As I drew close, I detected a glint of recognition in his eyes.

"That's right. You know me. Remember the cardboard tower I built—"

Mace snatched the booze from my hand. "Maybe. You're that architect guy, ain't ya? You're nuts, you know that?"

"You could be right," I admitted with a grin, "but I'm not here to cause you any harm. Wouldn't you like to go someplace warm, someplace safer than this?"

"What about my stuff? Can't leave it here. They'll steal it."

"We'll bring it with us. We'll take good care of it. Come on. I'll help you pack your things." I reached down to help gather his possessions.

"I can do it." Mace snatched the frayed backpack out of my hand. "Ain't no call for you to touch my stuff."

"Sorry. My bad." I stepped back, well beyond arm's reach. "Take your time—no rush."

"To your health." Mace twisted the cap off the bottle and downed a generous swig. He crawled out of his cardboard lean-to and, still kneeling, turned around to stuff half a dozen unrecognizable objects into his backpack. After collecting the remainder of his worldly possessions, he tied the pack's top flap shut with a length of twine and stood up. "Where are we going?"

"My place. Climb in; we'll be off."

"Hold on. You got a truck?"

"I do."

"This is yours?" He hesitantly slid in on the passenger side.

"Yep."

"Hot damn. Good hooch—a truck to boot. Who died and made you rich?"

"Nobody yet," I replied under my breath. As I keyed the diesel to life, it occurred to me that I was indeed grateful such was the case. After signing the papers, I continued visiting Grace, usually two to three times weekly. I now regarded her as a friend.

"Nice rig." Mace unscrewed the cap on the bottle and downed another gulp. When he offered me some, I declined. Hunkered down on the truck's bench seat, he looked at me as if I had sprouted a third ear on top of my head.

With the windows rolled up against the cold and the heater blasting, the cab's air suddenly became overpowering. I had forgotten that Mace stank to high heaven. With all my heart, I hoped he would accept my hospitality and take a shower.

Rather than head directly home, I took a slight detour. At Emil's Market, I bought a toothbrush, some mouthwash, deodorant, plus anything else I could find with a pleasant fragrance.

As we pulled away from Emil's, I gave up on holding my breath. "You like hamburgers?" I said with a hefty outrush of air.

"Sure."

"Good 'cause that's what's for dinner."

Six days later, Mace was feeling better. The retching had tapered off, and his shakes were less noticeable. At the outset, I had made the mistake of offering food too rich for his alcohol-soaked digestive system. As a consequence, he had vomited so violently that I had nearly panicked and dragged him off to the hospital. But meager helpings of toast and rice, softened with milk, had eased his distress until he could gradually take solid foods again.

During Mace's recovery, I had attended him regularly, even holding his head when he puked in the toilet. While serving as his nurse, I had learned a few things about the man: His last name was Larson. He had once worked as a high-powered accountant, and apparently, the death of his only daughter had triggered his self-destructive spiral. Beyond that, the details of his life were a blur. To me, though, he no longer seemed the same hollow man with whom I had once tried to drown my sorrows.

Mace had also cleaned up nicely, and to my great relief, he no longer stank like an unwashed garbage collector on a hot summer day. With his hair and mustache trimmed and decked out in clothes appropriate for winter, he looked like any ordinary bloke you'd bump into on the street. I'd been forced to guess when it came to sizes, but I'd done reasonably well, except with his shirt, which was too long in the sleeves. Only the tracery veins on his cheeks, the fine tremor of his fingers, and the jaundiced tint that colored the whites of his eyes spoke of his alcoholic history.

As I stood in the kitchen, a noise from Hannah's studio informed me that my guest was awake and would soon want his breakfast. As his physical condition improved, so had his appetite. I opened the refrigerator and took out a package of bacon and a carton of eggs.

No longer blessed with a wife willing to prepare my meals, the cooking duties had fallen to me. To Mace's credit, he had accepted everything I set before him without complaint, no matter how badly burnt or unrecognizable.

Rather than force my guest to sleep on the couch, I had emptied Hannah's studio and brought in a trundle bed. After boxing up her sculpting tools and carefully packing the blocks of marble she had sequestered for future projects, I had donated Hannah's entire workshop to the ladies' auxiliary at St. Anthony's. Giving away Hannah's treasures had aroused the uncomfortable sensation that I had crossed an intangible threshold. Though wary of accepting unusual donations, the women had promised to seek an artist who would appreciate the marble and put the tools to good use.

Parting with items my wife had dearly cherished was undoubtedly one of the most demanding chores I had ever attempted.

However, I had kept her last piece, the forlorn angel, for myself, having promised that it, too, would one day find a good home. The beautiful little statue sat on the floor in a corner of the living room. It was the first thing I saw whenever I entered the apartment.

"How'd you sleep?" I asked Mace as he stumbled into the kitchen, puffy-eyed and still unsteady on his feet.

"Off and on. Least the night terrors ain't so bad." He crossed to the cupboard to retrieve a drinking glass, which he filled with water from the faucet. "I used to hate this stuff." Without pausing to take a breath, he downed the entire glass. "Now I can't get enough. Go figure." After finishing every last drop, he filled the glass again before sitting at the table.

"How do you want your eggs?" I cracked six eggs into a skillet with a spatula, just like I had watched Hannah do it, except I broke every yolk. "How about scrambled?" The eggs sizzled when they made contact with the preheated pan.

"You should start with the bacon," Mace suggested. "That way, the eggs don't get all brown and rubbery."

I glowered at my guest, who sat with his elbows propped up on the glass tabletop. In turn, he shifted his gaze to the textured ceiling. With his chin in his hands and a hangdog expression, he looked like an abandoned puppy with a mustache.

"You want to do this?" I offered.

"Nope. Wouldn't want to deprive you of all the fun you're having."

"Didn't think so." Without fanfare, I shifted the skillet with the eggs to a cool burner and hauled down a second skillet from the cupboard beside the stove. With care, I laid out eight strips of bacon, four apiece.

"Why are you doing this, Justin, being kind to me and all? It's not like you have cause."

"I was wondering when you'd get around to asking." After the strips of bacon began to simmer, I stirred them around so they wouldn't stick to the pan. "Truth is, I need your help if you're willing."

"My help?" My guest seemed legitimately surprised. "Doing what?"

I pointed out the window toward the snow-covered lot across the street. "See that piece of property with Monroe Creek running through the middle? I intend to clean it up, but I can't do it alone."

Mace rose from the kitchen table and stepped to the window to peer out, squinting against the brightness of the winter morning. "Why?"

"Why do I intend to clean it up, or why can't I do it alone?"

"Both, I imagine."

"I intend to clean it up because I want to turn that ugly plot of ground into a park that I can donate to the county. Why I can't do it alone should be obvious. Surely, before the snow started falling, you must've noticed all the debris, especially the rotting planks and timbers. They're too big for one man to handle by himself."

"Can't say I paid much attention to that particular piece of ground." Mace scratched behind an ear. "Why should you give a damn? What's in it for you? Besides, the owner won't let you mess with it. They don't like us tramping on what belongs to them. The police will crack your skull if they catch you trespassing."

"No, they won't."

"Yes, they will. I've been thumped around enough to know what I'm talking about."

"You're wrong. The police won't do a thing."

"A lot you know. You may have hung out with us vagrants and boozed with us, but you were never one of us. Remember, you had a roof over your head and a warm bed every night. You have no idea what being homeless is all about."

"For a time, I too was homeless, and I do know what it's like. But that's not the point. The police won't interfere because I own the lot. It's mine. I have a deed that says I can do with it as I please."

My guest actually laughed. "And people call me crazy."

"It's true, Mace. I own it and can prove it to you if I need to. What I'm asking is would you be willing to help me turn it into a park?"

For several moments, the man regarded me as if trying to decide which of us was more screwed up. Eventually, he cocked his head. "You're serious, ain't you?"

About to answer in the affirmative, I noticed out of the corner of my eye streams of smoke drifting up from the pan that held the bacon. Hastily, I grabbed the handle and shifted the skillet away from the burner, singeing my palm.

"Yep," Mace affirmed, "you set the fire too high. Saw it right off."

Using a potholder, I maneuvered strips of bacon around so they'd cook evenly, ensuring the burned areas were away from the heated metal. I then returned the pan to the burner after readjusting its controls.

Having become bored with monitoring my culinary efforts, Mace returned his attention to the lot across the street. He continued to gaze in silence while I finished preparing our breakfast. Only when I set our plates on the table did he turn around.

"Why a park?" he said. "If you own the land, why not sell it? A plot like that has to be worth a fortune." He again sat in his chair and reached for the fork beside his plate. His mood had become more serious.

"It's complicated. One of the main reasons is that my wife deserves a memorial, something other than a gravestone. When people use the park I intend to design, I want them to think of her."

I tasted the eggs. They needed salt, so I rose from the table to retrieve the shaker from the counter and then sat down again.

"What about you? Isn't there someone you'd want people to remember?" I had cushioned my words in a compassionate tone of voice, though I strongly suspected I already knew what answer the man would give.

"My daughter, Amanda."

"How old was she when she died?"

"Eight."

"Tell me what happened."

My guest dropped his fork onto his plate.

"She was your only daughter—"

"Yes."

"It's okay, Mace. I'm your friend. No need to be afraid. You can talk about it if you wish."

"There's not much to tell. One day, I picked her up after school. On the way home, we were T-boned by a panel truck. Its front bumper crushed her side of the car. She died at the scene—never had a chance."

"That must have been terrible beyond imagining, but it's not the whole story, I suspect?"

Mace speared me with a look of pure resentment. For a moment, I thought he might attack me or bolt from the apartment. Instead, as some of the tension bled out of his neck and shoulders, he shook his head. "No. It's not."

"What really happened?"

Silence.

"Isn't it time you face the truth?"

"Screw you."

"Don't you want to put your pain behind you? I know you do."

"The truth? You want the truth? I was drunk. I ran a stop sign right into the path of that panel truck. I'm the reason Amanda died." The strain of holding himself together showed in his countenance.

As meekly as possible, I acknowledged his agony. "I understand how you feel. My wife is dead because I also made mistakes. Her blood is on my hands. She fell and broke her neck because I couldn't deal with what had happened to us. And as much as I wish to bring her back, I can't. What I can do, though, is make the best of whatever life is left to me and honor her memory by living the way she would want me to. That's why I intend to turn that wretched lot into a beautiful park, to remind me always to treasure her life. Will you help me do that? For Amanda's sake?"

"I don't know how much help I'd be."

"Anything is better than nothing."

"Look at me. You think I'm in any condition to lug planks around?"

"We'll do it together. And we'll get stronger. Do you think your daughter would appreciate having a park as a memorial? I know Hannah would."

"A park? Yeah, Amanda loved going to the park."

"Then there you are. Worth a try, isn't it?"

"A memorial park, you say? All right, I'll help—best I can."

"It means staying sober."

"I figured that much. When do we start?"

"Not today. I have a promise to keep. And tomorrow is Sunday. I thought I'd go to church. You can come with me if you want."

"Where?"

"St. Anthony's."

"Catholic services? No thanks. They go on and on forever. And there's all that kneeling."

"All right, but come Monday, we start clearing up the lot."

Mace nodded as if finalizing a business transaction. "You're on."

"Listen," I said, "I'll be away for the rest of the day. Will you be okay here on your own?"

"Sure."

"You're not going to take off on me, are you?"

"And do what, head out to the streets so I can freeze my ass off? I don't think so."

"Just wondered."

When I'd been forced to confront my loss, grief had driven me to attempt suicide by train. Perhaps Mace's grief had progressed beyond that stage, and he was now in the acceptance stage. I sincerely hoped so.

After breakfast and after the dishes had been washed and put away, Mace announced that he wanted to lie down for a time. I wished him well and then jotted down a number where I could be reached. It was Erin Fairchild's number. I had committed to building grow tables and shelves for her zinnias.

A forceful twist of my wrist snugged down the final crosshead screw. I returned the screwdriver to its slot in my workman's pouch. "That should do it." I looked at Erin.

She returned my nod, and we took hold of opposite ends of the sturdy wooden table we had just assembled. Heaving as one, we stood the bulky construct upright, settling it into place with a heavy thump.

With four-by-fours for legs and a raised lip around the edge of its 4×6-foot top, the waist-high table could easily accommodate three dozen potted plants, maybe more. Doubled sheets of heavy-duty plastic stretched over a layer of tar paper protected the table's surface. A bead of silicone sealant caulked every seam. It was the third and final table we had built together, and I felt good about what we had accomplished. Erin had a knack for carpentry and assisting without getting in the way.

She stepped back to admire our handiwork. With a grin, she ran an appreciative hand along the lip of the table. "These will do nicely." One thing I had noticed about my employer was her unshakable good humor. She had even laughed after hammering her thumb, but with tears in her eyes.

Erin looked around. She had mentioned that she would dearly love to have two additional tables, but space in the basement was at a premium. A row of new pine shelves lined one wall. They would hold her gardening supplies. A potting table was slated to occupy the last empty corner under the grow lights. There wasn't any more room.

A beam of sunlight spilled through the basement window set at ceiling level. The clouds outside were parting, hinting at a colorful sunset. We had been working steadily throughout the day, having decided to skip lunch. Despite our best efforts, however, we weren't going to finish as planned. One more Saturday would be required with the potting table yet to be built.

"Don't fret the mess." Erin indicated the clutter on the floor and the pile of sawdust we had tried to corral. "I'll deal with it later."

"That means we're done for today. Same time next week?"

"If you're available." Erin bent down to gather up several of the tools we had used. When she straightened up, she offered, "Would you like to stay for dinner?"

"Why are you always trying to feed me?"

"You know what they say, the way to a man's heart—"

"Is through his fly."

Erin grabbed a scrap of tar paper, wadded it, and hurled it at me.

I ducked. "I'd love to stay, but I shouldn't." I returned a pair of channel-lock pliers to the multi-drawer tool chest. "I must tell you, I admire how you care for your tools. Everything in its place, all in good working order. Not many are so meticulous."

"Don't change the subject. Aren't you hungry?"

"Yes, but—"

"I'm a good cook."

"No doubt, but—"

"But what?"

"I have a house guest."

"Oh. In that case—"

"Not that kind of house guest. A fellow I met some months ago has been down on his luck. I'm helping him get a fresh start. He's been staying at my place and is not in the best of health. I should check on him."

Erin thought momentarily and then gestured as if struck by a flash of inspiration. "You have a landline. I know you do because you called me, and I have caller ID. So phone home, see if everything's cool."

Despite myself, I was forced to return her smile. Not only was her lightheartedness infectious, but I marveled at how easily I had been manipulated.

I borrowed Erin's cell phone and dialed my apartment. Mace answered, and we spoke briefly. After hanging up, I looked at my employer. "What's for dinner?"

"That was delicious." I folded my napkin and laid it on the lace tablecloth. Mint green candles in tall silver candlesticks bracketed the purple zinnia that had served as our centerpiece. "You are a woman of many talents," I declared with admiration.

"Glad you enjoyed it."

Chicken breasts in a white sauce accompanied by steamed vegetables and an excellent Zinfandel were a far cry from the mac and cheese I had planned. We engaged in lighthearted conversation throughout the meal, transitioning easily from one topic to the next.

Erin rose from her chair, and I followed suit. When I reached for my plate to help clear the table, she said, "Let's leave these. I'll clean up later."

She was about to refill our wineglasses when I said, "I think I've had enough wine. Might I have something nonalcoholic instead?"

"Not a problem." She stepped into the kitchen and returned with a glass of club soda.

We carried our respective drinks into the living room. When I positioned myself on the settee, she sat beside me, close enough that our legs touched. Already snug up against the armrest, there was no way I could scoot over to open a space between us.

After sipping her Zinfandel, Erin leaned forward and placed her wineglass on the ash coffee table. I did the same with my water. A cozy fire crackled in the fireplace, creating a cheery contrast to the wintry night outside. I sat staring into the flames that danced above the blackened hickory logs. Sparks shot upward when a log collapsed into the embers. Smoke rose in ghostly streamers before disappearing up the chimney. Tongues of flame swayed in sensuous rhythms, keeping time with the beating of an unseen heart.

Then the screams began, not strident wails as before, but loud enough to banish all other sounds from my ears. Transfixed, I stared helplessly while Liberty Tower One disappeared in gouts of flame. My heart began to pound heavily in my chest.

A hand gripped my forearm. "What's wrong?" said a voice in my ear.

Ripped away from my nightmare, I gazed at my hostess with unseeing eyes. Gradually, I began to recall the day's events. Time started flowing forward again.

The pressure of Erin's hand on my arm tightened. "Are you all right?"

"Flashbacks—they come and go. Nothing to worry about."

Her concern was evident. "Anything I can do?"

"I don't think so. They don't come as often. Time heals all wounds, right?"

"It was the fire, wasn't it? You were—I should have known."

"How could you?" Leaning forward, I retrieved my club soda. I drained half the glass in one long swallow and returned it to the table. Feeling marginally calmer, I sat back and regarded Erin. For a while, we looked at one another. Her obvious concern eased my distress.

Strands of her auburn hair sparkled in the firelight. Her eyes drew me in. I felt myself drifting. The contours of her face and the freckles bridging her nose stirred my imagination. "You are beautiful," I whispered, "inside and out."

The tips of Erin's fingers caressed my cheek. I leaned over to kiss her on the lips, tentatively at first, then with increasing ardor. Long-dormant desires began to stir. I reached out to draw her closer.

Without warning, Hannah's image arose from my memories. Suddenly uncomfortable, I withdrew my hand from Erin's shoulder.

The mood shattered. Erin pulled back, breaking contact wherever our bodies had touched. A flush of insecurity colored her cheeks.

"It's not you," I declared fervently. "I thought I was ready—" I wanted to comfort her; to tell her how urgently I craved her affection, but I couldn't. The moment had passed, and there was no way to rekindle our intimacy. "I need more time," I offered in way of an explanation.

"Why?"

"So that when we're together, it will be just the two of us."

She sat quietly, as if measuring my meaning, and then nodded to indicate she understood. My sense of humiliation for having disappointed her began to ease.

After exchanging awkward goodbyes, I was about to leave, but then turned back. "About next Saturday," I said, "do you still want my help building the potting table?"

"Only if you promise to keep your hands off me." Her deadpan expression lingered but a few seconds before morphing into an infectious laugh that made it clear she was kidding.

With our relationship partially mended, I kissed Erin's cheek and stepped out into the night, my winter coat cinched against the frigid wind. *Idiot*, I scolded myself as I tramped back to my truck. *Why is it so hard to let Hannah go? Why can't you just get on with getting on?*

Some days turn out pretty much like you'd expect.

CHAPTER 17

Plump droplets melted off icicles hanging from the eaves above Grace's balcony. They fell like tiny bombs, exploding in puddles rimmed by thin edges of receding ice. Spring was on its way. I had sensed the air change when I entered the Manor. Most of the snow had disappeared from surrounding rooftops. Dawning rays of the late winter sun reflected off what few patches of ice remained. I would have opened the sliding glass doors and invited the morning breeze in if not for Grace, who sat beside me in her wheelchair, her familiar crocheted blanket tucked snugly around her lap and legs.

During the weeks we had been visiting, Grace's heart condition had progressed, further diminishing her endurance and leaving her vulnerable to strife, both physical and emotional. For that reason, I had decided to tread lightly, only occasionally probing issues that had triggered her dissociation from the world. I still felt that within that dynamic lay the key to understanding why she had chosen me as her beneficiary, rather than having chosen her grandson. It felt uncomfortable not knowing the twists and turns of her reasoning.

There was one topic to which Grace frequently returned with malevolent glee. As we sat side by side, gazing out upon the emerging day, she regarded me out of the corner of her eye. "Did you happen to encounter Ms. Fairchild on your way in?" The teasing in her voice came through loud and clear.

"I did. She told me she caught you flirting with Henry Blaine again." I had, in truth, tracked Erin down to confirm our next date. Having long since completed all her remodeling projects, we had decided to spend our Saturdays together anyway, doing whatever came to mind. However, our relationship was still platonic, not for lack of encouragement on her part.

"My nurse did not say that; besides, I was not flirting. Henry asked which anti-wrinkle cream I use so he could pick a different brand, and I asked him how many pennies he'd found in parking lots, all hunched over the way he was."

"Good for you. At least you're not ignoring the world like you were."

"You and Ms. Fairchild, have you two…you know?" Grace's eyebrow lifted in an expression of conspiratorial encouragement.

"No, and if we had, I wouldn't tell you. And while we're speaking of ignoring people, did you talk to Warren? I can't imagine why he hasn't been raising a fuss. I had expected him to do something by now. Why is he waiting?"

"Probably because he doesn't know."

"You haven't told him?"

"Of course not. Why should I?" Grace said with indignation.

"He's your grandson. Doesn't he have a right to know you've changed your will?"

"I love my grandson. Don't for one minute think I don't, but he's not going to understand that what I'm doing is for his own good. Besides, it's my will."

"What do you imagine will happen when he finds out? You can't keep your affairs secret forever."

"I'll cross that bridge when I come to it—if I come to it. Besides, he won't find out anytime soon."

"Why not?"

"Because he's traveling. His HMO sent him to Colorado to open a branch office. He won't be back for at least a month."

"How long has he been gone?"

"Since late November."

"How do you know this?"

"Jennifer Liscombe, his fiancée, told me."

"She came to see you?"

"No, she called."

"Have you ever met the woman in person?"

"Not yet, but I've learned much about her."

"How? The same way you learned about me? Through the investigative services of Ingersoll, Lake, and Johansson? So, what do you think of this Jennifer Liscombe?"

"Warren could do worse."

"You approve?"

"If she makes Warren happy and will treat him well, yes."

"Really. He thought you'd be so British that she couldn't measure up. Maybe you're right about his judgment. By the way, when is the last time you spoke with Mr. Ingersoll?"

Grace thought for a moment. "A week ago yesterday."

"Then you haven't heard about our problem with the county?"

"What problem?" Grace shrilled with alarm.

"Don't get upset. It's nothing I can't handle."

"What problem?"

Looking out through the sliding glass doors, I watched a medium-sized bird land on a telephone wire. Most likely a robin, but the bird was too far away to be confident. If so, it had to be the first robin of the season, at least the first I'd seen, even working outdoors cleaning up the lot for hours on end.

"The county planning office told me that even when the park is finished and fully landscaped, the commissioners won't take title unless it includes some special feature, a civic attraction as they put it."

"Like what?"

"A baseball diamond or a basketball court—something other than picnic tables and walking paths. It has to be something unique that sets the property apart."

"Monroe Creek isn't enough for them?"

"Apparently not. It has to stand out from the natural terrain, but don't worry. I'll figure something out."

"I trust you will. That's one reason I chose you; you like finding unique solutions."

I looked at Grace and noted the pallor around her nose and mouth. "Are you okay? Do you need to go back to bed?"

"Not yet. Seems like the only reason I wake up in the morning is to take a nap. Here I am, eighty-two years old, and I sleep more now than when I was a baby. Why do you think God lets us live so long?"

"Perhaps there's something important He's hoping we'll learn about ourselves."

Grace ignored my attempt to draw her out. Instead, she said, "How's the work progressing? How far along are you?"

"The basement is nearly filled in. It's been slow going, hauling one wheelbarrow at a time, and we've almost finished smoothing the hillocks over by the bluffs." I recalled brutal days of hard labor, but now I felt pleased for having put forth the effort. "Mace is stepping up more and more, and I think he's nearly lost his craving for the booze. Leastwise, he hasn't threatened to get drunk in over a week."

"Did he take the third-floor apartment in your building?"

"Yeah, he's pretty well settled in. Thanks for your help with that, by the way."

"No problem. Rux will pay his rent if he stays sober and continues helping you. What about clearing away the weeds and the surface debris?"

"We can start on that soon, plus grooming the creek bed after the snow melts, maybe as early as next week."

Emphatically, Grace announced, "When you've finished filling in the basement and the house is no more, I'll want to see it for myself. You're going to take me to visit the property. With my own eyes, I want to ensure every last trace of The Homestead is gone."

"Grace, you're not strong enough."

"I'll be the judge of that. If it's the last thing I do, I want to know that the evil that house represents has been obliterated."

"I doubt Ms. Lonergan will give her permission."

"I don't need her permission. I came here voluntarily, even though I chose not to speak. I'm not a prisoner. I can come and go as I wish. I'm counting on you to make this happen."

"Are you sure it's the right thing to do?"

"You're damn right I'm sure," Grace snapped.

"Very well. I'll do my best."

Grace smiled and reached across to pat my hand. "Good enough for me."

"Your life in Branford Gardens must have been awful to leave such bitter memories."

"You have no idea. Trevor, my husband, was a vile, abusive man. Andrew, my son, was no better. There was nothing they wouldn't do to satisfy their lust for money and power. They set out to destroy everything that got in their way."

"Including Max O'Bryan?"

"Especially Max. They swore an oath to kill him and his family. They would have too, had they lived."

"Is that why Max left town? Because of their threats?"

"Yes, but he wasn't afraid for himself. He wanted to stay. He told me so, but he had to protect his wife and son. Even though Trevor and Andrew were gone, Max feared their friends would make good on their oath. He was wise to take the threat seriously. A police lieutenant and a political crusader were gunned down not two weeks later."

"Did Father Samuel O'Bryan, Max's son, ever come to see you? You know, he's a priest now, assigned to St. Anthony's, that gothic eyesore on the corner of Myrtle and Century Boulevard."

"I know where St. Anthony's is. I remember when they built it—even attended mass there—once. And no. No priest has visited me, certainly not Max's son. I would've remembered."

"Would it be okay if Father Samuel dropped by? He needs to hear what you just told me."

"Yes. That would be all right, so long as that's all we talk about. What's he like, Max's son?"

"You can judge for yourself, but I consider him a good friend."

"Like I did his father." Fatigue showed in the old woman's features. It was time to conclude our visit, but there was one last item remaining, something I had wanted to ask for quite some time. With fingers crossed, I said, "Do you still have your mother's locket?"

"It's in the top drawer there." Grace tilted her head toward the nightstand beside her bed.

"Might I see it? Would you mind?"

"I don't suppose it would do any harm."

I retrieved the locket and pressed the clamshell halves open. Anna Tate's image still regarded troubles that she alone could see, just beyond the limits of the camera's lens. "What's your fondest memory of your mother?" I asked without looking up, not expecting an answer.

"My fondest memory…hmmm. Has to be when we went horseback riding. It was a beautiful day, warm and bright. The air was clear, and we laughed together so hard that we could barely stay in the saddles. I'll never forget that day."

"How old were you?"

"Nine, I think. It was a long time ago."

"Your mother never remarried?"

"She died three years later—pneumonia. Back then, they didn't have antibiotics. What is it you see in her locket?"

I glanced up to find Grace eyeing me shrewdly.

"Hope, I suppose. I've thought about it—why I'm so intrigued. Right from the start, from the very first moment I beheld your mother's image, I've had the impression she had it all figured out, that she understood why life is the way it is, and she was at peace with knowing. I want that. I want to get to a point where it all makes sense, and it's okay."

"You will."

"I hope so," I said with uncertainty. "Will you?"

"That depends."

"On what?"

"On how soon you eradicate The Homestead." Grace reached for the call light to summon the nurse's aide to put her back to bed. I returned the locket to her nightstand. Before the aide arrived, Grace grabbed my hand and squeezed my fingers lightly. "Don't forget. I want to see the land when it's bare. It's important that I do this."

"I'll take you, provided you're well enough."

"You'll take me there no matter what. I trust you in this. Don't let me down."

The aide appeared in the doorway, but Grace continued squeezing my hand. "Promise me," she pleaded.

"I'm not about to do anything that might end your life."

"Promise me." Despite the aide's urging, Grace refused to loosen her grip.

"All right, I promise," I said at last, "but you better not die on me. You got that?"

"I'll do my best."

The strength finally bled out of Grace's grip, and she relaxed her fingers. I gave her hand a gentle squeeze before letting go.

"Good enough for me," she said. "See you again in a few days."

"I'll be here. I promise."

Father Samuel wasn't at home when I knocked on his apartment door, so I used the spare key he had given me to let myself in. Our friendship had grown since our near-death experience to the point that the priest now trusted me to visit his apartment whenever I wished. I especially appreciated being able to consult his modest library when searching for answers to questions that troubled me. We had enjoyed debating theological issues on stormy nights, with winter's bitter wind howling above rooftops and along streets and alleyways. As a result, my understanding of the Scriptures had increased substantially, especially the Gospels.

I stepped inside and set about to make myself comfortable.

"Back for another sojourn in the Word?" Father Samuel said as he entered through the front door.

About to settle into a corner of the couch, I looked up.

He wiped his feet on the mat just inside the threshold to clean the mud from his shoes. He shed his heavy overcoat and hung it in the hall closet. His mood seemed somber.

Stating the obvious, I observed, "You're wearing your church duds. Another wedding? Seems like there's been a rash of 'em recently."

"A funeral. Sadly, there's been a rash of those, too. Billy Wirth, did you know him? Ten years old, son of Rita Wirth?"

"Rita Wirth? Isn't she the woman hired as a cook at Gresky's Bakery? Been there a few months?" I remember that she took the job Hannah had held for just one day. "I recall meeting her when I stopped in to thank Spiros for his kindness to my wife. What happened to Billy?"

"Asthma." The priest shed his vestments, folded them neatly, and draped them over the back of a chair. "Rita thought she had a back-up inhaler, but when she looked, she couldn't find it. The hour was late, and the Cost Right Pharmacy was already closed. Rita didn't own a car, so they waited for a bus. By the time they got to the hospital, the kid was in bad shape. The ER team worked on him for an hour but could do nothing to save him. Billy was Rita's only family. Her husband died last year." The priest slammed his fist into a wall. "Damn the monsignor. Why can't he see the need?"

"He still refuses to let you bring in your medical clinic?"

"The man is as movable as a brick wall and just as smart."

"Ouch. Keep it up, and you'll owe a bunch of Hail Marys."

"No doubt, but you're right, I should let it go. In the final analysis, it's God who provides, not me. I'm only here to serve."

"So you've said before."

The priest headed for the kitchen. "Did you eat?"

"I brought Chinese. It's on the counter."

"Nice. By the way, what happened to your truck? I noticed your windshield is a tad shattered."

"Vandals."

I followed the priest into the kitchen, stepping to the cupboard to retrieve two plates.

"A couple of the vagrants I kicked off the property are ticked off at me because I'm destroying one of their favorite places to get high. A scrawny fellow confronted me two days ago. He ran off when I threatened to bash him with a shovel. So now he's taking his hostility out on my truck. I hope he doesn't start stealing my tools."

"Did you report him to the police?"

"No, I'll handle it. Maybe I'll hire him and put him to work."

"You know, most people think you're insane, lugging wheelbarrows of dirt around in the dead of winter. How's it going, by the way?"

"We're almost finished with phase one, but there's a problem. It might be serious."

"What sort of problem?" The priest ladled a helping of sweet-and-sour pork onto his plate. He then added fried rice and a fortune cookie.

"The county commissioners won't accept ownership of a park that doesn't have some unique feature, such as a tennis court or a soccer field. Even a running track would do."

"The lot's big enough, isn't it?"

"Space isn't the issue. The limiting factor is Monroe Creek. Because of environmental concerns, the Army Corps of Engineers is reluctant to issue a permit for any feature that alters surface drainage. Monroe Creek ultimately empties into Lake Winachino. They're afraid a sports complex would pollute their watershed."

The priest looked up in amazement. "You're kidding. All the crap that flows along that creek." He set his plate on the table.

"I pointed that out, but the Corps' comeback was 'We're not going to let you make a bad problem worse.' Oddly enough, if I were proposing to build an office complex, they wouldn't have the same issues—eaves with gutters and downspouts can divert runoff to underground cisterns. Still, their stance seems somewhat irrational. Anyway, the bottom line is I will have to devise a different solution."

"Like what?"

"That's the problem. I have no idea."

I finished serving myself, and we sat down.

Father Samuel blessed our food and then looked across the table at me. "If you can't satisfy the commissioners and they refuse to take possession of the park—"

"I won't inherit the McFarland estate. It'll all go to charity."

"All that money. Man. What sort of charity, by the way?"

"Several, probably. Her will doesn't mention any by name. Apparently, her trustee, Rux Ingersoll, has complete discretion. He'll decide how the estate will be distributed if I'm disqualified. The only stipulation is that the money must go to organizations that benefit Branford Gardens' citizens. How the citizenry is to benefit isn't spelled out."

"I still can't understand why Grace should favor you with such a magnanimous gift—not that you're not worthy. That's not what I meant. It's just that…well, I'd have thought she'd do anything to keep the wealth in the family." Father Samuel stroked his beard. "Anyway, you're a bright fellow. I'm sure you'll put it all together."

"That's what Grace said. This reminds me of why I'm here; you need to see her. She told me things about your father that you need to hear."

"What things?"

"I'll let her tell you."

"Grace McFarland was my father's sworn enemy. That makes her my enemy too. Why should I believe anything she might choose to tell me?"

I rose from the table to retrieve the leather-bound album from the bookshelf in the living room. Returning to the dinette, I laid the album on the table and flipped through pages until I found the group photo I was looking for. Leaning over, I pointed to the woman engrossed in conversation with the priest's father. "If I'm not mistaken, that's Grace McFarland. Does she look like she's your father's enemy?"

"That's her?"

"You didn't know?"

"No, I didn't." The priest studied the photograph.

"She's expecting you to visit her," I said mildly. "But don't wait too long. She's not in the best of health."

Rather than close the album, Father Samuel left it lying open on the table. "Fine. I'll visit her, listen to her story—maybe even offer to hear her confession."

Good luck with that, I thought, but kept that sentiment to myself.

Before I could resume my meal, Father Samuel said with a twinkle in his eye, "While we're discussing matters of a personal nature, how's your girlfriend?"

"She's fine." I gave a nebulous wave of my hand, hoping the topic would wither for lack of encouragement.

"How serious are you about this girl? From what I've heard, she'd be quite a catch."

"Is that what your spies told you?"

"It pays to stay informed."

I pointed to the group photograph lying faceup in the album. "You're right. It is good to be informed."

"Don't change the subject. Are you guys serious?"

"By serious, you mean…?"

"Committed."

"No."

"Why not?"

"What are you driving at?"

"You know exactly where I'm headed."

"If you're about to tell me I need to get on with my life, that losing Hannah was a tragedy, but it's time to get over it, forget it. I've already told myself as much."

"What's holding you back? And don't dredge up some pathetic psychobabble to placate me. Why can't you commit to someone you obviously have sincere feelings for? And yes, my spies have been watching you. So, what's your problem?"

"I don't know."

"Really? There has to be a reason you're keeping this woman at arm's length. You need to figure out what it is, for your sake and hers. Come on, tell me. What goes on inside your noggin when you're with her?"

"You're asking because you feel an overpowering need to be supportive, right?"

"I'm concerned because I'm your friend. Tell me what you think when you two are together?"

"What I think is that I don't want to ruin Erin's life the same way I did Hannah's. Satisfied?"

"Is that it? Is that your issue? You and Hannah lived through a terrible catastrophe, but she stuck with you because she loved you, just as you loved her. What happened to your wife was not your fault."

"You don't understand." I briefly closed my eyes. Flames begin to flicker and weave together. I snapped my eyes open before the fire could flair into an inferno.

The priest softened his approach. "People who commit to one another agree to share the bad and the good. Hannah made that commitment of her own free will. You can't blame yourself."

"But I am responsible."

"How do you figure that? The coroner's inquest ruled otherwise."

"I'm just as guilty as if I struck a match. I knew Daren, my framing subcontractor, was cutting corners to save money. On the day they sealed the walls, I discovered he had failed to install several fire-suppression baffles. I could have demanded that he rip out the drywall and do the job right, but that would have meant an additional three days' work, and we were behind schedule and over budget. So I looked the other way. My greed killed seven people and ruined my marriage. Hannah's death was a direct result of the choices I made."

"Oh lord," the priest whispered.

"There you have it. You're the first person I've told. Even Hannah didn't know."

The priest commented softly, primarily to himself, "So that's why you reimbursed the victims, gave away everything, and went bankrupt. You were seeking absolution, trying to buy a clear conscience. And that's why you drank so much and picked fights—to punish yourself." He looked at me. "Now it all makes sense."

"Are you going to tell the authorities, have the coroner reconvene his inquest?"

"And stir that pot again, remind people of who and what they lost? Heavens no. You made a mistake, that's clear. You had a moral duty to ensure your condos were built according to code, an obligation you failed to honor, but none of us is perfect. We all suffer from flaws in our human nature. You're as much a victim of that fire as anyone who perished, as much a victim as your wife. You need to realize that some mistakes can't be undone. They can only be forgiven."

"How can anyone be forgiven for placing money ahead of people's lives?"

"By confessing, as you've just done, and by accepting the payment for sin that God has already made on your behalf. His son's sacrifice on the cross paid your debt. Because of Him, you are forgiven."

"It can't be that easy."

"It is—through faith. Jesus atoned for our transgressions, payment made in full. All you have to do is accept His gift."

"You're saying God will forgive me?" It seemed an impossible notion after so much anguish and so many deaths.

"I'm saying He has already forgiven you. That is if you want to be forgiven. Do you?"

"Of course—with all my heart."

"Are you sure?"

"Yes, I'm sure."

"Will you accept Jesus as your Savior?"

I recalled passages I had read in the Gospels. Suddenly, the words were starting to make sense. The message I had received, but never understood, was beginning to sink in. With profound amazement, I realized that my soul could be washed clean. "I will."

"Then the good news is that in God's eyes, you are now forgiven."

A sense of lightness of being that I had never experienced before came over me.

Father Samuel continued, "So now the question is, can you forgive yourself? Or are you so arrogant that you place your judgments ahead of God's?"

And there it was, the crux of the matter. I sat back momentarily and thought about what the priest had said. I reviewed in my mind everything I had learned in my studies of the Bible, especially the parts about salvation as described in the Gospels.

All at once, I understood. It was like somebody had flipped the switch. If God no longer judged me guilty, who was I to hold myself accountable? Relief surged through me, the likes of which I never could have imagined. After so much grief and all the misery and pain, I suddenly felt free—redeemed.

I closed my eyes and waited. Nothing happened. I waited a while longer, but the flames were gone. So were the screams. All that remained was a glimmer of hope.

I had arisen early in anticipation of another productive day. Looking out of my kitchen window at the lot across the street, it was easy to mark our progress in transforming a community eyesore into a park. Like lines drawn on a battlefield map, the demarcation between tangled foliage and cleared ground was advancing steadily, and our side was winning, except for the patches of new growth springing up behind us, a complication I had not anticipated. Weeds are tenacious, and it was becoming apparent they had no intention of surrendering at the first application of a shovel, an axe, or a hoe.

Like an orange beach ball, the morning sun balanced atop structures to the east. A few clouds drifted overhead, illuminated from beneath by the sunrise. I opened the sash to sniff the air. The chill was gone, and for the first time since the snows had begun to recede, I could declare with absolute conviction that spring had arrived.

The rising sun illuminated the trees along the banks of Monroe Creek, casting long shadows. New buds graced the ends of each twig. *Odd*, I thought, *how a watercourse could simultaneously be an asset and a detriment*. The creek was cleaning up nicely and would contribute to the park's beauty when fully landscaped. On the other hand, if not for Monroe Creek, I would have already solved the problem that bedeviled me—how to placate the Chillwind County commissioners.

A knock sounded at my front door. "Be right with you," I called out. As the weather had improved, Mace, too, had quickened to the task at hand. The bounce in his step and his willingness to push himself had paralleled improvements in his physical condition. Both of us were stronger and in better health, strengthened by a diet suitable for the manual labor we had endured.

I closed the window and grabbed the thermos of coffee I had brewed. It would see us both through the morning. On my way to the front door, I remembered how, as an apprentice carpenter commuting to various job sites, I had been swallowed up by the urban hustle. These days, going to work meant crossing the street.

After closing and locking my front door, I looked at Mace, who stood near the stairwell. "You ready?" I said.

He seemed rather handsome with his hair combed and his mustache trimmed and decked out in clean duds. Who would've guessed?

"On your six," my helper replied smartly. As we headed downstairs, he said, "I think this is the day we'll finally bury that basement."

"Good chance—assuming we push ourselves. How you doing, by the way?"

"You mean, do I still have cravings? Don't worry about me. I've learned how to ignore them."

"One day at a time."

"Right—one day."

Old habits die hard, especially self-destructive behaviors. Mace was having a hard time coming to grips with his role in his daughter's death. Still, I felt confident that, eventually, he would succeed.

I opened the front door and followed Mace out onto the stoop. As we crossed Beach Street, he jerked a thumb toward Myrtle Avenue. "Did you happen to notice? A fair number of merchants are sprucing up their shops—slapping on fresh paint and patching broken windows and doors. The pawnshop even installed a new awning. Yesterday, I saw what they were doing on my way to the hardware store. Do you think it's because of us?"

"What do you mean?"

"Well, they see us out here almost daily, clearing weeds and hauling out the garbage. Maybe it gave them the urge?"

"I doubt that. Probably just spring fever."

"Not a chance. I've lived in this ghetto for seven years, and it's never happened before."

"Do you honestly believe we're the reason?"

"Monkey see, monkey do."

"We're not that influential. Trust me." I unlocked the trailer and winched down the rear door that served as a ramp. "So, should we forget the weeds today and finish covering over the basement?"

"What do you think?"

I regarded the lot. "You're right. Let's do it," I declared decisively. Thinking about finally obliterating The Homestead reminded me of my commitment to Grace, a commitment I yearned to disavow but couldn't.

We gathered the wheelbarrows and tools we would be using from inside the trailer. When we emerged, a man was standing on the sidewalk. He looked to be in his early thirties and reasonably fit. He extended his hand. "Hi. I'm Tony Mallow, your downstairs neighbor."

"Oh, hello," I replied. "It's a pleasure to finally meet you." I returned his handshake and indicated my companion. "This is Mace Larson. He lives on the third floor."

"I know. I've been watching you guys come and go." Tony offered Mace his hand as well. "How you doing, man?"

"Doing fine," Mace replied. "You?"

"Good." Tony stepped back to survey the partially cleared property. "I thought I should tell you how much we appreciate what you're doing here. As you may know, I work nights, and it bothered me when Judy was home alone—with all the stuff that goes on out here." He indicated the empty lot. "We both feel safer now. Anyway, I wanted to thank you, and I'd like to help if you'd let me?"

"Seriously?" I said with amazement. "You're offering to lend a hand?" My neighbor seemed fit enough—perhaps a little on the thin side, but the wiry guys will surprise you. I had learned that they're often stronger and quicker than they look.

"I won't be a bother."

"It's not like clerking. You'll get all muddy."

"Not a problem."

"I can't pay you. I already have an assistant."

Tony shook his head. "I'm not looking for a job. I want to do my part."

"Well then, sure. Okay. Grab some tools. A flat shovel and an axe work well for clearing weeds, or you can use a scythe. If you want, you could grab a rake. We're going to finish smoothing over the basement."

"I'll do the weeds." Tony stepped onto the ramp but hesitated. "By the way, Mr. Moore—"

"Justin. You'll make me feel like an old man."

"Justin, I need to apologize. When your wife died, me and my family should have stepped forward, but—"

I raised my hand, palm out. "I totally understand. It wasn't your concern."

"But it should have been. That's the point. Anyway, we're truly sorry for your loss."

"Thank you."

Tony picked up an axe and a shovel. "Where should I start?"

"How about that thick clump over by the creek." I pointed. "You feel like taking it down?"

"You bet." Tony slung the shovel over his shoulder and headed off.

Mace turned to face me. He pushed his lower lip out in a way that could have said either "How about that?" or "I told you so."

"Yeah, right!" I exclaimed in protest. "What we're doing here isn't going to change things, not long term. You're not that naïve."

"Cause and effect, man—butterflies and storms."

I cocked my head as I considered his comment. Mace had given me something positive to think about. I grabbed the wheelbarrow and said, "Let's get 'er done."

"On your six."

Grace McFarland sat beside me on the bench seat of my renovated pickup. Her wheelchair was folded and stowed behind us in the truck bed. With Erin's help, we had gotten the old woman settled into the cab. In the process, Erin had covertly shared her apprehension. Her concern for Grace's health was as fervent as my own. When it had finally become clear that Grace was not about to be dissuaded, Erin waved goodbye and admonished us to stay safe.

Despite my foreboding, Grace and I were now on our way to The Homestead, or rather the empty lot where it had once existed.

Traffic along Westridge Boulevard was stop and go. With caution, I slowly navigated our way through Logan Heights. When the congestion thinned, I glanced at the old woman. "Anything seem familiar?"

"There are more dress shops than I remember—same number of jewelry stores." Staring out through my new windshield, Grace regarded the cityscape ahead. Her facial expression was grim. With a blanket draped over her shoulders and another bundling her legs, she looked like an old squaw I'd once seen in a photograph of the Wild West.

Grace and I had escaped just as lunch was being served because we knew Ms. Lonergan would be in the cafeteria assisting residents. As a consequence, neither of us had eaten. Having planned ahead, however, I pointed to the brown paper bag on the bench seat between us. "There are two sandwiches in there, ham and chicken salad. Take your pick."

"I'm not hungry."

"Would it trouble you if I ate?"

"Suit yourself." Grace didn't bother glancing in my direction. This was her first outing since entering the Manor, and she was probably afraid she'd miss something, though I suspected other emotions were also at play.

Not wanting to appear impolite, I changed my mind. "Guess I'll pass," I said, though I was starving, having also skipped breakfast.

The light ahead turned red. Gently, I applied the brakes. We came to a complete stop.

A woman in a miniskirt crossed in front of us. During the night, ambient temperatures had plummeted. I was forced to admire the woman's fortitude, if not her judgment. It seemed northern Illinois was about to take another run at winter. The storm that had rolled in had pelted streets and sidewalks with freezing rain. I had almost canceled our outing but had relented for fear of how Grace would react.

I looked at my passenger. "Why are you doing this?"

"I've told you a dozen times, I want to see for myself."

"I showed you pictures. Did you think they were staged? Haven't your minions at Ingersoll, Lake, and Johansson updated you on our progress?"

"It's not the same."

"Why not? What will seeing it firsthand accomplish? What is it you need?"

"A pair of earplugs if you don't shut your yap."

"Fine. I can take a hint." I squeezed the steering wheel with both hands and waited for the light to change. Then a thought came to me, a question I had previously intended to ask. I turned to Grace again. "Did Father Samuel come to see you?"

She shifted her eyes away from the road before us for the first time. "The boy's a lot like his father, though not in the way he thinks. He believed his father was a coward. I took great pleasure in setting him straight, which is what you had intended, I expect."

"I'm glad you two had a chance to visit. Did he talk about me at all?"

"Not really, though I did press him."

"I thought you might. You like him, don't you? I sure do. He and I have become good friends."

"Yes, I like him. I like him as much now as I did when he was a toddler."

"That's right; you knew him back then. And his mother?"

"Ruth O'Bryan? Yes. I knew her. You can go now."

"What?"

Grace pointed to the light, which had turned green.

"Right." I eased the truck into gear. "What was she like?"

"Ruth? A city girl through and through. Funny, I always felt that Samuel would wind up married to the church. Even as a child, he crossed himself often without reason. I presented him his first rosary, you know. He still has it."

"Didn't you tell me you weren't Catholic?"

"I'm not, but he was, like his father."

"Until Max converted to Judaism, right? I remember Father Samuel mentioning that his dad had renounced the Church. Must be tricky for a priest to have a father who converted to Judaism. When you spoke with Father Samuel, did he remember you?"

"Yes and no. Three-year-olds don't retain much of anything. Though he did recall I was the one who gave him his rosary. Look, this trip is difficult for me. Do you think we could drive and not talk for a while?"

"Sure, but one last question, okay?"

"If you must."

"Did Father Samuel ask about your family, particularly your husband and son?"

"Why?"

"Well, they're the reason his father fled to Iowa. If I were Father Samuel, I'd want to know what made them tick."

"Their names might have come up, but we never discussed them."

"Or Warren?"

"No. Are we done?"

"For now."

Grace chose not to respond when I flashed a charming smile.

As I returned my attention to my driving, I could make out the eastern bank of Monroe Creek through the gap where Westridge Boulevard spilled out of the bluffs of Logan Heights.

I would have continued our conversation, but Grace McFarland could be a stone fortress when she chose to be. I thought about telling her as much, but she was also my friend.

As we began our descent, Branford Gardens didn't seem quite as dreadful as when Hannah and I had first arrived. New splotches of color created intriguing patterns. Like a brick wall seen from afar, the individual elements had lost their ugliness.

Grace sat bundled in her wheelchair. I had parked her on the sidewalk and now stood beside her. She had begged to be moved closer, but I had refused. The ground was slick and muddy from the previous night's storm. I had no intention of getting her wheelchair stuck in the mire. As a compromise, we had settled on a vantage point as near as possible to where the house's foundation had been.

A stray dog bolted across a patch of open ground, only to disappear into a run of foliage still waiting to be cleared. If not for the labor Mace and I had invested, the cur might never have been seen. Much effort had gone into accomplishing as much as we had, but Grace seemed profoundly unimpressed by the expanse of weeds that had been removed. Perhaps her lack of appreciation stemmed from her being focused on the spot where the McFarlands' great house had once stood.

"Are you sure that's the place?" she said for the fourth time. "That's where it was?"

"Like I told you, every trace has been obliterated. We even used sledgehammers to knock the lip off the basement walls so the ground would lie flush with the rest of the terrain." My gaze scanned the area where I knew the house's foundation had been covered over.

Thirty yards to the west, the faint outline of a dark circle approximately ten feet in diameter caught my eye. Mace and I had tried to hide the site where Trevor had intended to build an ornate fountain, but the rain must have thinned the dirt. I hoped Grace wouldn't notice its contours. I could fix the defect later.

Grace's husband had intended to erect a magnificent water feature in front of the great house to showcase his artistic persona. The fountain had never been finished. Only the plumbing had been laid in, plus the ground-level tile work that Mace and I had attempted to conceal beneath an inch of earth.

Picturing how the McFarland fountain might have stood gave me an idea—a brilliant idea, actually. I nearly whooped out loud. Instead, I bit my tongue while I brainstormed possibilities.

Grace said, "I can't believe it's gone after all these years. Are you certain? There can be no mistake?"

"I promise you, the Homestead where you and your family once lived no longer exists. Every trace has either been burned, buried, or hauled away."

Suddenly, feelings of indignation and regret welled up within me. I was looking at the exact location where Hannah had died, and there was no evidence of her passing. It felt wrong that there was no marker or memorial.

"When you were…that is, in the basement, you must've hauled stuff out before filling it in. Did you—was there anything unusual down there?"

"Like what?"

"Did you find anything strange? Out of the ordinary?"

"Did I stumble across another tortoiseshell treasure box or another locket?"

"No, that is definitely not what I mean. Never mind. You would have mentioned it if you'd found something."

"What might be down there, I wonder?"

Grace clutched a fist to the center of her chest. Her face contorted in a grimace of pain. The color drained from her cheeks.

"What's wrong?" I said with alarm.

The old woman reached out and grasped my hand for support. Her breaths came in quick, shallow gasps. For a moment, I thought she might lose consciousness. Feeling helpless, I watched for a time. Just as I was about to holler for help, her discomfort seemed to subside.

She stared up at me, her hazel eyes brimming with tears. "I'm okay. I need to lie down."

"My apartment is across the street."

"You live on the second floor, and I'm in a wheelchair."

"I'll carry you. You're not that heavy."

In fact, at the foot of the stairs, when I bent down to lift her out of her wheelchair, she felt remarkably light in my arms, old age having leached away the substance of her body.

Grace lay stretched out on my living room couch. I had endeavored to make her as comfortable as possible by placing a pillow under her head and tucking blankets around her torso and legs as I had watched Erin do. I had even provided a glass of water, for all the good it would accomplish.

"That was the worst one yet," Grace admitted when the pain had nearly disappeared.

I had repositioned my armchair so it was in her line of sight. That way, she could see me without craning her neck. "How are you doing?" I asked.

My trepidation must have registered on my face. Grace offered reassuringly, "You needn't worry. Whether we like it or not, nature will take its course."

"You should let me call the Manor. Someone there must know a doctor willing to make house calls."

"In this neighborhood?"

"Well then, let me call an ambulance. They can take you to the hospital."

"To what end? Modern medicine, with all its marvelous technology, can't make me any younger. Just let me rest a bit."

I kept a silent vigil while Grace closed her eyes and tried to relax, though I could tell she was afflicted. During my periodic visits to the Manor, there had been occasions when this topic or that had caused her distress. Her uneasiness seemed substantially more intense this time, and I was truly worried.

After quite some time, she opened her eyes to look at me. "Promise me something."

"What, to take you on another field trip?"

"Promise you won't think badly of me when I'm gone."

"Why should I think badly of you? I like you, even though you can be as charming as a sheet of double-aught sandpaper at times."

"You're saying I'm abrasive?"

"I'm just teasing. Look, you're my friend. Why should you worry that I might think negatively about you?"

"Because of what I'm about to tell you. Somebody needs to know what happened."

"Maybe now is not the best time—"

"This may be the only chance I get. I'd planned on taking what I know to the grave. I thought seeing the lot vacant, with the house gone, would bring closure. It didn't. Nothing has changed. That's why I need to speak now. How much do you know about my relationship with Max O'Bryan?"

I leaned forward in the armchair and braced my elbows on my knees. "You two were friends. I also know you held him in high regard. You said so."

"Did you ever wonder if we were lovers?"

"The thought may have crossed my mind, but I'd never say anything to his son."

"Well, we weren't. I loved Max, and our relationship was on the up and up, but that's not how Trevor saw it. He was a very jealous man. One evening, Max and I attended the same reception, a get-together honoring the retirement of a publisher we both knew. Somehow, a picture of us talking found its way into the society pages of the *Westlake Gazette*, Max's newspaper. Max and I thought nothing of it. We'd been faithful to our respective spouses. Trevor, however, was livid.

"Like The Homestead, to Trevor, I was his property, and heaven help the guy who tried to take what was his. When Trevor came home, he barged into my bedroom upstairs. Blinded with rage, he cursed me wildly. He called me an adulterer, a whore, a slut, and as many other vile names as he could dredge up."

"Did he hit you?"

"Yes, with his fist. It wasn't the first time, but it was the last. You see, Trevor already hated Max. More than once, he had threatened to destroy him. This time, he threatened to kill him. Half-drunk and out of his mind with rage, he headed downstairs. I couldn't let him leave in that condition. I couldn't take the chance that he might kill the man I loved.

"So I grabbed the pistol I kept in the top drawer of my dresser and fired a single shot. It struck Trevor in the back of his neck. He died instantly. I dragged his body down into the basement. We'd been having plumbing problems, and the workers had torn up a section of the concrete floor. Perhaps you noticed? I never got the chance to patch it properly. Turns out it was just the right size for a grave. I buried my husband with my own hands and then cleaned up where he had died."

I recalled the patch of earth I had discovered. While preparing the basement, I had shifted aside the pallet I'd used for a bed. At the time, I hadn't paid much attention to a rectangle of bare earth, just another unfinished project common to most houses. A shiver ran through me when I realized I had spent several nights sleeping on top of Trevor McFarland's corpse. "Does Father Samuel know any of this?"

"No, and you will never tell him. Agreed?"

"Don't you—"

"Agreed?" Grace demanded.

"All right. I won't. What happened then?"

"I started a rumor that Trevor's cronies had divested themselves of a liability. The police never had reason to suspect the grieving widow."

Something in Grace's manner told me there was more to come. "That's not the end of it, is it?"

"No. Andrew came home a week later. He'd been away on business. Like his father, Andrew hated Max, and when he learned about the photo of me and Max together, he was furious, but unlike his father, he was deadly calm. He always was the more calculating of the two.

"Andrew had already bought into the story that his father's death had been a hit, a murder committed to protect the organization. But rather than blame his father's partners, he blamed Max and, like his father, vowed to kill him. So, I shot him too, a single bullet to the brain. The police had no trouble accepting that my son had died at the hands of the same violent men who had caused my husband to disappear.

"Betty, Andrew's wife, up and left the following day. She just took off. I think she was afraid they would come after her next. I later heard she drank herself to death somewhere in Utah.

"Two weeks later, when Warren got home from boarding school, and after the funerals, I set fire to the house. You won't understand this, but I enjoyed watching it burn. Then Warren and I moved to England. You know the rest."

"Was that when Max relocated to Iowa?"

"Yes. I understand he's still alive, but we'll never see each other again. He never learned the truth about what happened. I do not doubt he was genuinely afraid for his family."

Shocked by what I'd heard, I studied the old woman lying on my couch. Then I realized my knees were sore where my elbows were digging into them. I sat back and tried to digest Grace's confession. A double homicide, arson, and lying to the police—who could have guessed such a refined woman could be capable of such horrendous acts? Admittedly, there had been provocation. Still…

I needed time to think. "I'll be right back." I rose from the armchair and headed into the bathroom.

"You promised," Grace pleaded as I turned away, "not to think badly of me."

I stopped to look back. "Maybe I understand why you did what you did, but it's going to take time to put things into perspective."

"All I ask is that you remember me fondly." Her voice sounded thin and reedy. With great effort, she lifted her head off the pillow.

"Grace, it's not my place to judge you, and even if it were, I would forgive you. And I know God will, too. Besides, you're my friend. I will never forget you. That's a promise I'll have no trouble keeping."

"Good enough for me." She rested her head on the pillow with noticeable relief and closed her eyes.

Several minutes later, when I emerged from the bathroom after doing my best to sort out the ins and outs of what I'd learned, Grace McFarland was dead. Her heart had simply stopped beating. Thankfully, she was now at peace.

CHAPTER 18

Three weeks after Grace's passing, Erin Fairchild's silver SUV pulled to the curb and parked forty yards from where I stood overseeing work on the fountain. Her Jeep was a boxy gas hog, but with superior road clearance and four-wheel drive, it was well suited to winter road conditions. I knew because I had borrowed it to run an errand before the snows melted.

A glance at my new watch told me Erin was running late, as usual, not that it mattered. No one would notice her tardiness other than me, and I didn't mind.

I waved and headed toward the sidewalk to greet her.

"Glad you could get away," I said, bestowing a quick kiss on Erin's lips. Her eyes sparkled like her dangly earrings. Both were deep-sea blue. For me, even a tentative display of public affection was an improvement. I was learning. Our private embraces were becoming downright steamy, though we still hadn't graduated to the next level of intimacy.

"Wasn't easy getting away," Erin admitted. "I told Daisy I needed to check on a sick friend. I don't think she believed me."

Rather than scrubs, Erin had on calf-length boots, jeans, and a pale-yellow blouse under a denim jacket, her gardening uniform. I assumed that she had stopped off at her house to change.

Erin smiled brightly at Mace, who was gathering fallen twigs and broken branches from the banks of Monroe Creek. He waved back.

The coroner's autopsy had confirmed Grace's cause of death. She had died from a heart attack. Father Samuel had officiated at her funeral. Rux Ingersoll, me, a handful of Harwood staff members, including Erin, and one Harwood resident, Henry Blaine, had attended. Citing pressing business obligations, Warren had chosen to stay away.

Unfortunately, Warren wasn't the only one with issues. Greta Lonergan still blamed me for her patient's demise. In her mind, I had put Grace at risk by spiriting her away from the Manor. At the memorial service, caught up in the passion of the moment, the nursing supervisor had come near to accusing me of manslaughter.

The best falsehoods are often built upon a kernel of truth. Grace might have lived a few days, weeks, or months longer had I denied her request to visit The Homestead. Perhaps I was responsible, from a certain point of view. The problem was that I could not defend myself. No matter what, I would never violate Grace's trust and reveal her secret, not to anyone, which meant shouldering Ms. Lonergan's condemnation without protest.

"Wow, that's beautiful." Erin headed for the emerging fountain with evident admiration. "It's coming along. I love how the blue and turquoise tiles complement one another and show off the gold lettering."

That particular combination of colors had been Mace's idea. From the moment of inception, progress on the fountain had moved swiftly ahead. My inspiration, birthed during my visit with Grace, had evolved into a three-tiered design with water sprays and shimmering flows cascading down from each level. I had designed the fountain, personally refitted the plumbing, and erected its internal skeleton. And now the stone masons were doing a remarkable job setting the three-inch tiles precisely in place.

The county planning office had jumped at the idea of acquiring a park with a landmark water feature as the principal attraction. The Army Corps of Engineers had promptly issued a permit since a fountain would have zero environmental impact. I even overcame Rux Ingersoll's misgivings by pointing out that Trevor McFarland had never actually built a fountain. Our design would never remind the community of him, in compliance with Grace's wishes.

Intrigued by the notion of a local park, the citizens of Branford Gardens had begun stepping forward in increasing numbers to offer assistance. The idea of turning the fountain into a community memorial had taken root rather quickly. It seemed everyone had a friend or loved one they wished to commemorate. Mace had immediately nominated his daughter, Amanda.

Rux had proposed letting each resident nominate one name to be inscribed in gold letters on a memorial tile. He had also insisted that, to honor Grace's request, her name should be excluded, both from the fountain and anything related to the park itself. Reluctantly, I agreed.

My contribution, my offering of remembrance, was Hannah's forlorn angel, modified to stand atop the fountain, wings outstretched and arms reaching toward heaven. It seemed the perfect memorial, precisely how Hannah would have wanted people to celebrate her life.

Erin had strongly agreed, though the two women had never met. In ways I couldn't comprehend, I sensed Erin was developing a transcendent bond with my departed wife. Women can be spooky like that—no doubt about it.

Standing at my side, Erin gazed across the vacant lot, now barren except for the mature trees that lined Monroe Creek. "All these folks, they just volunteered?" Teams of two and three loaded the last piles of weeds into dumpsters at curbside or smoothed the ground where the picnic tables and walkways would eventually go. A larger group with masonry skills hovered around the fountain.

Virtually every helper was unaware that I owned the property, except for Erin and Mace, and both had promised not to tell. I intended to keep the matter secret till after the county had taken title.

I draped an arm around Erin's shoulder. "Pretty amazing, huh? I think the idea of a memorial park touched a communal nerve." People who, until only recently, had gone out of their way to ignore each other were now working together. Neighbors who for years would pass on the street without speaking were talking. "All it took was a common sense of purpose, a feeling of belonging. By the way, did you get a chance to tour the neighborhood as I suggested?"

"Not yet."

"You should on your way home. You'd be impressed. Branford Gardens isn't the slum it used to be. Even the alleys are being cleaned up."

Thinking about alleys reminded me of the empty cardboard box I had clutched in my hands and its message of condemnation. My feelings of emptiness were nearly gone. So was the guilt—mostly. Even so, I sensed my life was moving in the wrong direction. It was a premonition I had been unable to shake for some time.

"What's the matter?" Erin said with concern. "You look troubled."

"I am, sort of—not that I can explain why."

"Is it the fountain? I thought you were happy with your design."

"I am. That's not it."

"You can't be upset with the way the project is moving forward."

"I'm not, but every day brings me closer to being rich."

"And that bothers you?"

"Yeah, a little. It's too easy."

"For real?"

"Tell me something, would you still want me if I wasn't the beneficiary of the McFarland fortune?"

"I know that look. What's on your mind?" Erin slipped out of my embrace and angled her body to face me straight on.

"Nothing."

"Don't shrug me off. I want to know."

"It's not important. I want to be sure it's me you care about, not—"

"Don't ever think that. I fell for you when you were poor, remember? Before any of this." Erin's arm inscribed an arc that encompassed the entire lot.

"I remember." Teasingly, I said, "You were just playing hard to get. They say a man chases a woman until she catches him." I chuckled. "Come on. Let me show you what I have in mind. You can decide if you still want to lend a hand."

I stepped to Erin's side and looped my arm through hers. Gently, I urged her toward the south edge of the lot while I laid out my ideas.

Because of her knowledge of plants and especially because of her green thumb, Erin seemed uniquely qualified to oversee the park's landscaping. And unless the supply of volunteers petered out, she, Mace, and I wouldn't have to do all the physical labor ourselves. Primarily, her job would be designing gardens, fashioning the irrigation system, and deciding which varieties of flowers went where. I assumed we would have lots and lots of zinnias.

"What do you think?" I said as we approached the perimeter. "Should we bite the bullet and go for sod, or would it be better to till the ground and plant grass seed?"

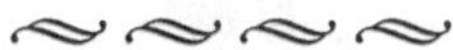

"I must admit," snarled a male voice from the landing above me, "that's a nice touch, finishing my grandfather's fountain. You found the perfect way to mock my family, didn't you, you cynical bastard?"

From the bottom of my apartment building's stairwell, I peered up into the gloom. A shadowy form hovered on the landing above. As my eyes adjusted to the darkness, I recognized Warren McFarland glowering down at me, his fists clenched at his sides.

It seemed the confrontation I had anticipated was at hand.

What I wanted at that moment, other than a couple aspirin, was a hot shower and a decent meal. From before sunup, we'd been planting shrubs and trees. I had spent most of the day stooped over, and my back ached horribly. Warren's timing could not have been worse.

In a voice muted by fatigue, I replied evenly, "You're angry, I can tell. I would be too, I suppose, if I were in your shoes. You must feel—"

"Don't presume to know how I feel. You can't begin to grasp how loathsome you are in my sight. I trusted you. I honestly believed you were my grandmother's friend. All the while, you were scheming to steal what belongs to my family and me. How dare you manipulate a frail old woman! You are a vile, despicable thief."

"I imagine this means you've spoken with Mr. Ingersoll? Just because you've learned the contents of your grandmother's will doesn't mean you know everything. And if your assumptions are wrong, your conclusions will be wrong. Perhaps you should withhold judgment until you know all the facts. But right now, I'm too exhausted to debate the issue. Tomorrow, when it's daylight, or better still on Monday, we can hash things out."

"We're going to deal with this here and now—not tomorrow, not in two days." It was apparent Warren had no intention of backing down.

I sighed. "Have it your way." Mentally, I prepared myself for battle.

Oddly, though, Grace's grandson was wearing a suit. If he'd come to pick a fight, he certainly wasn't dressed for combat. Besides, he hadn't seemed like a warrior at our first encounter. Even so, I decided it would be prudent to keep my guard up.

Cautiously, I headed up the stairs. As I drew near, I confirmed he was alone and not holding a weapon. In a fair fight, one-on-one, I felt confident that I would emerge victorious. His fifty pounds of extra flab would slow him down—just enough. The sad part was that fighting would solve nothing.

Sometimes, you have to get a mule's attention before you can bend him to your will. In my mind, I mapped out the moves I would use to counter Warren's assault and then respond with a vicious counterattack. When he backed up two paces rather than launch himself at my throat, I felt a great relief. Perhaps we could communicate like civilized beings after all.

While watching Warren for signs of aggression, I unlocked the door to my apartment. "Come in. No sense dealing with this out here."

After switching on the light, I waited for my unwanted guest to enter. He advanced to the center of the living room. I followed him inside. Rather than sit down, he stood monitoring my movements, as if he was the one wary of being attacked. I wondered if his opinion of me really could be that skewed.

I slumped down on the couch rather than stand toe-to-toe facing my adversary. *How would I feel*, I thought, *if my only living relative had abruptly turned her back on me without any explanation whatsoever?*

Mildly, I said, "You should know that your grandmother loved you right to the end. Regardless of what you may think, what she did was for your benefit, at least in her mind. I tried to convince her not to change her will, but she was stubborn. I'm sure you know that."

"Spare me. Nothing you can say will alter how I feel."

"Then why are you here?"

"To inform you that you're going to restore what is rightfully mine to me."

"I'm listening."

"You will deed The Homestead over to me, free and clear. Then you will convince Mr. Ingersoll to deposit the balance of my grandmother's estate into my account. All her assets are to become my sole and separate property."

"That's what you envision?"

"It will happen. You will make it happen."

"There's no way we can wind up with the land and her investments. Her will precludes it."

"You're going to find a way to see that they both come to me."

"Even if I wanted to, I couldn't. If I deed the land to you, the remainder of her estate goes to charity. That's what her will specifies. It's a provision neither of us can change. On the other hand, if I establish a park and donate it to Chillwind County, I can't very well deed the land to you, can I? Either way, my hands are tied."

"Oh, you will comply. You'll have no choice."

"I don't have a choice now. Grace has seen to that. Don't you get it? Look, I assume you've consulted a lawyer, who advised you that your chances of overturning your grandmother's will are virtually nil. Otherwise, you wouldn't be here. Putting all that aside, regardless of whatever legalities apply, I intend to be guided by your grandmother's wishes. They are what's important, and she made it clear that you will inherit no more than one dollar, and that's all."

For a moment, I thought Warren might explode. His face became engorged with blood. Even the bald spot in his Friar Tuck haircut turned bright red. Then, slowly, his anger began to subside. "One dollar, the supreme insult. How could she? Funny, there was a time when I believed she loved me."

"She did love you. That's what I've been telling you. Hear me out. She loved you and wanted to protect you. She thought she recognized something in your character. She wanted to keep you from being corrupted by unearned wealth, like your father and your grandfather before him."

"Leave my family out of this. This is between you and me."

"You need to face the truth about—"

"Would you like to know why you will do as I tell you? Because if you don't, the police will reopen the investigation into your wife's death."

"What?"

"I'm prepared to produce a witness, a fellow who will swear he was lurking in the weeds the night your wife died. He overheard the two of you arguing. He also heard you threaten her life." Warren's menacing grin set my teeth on edge. "That's right. That would mean Hannah was alive when you encountered her beside the basement."

"Who is this liar? Some homeless vagrant, a bum you fished out of the gutter?"

"Do you think the police will assume that just because a man is homeless, he's automatically a liar? My witness will testify he was curled up nearby, out of sight, and trying to sleep. He will say that you and Hannah were arguing near the basement wall where they discovered her body. Mrs. Mallow has already told the police you were agitated when you set out to look for Hannah. The obvious conclusion will be that, in a fit of anger, you deliberately pushed your wife, and she fell to her death. They will conclude that you lied to cover up your evil deed. You, sir, will be charged with murder."

"You gutless son of a bitch." I sprang off the couch and surged forward, but checked myself before smashing his nose; adding assault to whatever charges he intended to cook up would be foolish. Instead, I yelled directly into his face. "I loved my wife. Why should I kill her?"

"I loved my grandmother!" he screamed back. "But unlike you, I'm not a violent man, or have you forgotten all the fights you instigated and all the drinking? What jury would buy the theory that you don't have a temper?"

The words that came out of Warren's mouth dripped with venom.

"You know, it's dangerous when you're around. People tend to die. Maybe you've noticed. Perhaps the authorities will reopen their investigation into that fire that just happened. Who can imagine what new evidence might be brought to light?

"They may even conclude you harassed my grandmother until her heart gave out. In the eyes of the law, that's manslaughter. Grandmother's doctor repeatedly cautioned her not to become overly excited. You knew that. Ms. Lonergan told you so. Daisy will swear that you manipulated her patient from the start, even though she warned you to stay away. More than that, she's willing to describe how you kidnapped Grandmother on the day she died. Do you see a pattern emerging here?

"Think you can withstand the public wrath that will rain down on your head? Half the world already believes you're a murderer. It won't take much to convince the other half. If I were in your shoes, with your reputation, I'd think long and hard about cutting my losses. You'd be well-advised to do precisely as I say.

"Now, I realize this may take some time, and there's no reason you shouldn't finish what you've started since it will only enhance the value of my property. So you have one month from today to restore the McFarland fortune to me. Otherwise…" Warren raised his hand and craned his neck to mimic a man being hung. He spun on his heel and was outside before I could respond.

The best fabrications contain a kernel of truth. The more I studied Warren's lies, the more I realized I was in serious trouble. As outrageous as his allegations were, I could no more prove my innocence than I could comply with his demands. Either way, I was screwed.

I looked toward heaven and lifted both hands, like Hannah's angel. "Why?" I cried out in protest. "Haven't I changed enough to suit you? What possible good can come of this?"

In response to my frantic pounding, Father Samuel opened his apartment door wearing paisley pajamas, a gray terrycloth robe, and slippers. Rather than wait to be invited in, I barged past him. For thirty-six hours straight, I had struggled with how to respond to Warren McFarland. My date with Erin that morning had turned into a total disaster because of my preoccupation and because I had no desire to involve her until a solution had presented itself. Denials and reassurances are of little value when those who love you sense something is amiss. Thank God patience was one of my girlfriend's primary virtues.

The priest yawned and knuckled an eye. "What time is it?"

"It's late—or early, depending on your perspective."

"What's up? You okay?"

"I need your help. I have to figure out what I'm supposed to do." I began pacing in Father Samuel's living room.

"I thought we had this conversation already."

"This is different. It's worse. Much worse."

"I see. You want some coffee? Forget I offered. You're wired enough already, but I need a cup." He headed for the kitchen to brew a pot. I remained in the living room, marching to and fro. On my second circuit, I sensed that his apartment felt different.

It took a moment to register. Then I realized the ornate artifacts and expensive knickknacks were gone. I stopped pacing but remained standing. "You redecorated?"

"I decided to simplify my life."

"But you like nice things. Why give them up?"

As the coffeepot percolated, the priest shuffled into the living room. "It's complicated." He settled himself on the brocade sofa and gathered his robe around him. "Mainly, it concerns not serving two masters, God and money."

"What brought this on?"

"Do you really want to discuss theological matters?"

"People don't change overnight. What happened?"

"It's too soon to know, but I think I'm rediscovering my faith, perhaps for the first time."

"Really? This is good, isn't it?"

"Oh, yes. Very good."

"Why all of a sudden?"

"Like I said, it's complicated."

"Is this a polite way of telling me to mind my own business?"

"Not at all, though I'm not sure I understand it, not entirely anyway. Whatever this is began when I went to see your friend, Grace McFarland, and we talked about my father. All those years growing up, I considered him a coward. And I suppose subconsciously, I felt I couldn't trust him, not completely. It's hard to rely on someone who is likely to run away at the first sign of danger. But after talking with Grace, my opinion of my father changed."

"I don't understand." I sat on the opposite end of the sofa and faced the priest. "What does this have to do with finding your faith?"

Father Samuel, who had been staring into space, blinked and looked in my direction. "It's called transference. I've been studying what happens. Without realizing it, I must have attributed to my Heavenly Father the same attributes I found offensive in my earthly father. If I couldn't trust my dad, how could I trust God? Instead, I found my security in owning nice things and trusting in my ability to provide for myself. That's not the way a priest's life is supposed to work. We're taught to rely on God completely. So I've decided to turn everything over to Him, including all my earthly possessions, and now I'm free. From this point forward, I intend to live by faith alone."

Struck by a burst of insight, I jumped up off the sofa. "That's it. Poverty!" I exclaimed. "That's the key." I began pacing again, mumbling to myself as my thoughts raced this way and that. "It could work. If I don't own anything, I'm out of the loop. It takes away Warren's motivation. What would be the point of coming after me other than pure revenge, which would hardly be worth it?"

"What are you talking about?"

"Hang on, please. I need to think this through." I continued pacing the path I had trod into the soft carpet.

"While you're wrestling with your demons…" Father Samuel rose from the couch and dragged himself into the kitchen, filling two cups with coffee. Returning to the living room, he set one out for me. "It would be impolite not to offer you some." He began sipping the other as he settled on the sofa again.

After a long interval, I halted and eagerly turned to face my friend. "The Catholic Church oversees charitable foundations, true?"

"Quite a number, though I'm not sure how many worldwide."

"What would it take to create a tax-exempt foundation right here at St. Anthony's?"

"That depends. What sort of foundation?"

"A foundation to provide humanitarian services to the citizens of Branford Gardens."

"What kind of humanitarian services?"

"We'll get to that. Just tell me what would be involved. What would need to happen to form such a foundation? And how long would it take? The abbreviated version, please."

"Well, let me think. After carrying out a feasibility study and securing the blessings of the bishop, or maybe the archbishop, perhaps even the pope, a truckload of paperwork would need to be submitted to the IRS. Every foundation requires a charter. That means filing a set of bylaws and other documents with the state. The Church would then appoint a board of directors, a chief executive officer, and so on and so on. The entire process could take quite a while."

"Do you think a beneficent contribution of eight million dollars would speed things up?"

"Eight million? Holy—yeah, I think so. What's going on? What are you up to?"

I began by sharing Warren's threat with Father Samuel, leaving nothing out. When I finished, we both agreed that Warren had done his homework, and how he had twisted the facts made his lies seem plausible, which was awful news for me.

We kicked around the pros and cons for a while as my plan took shape.

The notion that the priest might soon achieve one of his most cherished goals overcame his reticence, and he wholeheartedly signed on to my strategy.

"One thing," he said as we were about to finish, "are you sure you want to do this?"

"Not entirely, but it feels right."

"It means giving up everything, including whatever chance you might have had to regain your former life."

"I won't be giving up everything. Besides, that life is over. Anyway, like you said, I'll be free. Some things are more important than money."

"Touché. Have you talked to Erin?"

"Indirectly. I mentioned something tangentially related—sort of. Anyway, she has to be okay with it. I don't have a choice."

"There's always a choice. You remember when we spoke about free will, how God lets us decide who or what we will serve? Well, in my opinion, this falls into that category. You're on the right track, but only you can be certain. If you have a sense of peace about it, then full steam ahead."

I smiled. "Glad you're with me."

"Good. Then, let's talk to the monsignor. We can get the ball rolling." The priest stood up from the sofa. "I'll get dressed."

"There's a man I need to see first. It might be best if I went alone. His stamp of approval is critical, but not assured."

"In that case, I'm going back to bed."

"Good luck with that. I haven't slept in a couple of days."

"Yeah, I can tell."

"And you're all bright-eyed and bushy-tailed, are you?"

"Whose fault is that?"

"Right." I headed for the door. "I'll call you when I know where we stand."

"And I'll pray that the Holy Spirit guides you while you're while you're gone."

With newfound hope, I ventured out into the emerging dawn.

Twenty-six days later, I found myself sitting across the table from Warren McFarland in Rux Ingersoll's conference room. A lot more than a vast expanse of polished maple divided us, though Warren was starting to come around to my way of thinking. Rux had again excused himself and stepped out of the room, this time on the pretext of retrieving an updated copy of the bylaws for the Hands of Grace Foundation. I suspected he wanted us to finish hashing things out on our own.

Warren was being obstinate, though not nearly as much as before. The letter the lawyer had produced had helped tremendously. Until that morning, I had been unaware of its existence and still did not know what Grace had written to her grandson.

Drafted the day she had changed her will, the letter's contents had affected Warren deeply, as confirmed by the sadness in his eyes and the fact that he was having trouble gathering his thoughts. I wondered if she had confessed to him the same things she had admitted to me, though I strongly suspected I would never find out.

I gazed across the table and sighed. "Should we go over it one more time?"

Warren nodded as if not trusting his voice.

I tried to imagine what it would be like to deal with Grace's grandson without her posthumous missive to soften him up. Crafty woman. You had to admire her style. She had anticipated complications and yet had engineered countermeasures to guide the process toward the desired outcome.

I leaned forward, elbows on the table. "The Hands of Grace Foundation, as I said before, is a duly licensed nonprofit organization. It's tasked with aiding the citizens of Branford Gardens. Okay? The Catholic Church, specifically the priests of St. Anthony's parish, have already selected and installed a governing board and are now searching for a chief executive officer."

With vehemence, I continued, "In no way am I affiliated with the Foundation. It's a separate entity over which I have no control. However, I have negotiated an ironclad, irrevocable property lease. For the next twenty years, the Hands of Grace Foundation will have complete and unrestricted use of your grandmother's land, for which they are to pay an annual fee, approximately five percent of the land's appraised value, adjusted biannually. As to what's to become of that fee, we'll get to that in a minute. Are you with me so far?"

Warren nodded.

"Good, because here's where it gets somewhat complicated. Mr. Ingersoll has determined that contributing to the nonprofit Hands of Grace Foundation would be entirely in keeping with your grandmother's wishes. In that regard, and since he alone has sole authority to make such a determination, he has decided—pending the outcome of this meeting—to donate the entire worth of your grandmother's estate. And since bequests to nonprofit organizations are exempt from estate taxes, the worth of the gift adds up to somewhat more than $8 million. He can provide the exact amount if you wish.

"Here's the kicker, and this is where you come in. With your approval, I will deed the land over to you as encumbered by the twenty-year lease. As the new owner, you'll receive all annual lease payments, minus part of the first payment, which will pay back your grandmother's estate for the monies I used to develop the park. When the lease expires in twenty years, the land will be yours to do with as you see fit. In the meantime, the Hands of Grace Foundation intends to build a freestanding, multispecialty medical clinic on the property and oversee its operations. High-quality, low-cost care will be made available to the citizens of Branford Gardens and the surrounding communities.

"With your HMO background, especially since you're an expert in provider relations, it would seem that you are a perfect choice for a position as CEO for the Foundation, assuming you pass the vetting process, which I can't imagine would be a problem. Of course, your salary will be appropriate for your duties. You'll have to answer to the Board of Directors, but you'd be given a reasonable amount of autonomy. So, there it is. What do you think?"

Warren cocked his head with a look of uncertainty. Light from the recessed fixture overhead reflected off his bald spot. "And if I decide to cancel the lease?"

"You won't be able to, not without the consent of both parties. Mr. Ingersoll has seen to that. And the Hands of Grace Foundation will never agree."

"So, what happens to the clinic at the end of twenty years?"

"That will be up to you. All permanent structures still on the land when the lease expires will be yours. You can tear them down. You can sell them along with the property. Or you can write a new lease for the buildings and the land. That way, the clinic would remain open. The choice will be yours."

"What are you getting out of all this?"

I glanced out the window. A golden sun rode high in the sky above Chicago. "I've been invited to design the clinic, for which I will receive a standard architectural commission."

"That's it?"

"It'll be enough for a second start."

Warren leaned back and laced his fingers behind his head. "I never expected you to walk away. I assumed you'd fight me to the bitter end."

"Does that mean you'll accept our proposal?"

"I haven't decided."

"Keep in mind that since I failed to donate the land to the county, there is no way I can inherit the balance of the McFarland estate. It's beyond my reach. According to the terms of your grandmother's will, Mr. Ingersoll is legally required to give the money to charity as her executor. Neither you nor I will ever see a penny of it. Accepting this proposal is the only way you'll end up with anything.

"Look at it this way: at the end of twenty years, if you include lease payments, your salary, and the value of the land and buildings, you will have received nearly all of what the estate is worth now, but you'll have earned it. Whether or not the clinic survives and prospers for twenty years will be up to you as its CEO, which is exactly what your grandmother intended. Her foremost fear was that you would be corrupted by wealth too easily acquired."

"What about the money the Foundation is to receive?"

"It stays with the Foundation, which is the only reason the Catholic Church agreed to this plan."

Warren rocked forward to cast a malevolent scowl in my direction. "And if I refuse and produce that witness we were talking about, what then?"

"I will immediately deed ownership of the land to the Foundation instead of to you, and Rux will donate the money. You might cause me a great deal of heartache, but you'll wind up with nothing. So, what's to be gained?"

"Revenge."

"Is seeking vengeance worth losing everything?"

"It's tempting. How about this? I sue you and have the judge roll back the land transfer. I prove you coerced my grandmother, and on that basis, I can have her second will set aside."

"If you think you'll succeed, go for it. I'll bet, however, that your lawyer has already advised against that course of action. Remember, you'd be fighting Mr. Ingersoll and me in court, as well as his partners. I don't know about you, but I wouldn't relish taking them on. Also, don't forget the Catholic Church. They'll have a vested interest in any proceedings you initiate. You'll have to contend with them as well.

"Warren, you need to realize this isn't my doing. Your grandmother set this up. Besides, as much as she wanted to protect you, she wanted to help the citizens of Branford Gardens. She figured she owed them something. Surely you must understand that. Just imagine the good that will come from having a multispecialty medical clinic in the neighborhood. Wouldn't you like to be part of a worthwhile project?"

Warren's scowl faded. "I hope you don't expect my decision today."

"Take your time. The land isn't going anywhere."

A ray of early afternoon sunlight illuminated sprays of water that arced outward from the fountain's three tiers. Gold letters etched into the commemorative tiles glittered. Seven feet above the collecting pool, Hannah's angel gazed heavenward with an expression that, to my eyes, no longer seemed forlorn. Instead, I recognized solemn adoration in its upturned gaze.

Interpretation is a matter of perception. We see in the world what we see inside ourselves. Look with jaded eyes, and apathy is what you'll find. Look with hope, and fulfillment is your reward. This is one of the lessons I had learned.

Beyond the fountain, thirty yards to the northeast, away from where the McFarland great house had once dominated the neighborhood, the Hands of Grace Medical Clinic offered care to all citizens. I watched Warren disappear through the revolving door at the main entrance. Father Samuel, chairman of the foundation's Board of Directors, walked at his side. Yesterday, the clinic's ribbon cutting ceremony had drawn a huge crowd, including a high school band bused in from Logan Heights. Mayors from every surrounding community had been invited to speak. The folks of Branford Gardens had even elected Emil Schumann as mayor specifically for the occasion. Every official had pontificated about prosperity and community spirit.

Beyond Monroe Creek, the clinic's parking lots were partially hidden behind verdant trees and rhododendron hedges, now chest-high. Three wide bridges spanned the watercourse, permitting easy access to the clinic's entrances. Rows of brightly colored zinnias, like miniature fireworks displays, filled the flower beds that paralleled the walkways. Mace Larson had agreed to become the clinic's gardener. I watched him pull weeds from the tilled earth beneath a flowering hibiscus.

Toward the base of the bluffs, safely away from the creek and other hazards, a fenced-in children's playground rang with youthful squeals and shouts. The foundation's board of directors had voted to gift the community with a mini park just for kids. One thing about kids, only when you hear them at play do you understand how tragic their silence is when they're not around. I recalled previous days, full of fear, when anxious parents had kept their children indoors. Those days were now gone.

Under Warren's supervision, two family practitioners, an internist, two gynecologists, a surgeon, and a part-time radiologist had joined the clinic's medical staff. As of noon, the clinic was officially open for business. Ambulances were afforded easy access to the urgent care services at the rear of the building.

My fingers closed around the gold locket I carried in my pocket. I would keep it to remember Grace, my friend.

In my mind, I pictured the weed-infested lot that had seemed so vile. In musing about the evil it had represented, I was reminded of the most important lesson I had learned: Individuals never determine outcomes. That power is reserved to a higher authority. We can only influence the flow of events. How things turn out is not up to us; there are too many variables we cannot control.

So when tragedies occur, our best response is to build a monument to honor what was lost and move on.

I regarded the fountain again. I would love Hannah forever and would cherish her memory always. Yet, Providence had ordained that my life would continue along a different path. I stepped forward to catch a handful of water from one of the sprays. As water trickled through my fingers, I studied the adoring angel. It perfectly symbolized the longing that follows loss and the hope that all will be made right one day. I drew my hand back from the water. "Goodbye, Hannah," I said softly as I turned away.

My contribution to the inferno that took Liberty Tower One would forever haunt me. Nothing could erase that memory. Moving forward, however, I could ensure I would not make the same mistakes again. Therefore, the Hands of Grace Medical Clinic had been built strictly according to code. Every safety feature available would protect its occupants from harm. In some small way, I felt redeemed.

And if someone were to ask me why things happen the way they do, I'd say it's because they're supposed to happen that way. Experience shapes character. What we endure forces us to become the people we are meant to be. That part of my life was finally beginning to make sense.

Erin appeared just inside the revolving door. We had begun designing and building modular greenhouses, and our business was growing, literally and figuratively. It felt terrific again to be a part of something with a future.

When Erin waved to me, sunlight glinted off her wedding ring. Her last name was no longer Fairchild. It was now Moore, and she had registered as the first patient of Dr. Fleming, the female obstetrician-gynecologist. My bride of nine months held up two fingers and smiled broadly. After a moment of confusion, I let out a whoop of joy as I ran to her.

Erin threw her arms around my neck. "Twins. Can you believe it? We're going to need to add on another bedroom."

I kissed my wife with abandon. My heart was happy.

Some days are full of surprises.

The End

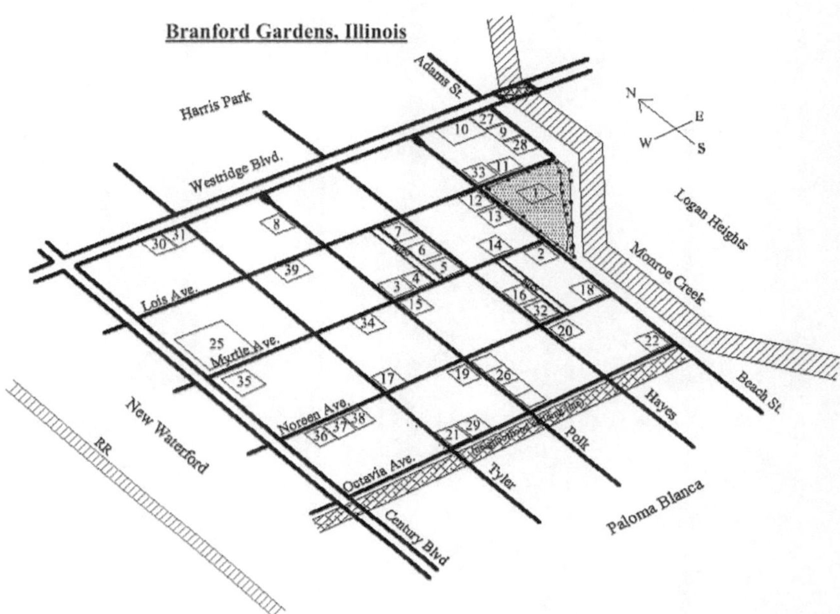

Branford Gardens - Site Index

1) McFarland Homestead
2) Justin Moore's Tenement Apartment
3) Gresky's Bakery
4) Occasional Flowers
5) Horton's Reality
6) Tempest Bar
7) Quick Spin Laundry
8) Lorraine's Beauty Parlor
9) Monroe Realty
10) Starways Bus Depot
11) Old Treasures
12) Benjamin's Appliance Repair
13) Argyle's Shoe Store
14) Speedy Images (out of business)
15) Carlisle Hardware
16) Big Water Pawn
17) Emil's Grocery Store
18) Best View Apartments
19) Bartoli Liquor
20) Groovy's Diner
21) Father Samuel's Apartment
22) Private Duplex
23) New West Guns & Ammo
24) Trattoria Napoli
25) St. Anthony's Catholic Church
26) Row Houses, Mostly Hispanic
27) Hadron Adult Movie Theater
28) Imagination Books (boarded up)
29) Rita Wirth's House
30) Apartments
31) Able Liquor Store
32) Save Your Soul Shoe Repair
33) Barton's Music
34) Kindred Spirits Boutique
35) Craig's Gym
36) Testament Apartment
37) Newland Apartments
38) Cost Right Pharmacy
39) Private Home

www.ingramcontent.com/pod-product-compliance
Lightning Source LLC
Chambersburg PA
CBHW020752310726
48969CB00002B/499